Praise f

With two parallel and delightful slow-burn love stories, *First Love, Second Draft* is a deliciously romantic story of grace, forgiveness, and reconciliation that readers are sure to love!

COURTNEY WALSH, *New York Times* bestselling author of *The Summer of Yes*

Full of charm, snappy dialogue and characters you root for, Kinzer's latest rom-com is a perfect read for the beach. I thoroughly enjoyed it.

RACHEL HAUCK, *New York Times* bestselling author of *Meet Me at the Starlight*, on *First Love, Second Draft*

What a witty and winsome read! Becca Kinzer has written a charmer in *First Love, Second Draft*. I loved the theme of second chances and the emotional journey of watching Gracie slowly open up and risk her heart. And the humor was a delightful bonus!

MELISSA TAGG, Christy Award–winning and *USA Today* bestselling author of *Wedding at Sea*

Becca Kinzer shines in her ability to write quirky characters and their zany escapades. *First Love, Second Draft* is the lighthearted beach read fans of Pepper Basham and Rebekah Millet will want to reach for this summer.

SARAH MONZON, award-winning author of *All's Fair in Love and Christmas*

This cute, quirky, and adorably sweet romance hit all the right notes of tender, funny, and downright charming.

PEPPER BASHAM, author of *Some Like It Scot*, on *Love in Tandem*

A sweet tale of misadventure and unexpected romance.

Love in Tandem was everything I hoped for. Becca Kinzer knows how to deliver characters I immediately care about . . . Not to mention she delivers on humor, swoony heart-stopping moments, and a happily ever after that still makes me grin long after reaching the end. *Love in Tandem* is one for the Top Ten lists.

A lovely debut by Kinzer that had me cheering for the unlikely, and yet so perfect, pair, Edith and Henry.

A charming rom-com. . . . This lighthearted jaunt checks all the boxes readers will expect.

FIRST LOVE, SECOND DRAFT

FIRST LOVE, SECOND DRAFT

BECCA KINZER

Tyndale House Publishers
Carol Stream, Illinois

Visit Tyndale online at tyndale.com.

Visit Becca Kinzer's website at beccakinzer.com.

Tyndale and Tyndale's quill logo are registered trademarks of Tyndale House Ministries.

First Love, Second Draft

Cover designed by Libby Dykstra

Edited by Kathryn S. Olson

Published in association with the literary agency of Gardner Literary LLC, gardner-literary.com.

First Love, Second Draft is a work of fiction. Where real people, events, establishments, organizations, or locales appear, they are used fictitiously. All other elements of the novel are drawn from the author's imagination.

The URLs in this book were verified prior to publication. The publisher is not responsible for content in the links, links that have expired, or websites that have changed ownership after that time.

For information about special discounts for bulk purchases, please contact Tyndale House Publishers at csresponse@tyndale.com, or call 1-855-277-9400.

Library of Congress Cataloging-in-Publication Data

A catalog record for this book is available from the Library of Congress.

ISBN 978-1-4964-8902-9

Printed in the United States of America

31	30	29	28	27	26	25
7	6	5	4	3	2	1

To my mother-in-law, Dianne Kinzer, who
is truly a character all her own.
And in memory of my father-in-law, Bill Kinzer, who
was one of the sweetest characters I've ever known.

1

October 1 headlines:

MARINERS CONTINUE WILD RIDE INTO POSTSEASON PLAYOFFS

SEATTLE MANAGER SHAKES UP ROSTER, SHOCKS FANS

WIN BIG OR GO HOME: PARKER GOES HOME

"No comment."—Noah Parker, Pitcher for the Seattle Mariners

2

Gracie loved Mona with every beat of her heart, but the occasional moment arose when she wanted nothing more than to smack her beloved sister in the face with a Bavarian cream pie.

Possibly cherry.

Actually, any pie would do so long as it got Mona to just. Back. Off. "Would you stop hovering? I'm fine."

"You're panting worse than a cocker spaniel in heat. You're not fine."

Gracie dropped her head back against the headrest. She hated it when her sister was right. Especially when her sister wasn't right. A cocker spaniel in heat? Please. But she might be onto something about the *not fine* part.

"I just need a second to catch my breath." And an even longer second to figure out how to maneuver into a standing position from the passenger's seat of her sister's car without splatting like a human-sized pie on the driveway.

A gentle breeze coaxed a handful of leaves from the giant maple tree next to Gracie's driveway down onto the windshield of Mona's red Nissan. Wouldn't be long before Gracie's entire five acres crinkled with red, gold, and brown.

Oh, how she'd loved cannonballing into a huge crunchy pile of leaves as a kid.

Now, on the other side of forty, Gracie didn't see any cannonballs left in her future. Especially not with a body currently suited for a woman twice her age.

"Well?" Mona's pointy-toed shoe tapped an impatient beat against the pebbled driveway. "Has it been a long enough second?"

"Just a half second more."

Mona huffed. Between her suit jacket, brown hair, and glasses, and her ever-present puckered-lip disapproval, she was the spitting image of Joan Cusack's uptight principal role in *School of Rock*. "You should've just gone to the rehab facility," she muttered.

"We've already gone over that."

"Well, maybe we should go over it again." Mona leaned down, the scent of rosemary punching Gracie in the nose. When her sister quit smoking two years ago, she'd exchanged her nicotine dependence for a fierce obsession with essential oils. Some days, depending on the scent, Gracie wished her sister had taken to covering her body in nicotine patches instead.

"Are you listening to me? I said at the very least, you should have moved into Dad's house until it sells. Friendly neighborhood. Middle of town. Shoot, even the dumpy little cabin you're trying to rent out next door would be a better option than your house. No stairs. One level."

"You sound like a Realtor." Gracie batted her sister's rosemary scent away from her face.

"I *am* a Realtor."

"Well, stop talking like one, and talk like my sister."

"Fine. You're an idiot. Better?"

"Perfect. Now get out of the way." Gracie swiveled her feet to the driveway and bit back a cry. The crisp October air brought no relief to the fiery sparks igniting her pelvis whenever she moved the wrong way—which was *any* way since her little horse accident. A little horse accident she prayed nobody had captured on video.

Writhing on the pavement outside her small hometown's grocery store on Main Street wasn't exactly Gracie's preferred method for going viral and rebuilding her author platform.

Ignoring the sweat beginning to ooze down her temples, Gracie reached for the open door in an attempt to find leverage as she splinted her sore ribs with her other arm. "And just so you know, my *adorably charming cottage* isn't even available right now. Matt found a renter while I was in the hospital. And before you start hammering me with a thousand questions, no, I don't know who the renter is, and no, I don't care who the renter is. He paid the deposit and that's all I care about. Now not another word until you get me into the house."

"And how am I supposed to get you anywhere when every time I touch you, you hiss at me like a feral cat?"

"You're the one with the claws."

Mona waved her red-painted talons. "You saying I lack a soft touch?"

"Yes, Wolverine. That's exactly what I'm saying."

A chime sounded. Mona whipped her phone out of her purse faster than a gunslinger at high noon. "What now?" she said in greeting as she hip-checked the car door right into Gracie's shins.

"*Ow.* Nice soft touch."

"Sorry." Mona's lips, as red as her nails, twisted toward the phone. "No, not sorry to *you*. I already told you the house wouldn't be ready for viewing until next week."

"Mona, before you badger that poor soul any further, can you at least help me stand so I'm not stranded in this seat?"

Her sister marched away, badgering the poor soul further and leaving Gracie stranded in her seat.

Terrific. Gracie closed her eyes and inhaled several tortured breaths as her sister paced back and forth, chastising the caller, then soon the entire male population—a common recurrence ever since Mona's boyfriend left her high, dry, and pregnant twenty-three years ago.

At this rate, Gracie would either be completely healed or completely dead before she even made it out of the car.

Gracie dropped her head sideways onto the headrest. Maybe she was being an idiot. Not about the rehab facility. Oh, no. Gracie knew about those places. They were the types of places a person enters and never leaves. Just ask her poor dad.

Last thing Gracie needed was to be surrounded by geriatrics watching *Wheel of Fortune*, all but forgotten by family who at first visited faithfully every day, then dropped their visits to three days a week, soon followed by weekends only, then eventually major holidays, weather permitting.

Just ask her poor dad.

Okay, maybe it wasn't as bad as all that. Up until her horse accident, Gracie had visited Buck every day. Still, the rehab facility had never been an option—not even when Gracie's orthopedic surgeon claimed it her best option for the next couple of days.

Gracie didn't need physical therapy sessions to get back on her feet. She needed a bestseller.

Gracie held her side, the memory of her conversation with her agent aching worse than her ribs. *Sales have been stagnant . . . Last book bombed . . . Need something new . . . Something fun . . . Get back to your earlier brand . . . Find that romantic zing . . . Make people laugh . . .*

Sure, sure, sure. Make people laugh. Find that romantic zing. Gracie could do that. She *would* do that. Soon as she figured out how to get out of this car without dying.

Her eyes drifted to the white two-story farmhouse with painted green shutters. A giant *Welcome Home* banner hung from the roof above the wraparound porch where it looked like people had already started dropping off casserole dishes.

As if she needed one entire casserole for herself, let alone twelve.

Another ache that had nothing to do with her bruised ribs squeezed her entire chest as she continued gazing at the home she used to share with her husband. The house that she could never bring herself to sell—even after he became her ex-husband.

Probably because she'd fallen in love with this property even faster than she'd fallen for her ex. *Noah, we have to get it. We have to. Just look at that view.* Gracie had motioned to the pink sunset fading over rows of farmland as far as the eye could see from the front porch swing, before dragging him to the back of the house so she could amaze him with the tree line. *It's like our own secret forest back here. Look, there's even a little cabin.*

Thankfully there wasn't a lot of competition for a run-down house on a property in central Illinois located in the middle of nowhere. Her hometown of Alda sat the closest, and that was a good twenty-minute drive away. Their pitiful offer got accepted. Then when they went through their pitiful divorce years later, this was the only part of their marriage Gracie wanted to keep.

Maybe because despite all the heartache, despite the bad ending, she'd dreamed up some of her best story ideas within the walls of that farmhouse. Stories bursting with zing.

More importantly, sales.

"Lord, please bring back the zing." Gracie was running out of time. And money. Even with someone renting the dumpy little cabin she'd transitioned into an adorably charming cottage, she was going to need more cash flow. Soon.

Really, what she needed more than anything right now was the second half of her advance—something she'd only receive if her editor accepted her full manuscript that was due two weeks from today.

Which meant Gracie should probably come up with a better ending for her rom-com story that was more *happily-ever-after*-ish, less *everybody-dead-on-the-stage-Shakespeare-tragedy*-ish.

"Oh, and God?" Gracie squinted toward the sky. "While I've got your attention, can you also get me through the front door without wetting my pants?" At the moment that request felt like a prayer of more miraculous proportions than the zing.

Holy hyssop. Did the front porch always have so many stairs? Didn't seem so when she could bound up and down them without any thought.

Today it was going to take thought. Lots of thought.

And now that she was giving it some thought, Noah really should have gotten around to fixing the porch step railing before she kicked him out of the house five years ago. She'd probably topple right off into the hydrangea bush the moment she put any weight on it.

"Ready to do this?" Mona dropped her phone into her purse with one hand, backhanding a leaf from her shoulder with the other.

If Gracie weren't so terrified about whether she was *ready to do this*, she'd tease her sister for going all Chuck Norris on a defenseless leaf.

The fact that Gracie didn't, must not have escaped Mona's notice. Her pencil-thin brows dipped in concern. "This is too much for you, isn't it? I knew it would be. We don't even have a walker. There's no way you're going to make it into the house. That's it. You leave me no other option . . ." Mona sighed and dug out her phone.

"Put that phone away. You are *not* calling the boys at the firehouse." For as long as Gracie could remember, probably ever since her sister heard firefighters were rumored to rescue kittens from trees, Mona believed all of life's difficulties could be handled by calling "the boys at the firehouse."

One of these days her sister really needed to acknowledge that firefighters weren't all boys. But that was a battle for another day. "Mona, I mean it. Put that phone away."

"Why? Wombat can toss you over his shoulder and carry you inside like *that*." Mona snapped her fingers.

Gracie whimpered. The thought of her bruised ribs coming into contact with anything, especially Wombat's beefy shoulder, tested her bladder control. "The last thing I need is a bunch of people showing up thinking they need to help me. Next thing you know, they'll be popping in and out of the house all week. I can't have that. Not when I need to be completely focused on finishing my story. *Alone.*"

"Uh-huh, and how are you going to do anything *alone* when you can't put any weight on your right leg? Or was it your left leg?" Mona began rummaging through Gracie's white patient belongings bag. "What did we do with your discharge instructions?"

"I'm weight-bearing as tolerated on both legs."

"Which would be great if you could actually tolerate any weight.

Here we go." Mona dug out a stack of papers, ran her finger down a page, frowned, and flipped to the next page. "So far it just keeps talking about how pain medicine can cause constipation."

Well, hurrah. One thing Gracie didn't have to worry about then, since she didn't plan on taking a single pill. Pain medicine had always made her nauseous. The only reason she'd asked Mona to swing through Alda to pick up her prescription on their way home from the hospital was to delay getting out of the car for a few extra minutes.

Sure, Gracie was anxious to get into the house, but that didn't mean she was anxious to experience the pain of getting into the house. But she'd certainly delayed long enough. Pain or no pain, it was time to finish her story. And she'd finish it on her own two feet.

Okay, her own two feet plus her sister's two feet. But no more feet than that. "I'm ready. Let's do this."

No sooner had the words left Gracie's mouth than the loud rumble of a vehicle approached from behind, drawing Mona's attention a brief second before she dropped her gaze back to the discharge papers. "Who's that?" Gracie asked.

Mona didn't answer. Gravel crunched and popped beneath tires as the vehicle drew closer on the long driveway leading up to Gracie's house. Too heavy to be a car. Sounded more like a tank. Or a . . .

No.

Gracie glared at her sister, who was still pretending to be enthralled by the discharge papers. "Mona, that giant truck I hear better be a FedEx delivery because I specifically told you *not* to call the boys at the firehouse."

Mona flung her hands, losing half of the discharge papers in the process. "Well, what else was I supposed to do? They insisted. You know how much those boys love you. And besides, we need the help. It's been thirty-two minutes, and you haven't even made it out of the car."

"It's been twenty-eight minutes, and I'm practically inside the house."

"Stop being so stubborn." Mona's phone began ringing.

"I'll stop being stubborn when I'm not on a deadline. Don't you dare reach for your phone. You are not taking that call until you tell them to leave. Did you hear me? I said you are *not*—"

"Mona speaking." Mona side-stepped Gracie's reach, answering with her professional Realtor voice, a voice that didn't betray the slightest hint her younger sister was currently hissing out ways she planned to murder her with pie.

"Hey, Miss Gracie." Wombat sauntered over, interrupting her pie tirade. He was wearing his volunteer fireman T-shirt, which Gracie was pretty sure he'd ordered online in bulk, along with tactical pants and red suspenders. It was his ensemble whether he was working as a tow truck driver, volunteering as a firefighter, shopping for groceries, or sitting in a pew at church. Should he ever get married, Gracie imagined he'd forego a tuxedo for his current attire.

He stooped down to gather her discharge papers. "Glad you're home. We hung the banner earlier, then figured we'd swing back by to see if you needed extra help with"—his eyes dropped to the papers—"constipation?"

Gracie snatched the papers and tossed them behind her. "I don't need help."

"She does. Can you get her into the house?" Mona spoke over Gracie, then pressed her phone back to her ear. "*Not you.* I told you the house wasn't ready. Now, you listen here, you little . . ." Mona marched off, leaving Gracie alone.

Well, *alone* not counting the four firefighters she used to babysit every summer when they were toddlers, and now fed at least once a month at the fire station, currently crowding around her, cracking their backs and rotating their necks.

"So how do you want to do this?" Wombat asked the other three. "I'll grab one thigh. You grab the other. You steady the head. Sound good?"

No. Being discussed like a turkey at Thanksgiving dinner did not sound good. Especially since Leo, the one she'd always had to hide the scissors from as a toddler, had an axe propped over his shoulder.

"Listen. You guys are so sweet. I mean it. You're the best. But

I'm good. Really. In fact, why don't you take a few of those casserole dishes with you? Maybe drop one off at the cottage for my new renter while you're at it? That would be the biggest help to me, because I'm telling you, I'm fine. See?" Gracie gripped the handle on the open car door and rose to a standing position.

Or at least tried to. Her rear end barely cleared the seat before a scream erupted from her lips.

All four men jumped a foot back. Leo swung the axe in front of himself like a weapon.

Okay, *fine* might've been a slight exaggeration.

Footsteps rushed to the car, kicking up pebbles and dirt before skidding to a stop in front of Gracie. "Wombat, hey. What's going on here?"

Oh thank goodness. Matt. Her kindhearted nephew. The one person on the planet who could hopefully bring a little sanity to this situation.

"Mom," he said to Mona. "You were supposed to call me once you left the hospital."

Mona lowered the phone and whisper-shouted to Matt. "I called Aimee."

"Why would you call Aimee?"

"She's your fiancée."

"How many times do I have to tell you, she's not my—" He clamped his jaw shut with a growl.

Gracie kind of wanted to do the same. "Matt, will you please help me stand? I promise I'll fine if someone will just help me stand."

Matt gripped her elbows and lifted her to a standing position.

Holy hyssop! Gracie clamped her mouth shut, afraid of what words might escape past her lips, none of them holy. Felt like a fifteen-pound bowling ball was sitting inside her pelvis.

After several awful seconds, the pressure began to disappear. The sweat drizzling down her forehead and into her eyes, however . . .

"See?" she gritted out between her teeth. "Perfectly fine."

"Oh boy. You look . . ." Matt scratched behind his ear, smart enough not to finish that sentence. "I don't know, Aunt Gracie, maybe we do need the extra hands to get you inside."

"That's why Mona is here," Gracie said in between pants that even she had to admit sounded an awful lot like a cocker spaniel in heat.

"Not anymore." Mona rushed to the driver's side door. "Sorry, Sis. That lunatic is demanding to see the house in Litchfield today. I need to drive over there before he climbs in through a window or something."

"Mona, no." Her sister wasn't leaving. Not with Gracie standing here. Outside. With half the Alda volunteer fire department.

No no no. This was not the plan. The plan was to get Gracie inside. Alone. With food. Water. A computer. And zero distractions until she had a manuscript bursting with zing. A manuscript with a much better ending than the one she emailed to her agent a few days ago, promising that everything was under control.

That promise would've carried a lot more weight if Gracie hadn't fallen off a coin-operated horse and landed in the ER later that same afternoon. "Mona, you can't leave me."

"I'll be back before you know it," she shouted through an open window as her car peeled away.

Matt tugged Gracie away from the spraying gravel. He wasn't holding her tight, but even the little bit of pressure hurt her ribs. Her back. Her pelvis. Her pride. Everything. A whimper slipped past her lips.

"Sorry," Matt said.

"No, it's not you. It's . . ." She buried her face against Matt's shoulder, unable to hold back the tears. Why couldn't anything in her life be easy? Ever? Sakes alive, she couldn't even climb on a toy horse without getting hurt.

Matt's shoulders shifted uncomfortably, probably because he could feel her tears and snot seeping through the cotton fabric of his long-sleeved shirt. "Hey guys, appreciate the help, but I think we're good here."

Still crying, Gracie flapped her fingers toward the porch. "Don't forget the casseroles," she whimpered.

She didn't have to tell the poor boys twice. They'd probably rather deal with a blazing fire than a crying woman any day. The fire truck's heavy rumble soon disappeared.

At last, peace.

Until the front door to the cottage squeaked open and clapped shut. *Oh wonderful.* Just what she needed. To meet the new renter with a blotchy face covered in snot. On the bright side, maybe the sight would scare him off from ever bothering her again.

"Is that the nice guy you told me about?" Gracie tried lifting her head to get a good look at him.

Matt squished her face back against his shoulder.

Clutching the back of her head with one hand, he began patting her on the back as if he were burping a baby and had no idea how to do it. Which in a weird way brought her more comfort than anything else had so far. She really did love her one and only nephew.

"So listen, Aunt Gracie. About the renter . . ." Matt cleared his throat, slapping her back now as if she were choking. "I know you said you wouldn't need any help, but—"

Footsteps approached, crunching over dry leaves. The closer the steps came, the faster Matt talked.

"The doctor said you're going to need help. Especially the next few days. Maybe longer. What if you fell? You could lay there for hours, and nobody would know. You could die and nobody would know. You need someone close by. Someone to help take care of you. And let's face it—my mom's not a caregiver. We all know that. You need someone who can help you up the stairs. Fix you food. Give you a bath. And that's not me. I love you, but I'm not giving you a bath."

Gracie finally managed to tug her face away from Matt's shoulder long enough to gasp in a deep breath. "Considering you just about suffocated me, yeah, I'd say you're not exactly caregiver material either."

Lucky for her she didn't need a caregiver at all. Which she was about to point out to Matt when he said, "So you understand then."

The back of Gracie's neck tingled. "Understand what?"

"Why I did what I did."

The tingles grew sharper as Gracie held her nephew's gaze. "What did you do?"

When a throat cleared behind her, Matt didn't have to answer. She knew. "You little Benedict Arnold." The back of Gracie's neck no longer tingled. It blazed.

If Gracie had a will, she'd write Matt out of it first thing tomorrow. She never did care for her one and only nephew. "Look me in the eye right now and tell me the nice guy you rented my cottage to is *not* my ex-husband."

Matt looked everywhere. The house. The maple tree. The snot stain on his shirt. Everywhere but her eyes. "He'll take care of you."

She shook her head.

"He still loves you."

She shook her head harder.

"He won't mind helping you out with a sponge bath?"

There weren't enough pies in the world to smack her nephew in the face with at this moment.

"Please, Aunt Gracie. Just give him a chance."

"A chance," she scoffed. "Are you crazy? Hey, where are you going? You can't leave me. Matt, don't you dare—"

Her evil nephew dared, backing out of her reach. Gracie didn't have time to stumble after him before two arms circled her from behind. When her knees buckled, she didn't know if it was because of the pain in her right hip shooting down to her groin or the much-too-familiar voice speaking next to her ear.

"Don't worry, babe, I've got you."

Gracie squeezed her eyes shut. This couldn't be happening. It didn't make sense. Somebody call back the boys from the firehouse. What was Noah doing here?

And how on earth was she already back in his arms?

Gracie glared at the sky, grinding her teeth as she grumbled, "This is not what I meant when I asked you to bring back the zing."

3

Noah kicked the door shut behind him as he scanned the interior of the house he still thought of as home—even if he hadn't stepped foot inside of it for nearly five years. "Place hasn't changed much."

"Except for the dirty boot print on the door," Gracie muttered in between panted breaths. Her thin frame sagged further against him with each step from the entryway into the family room, furnished with a new beige sectional and leather recliner. Other than that, same white shiplap walls. Same dark wooden floors. Same hodgepodge of black-and-white photos and musty-smelling books lining the built-in arched bookshelves.

She'd always been a sucker for old things. Noah joked once how it was a good thing he liked old things too since she was nearly two years older than him. Yeah, that was a joke he never made again.

He crept another step forward, his right arm wrapped around her waist. At the pace they were going, they might just reach the living room by New Year's Eve. "Cabin looks good. Matt told me a while back how he was helping you fix the place up."

"Just get me to the couch, will you? And it's a cottage."

"You eating enough?" Looked like she'd lost weight since the last time he saw her. Though that had been from a distance. Had he seen her since Matt's high school graduation? He didn't think so. Not unless social media stalking counted. "You feel thin."

"The couch, Noah. I don't need any commentary on the state of my figure."

"You need to take care of yourself is what you need."

"You know what—" Gracie pushed him away with the force of a soft breeze. "I can take it from here." One step later, she latched onto his elbow. "And by *here*, I mean *there*. On the couch."

He escorted her past the antique-looking steamer trunk that served as a coffee table. He remembered how excited she'd been to find it at an estate sale the first summer after they married. He also remembered how close he'd come to getting a hernia lugging it up the porch steps.

He lowered her to the couch and slowly swiveled her feet onto the cushions. She didn't make a sound, but judging by the lobster shade of red on her face, lots of sounds were begging to be released behind her pinched lips. He shoved a pillow beneath her head and gave it a few whacks.

"What are you doing?" Her words erupted with a blast of pent-up air.

"Fluffing your pillow. It's what nurses do. You need some chicken noodle soup or something?"

"I need you to leave."

"Sure." Noah plopped into the recliner next to the couch. "You can barely walk, but yeah, why don't I just head back to the cabin now."

"Cottage."

"And when you need to go to the bathroom, you'll . . . army crawl to the toilet?"

"That's the plan."

He yanked the lever to raise his feet and propped both hands behind his head. "I'm not going anywhere, babe, so you may as well use your energy for healing instead of fighting."

"Don't call me *babe*. And seriously, what are you doing here? Your team made it to the playoffs. And aren't you only five strikeouts away from the team's all-time strikeout record?"

"You still follow my career? I'm touched."

"Like I can go anywhere in a fifty-mile radius without hearing about your stupid team."

Noah grunted, massaging his left shoulder. "Well, you must've missed the part where I didn't make my stupid team's roster for the postseason."

For once, Gracie looked speechless. Probably the same way Noah had looked when he got the news from his manager.

Noah knew he was in trouble the second Dusty asked to speak to him in his office right after clinching the division title. His shoulder had been bothering him and he'd been pitching some truly terrible games lately. As much as it killed him to not get a shot at that record, Noah wasn't surprised Dusty wanted to make room on the roster for the younger arms who'd been on absolute fire the past several weeks of the regular season.

What Noah hadn't seen coming was the phone call the next day from Matt telling him that Gracie was trying to find a renter for the old cabin on their property. Sorry—*cottage*.

The idea of getting away from reporters and taking some time to figure out his next steps was tempting on its own. But once Matt let it slip that Gracie had been injured in an accident and could use the help, Noah couldn't pack up his Jeep fast enough.

For five years he'd been praying for a way to walk back into Gracie's life. Now he just had to figure out a way to stay in it. Which meant he needed to figure out what to do with *his* life now.

Sure, hitting forty put him well past his prime as a pitcher, but by most standards he was still young. Young enough to start another career if he wanted. Young enough to even start a family.

He still had time on his side, no doubt about it. Question was whether he'd ever have Gracie back by his side.

"You still haven't answered my question," Gracie said once she'd apparently recovered from her speechlessness.

Dust motes floated in a slant of sunlight from the bay window. A water ring marked the trunk's wooden surface. "Did you know heat gets rid of water marks? Saw a video of someone using a clothes iron on a dining room table, I think."

"So that's why you came back? To offer home remedy tricks you picked up online? Well, thank you, Noah. There's a stubborn stain on one of the bedroom carpets. Maybe you can tackle that next."

"Sure. Got any baking soda?"

She shot him the same look batters would give him when his pitch ran a little too close inside the plate. He gave her the same look he'd give back to the batters. All innocence. "Look Gracie, you need help. I'm here to help. Simple as that."

"Ha. Nothing's as simple as that. Not when it comes to us," she muttered as she tried propping herself on her elbows to readjust the pillow behind her. *"Don't,"* she said when he started lowering the footrest to help.

He lifted his hands in surrender and leaned back. After barely seeing her in person for five years, he didn't mind taking the opportunity to just drink her in while she was distracted doing . . . well, whatever it was she was trying to do with that pillow.

A few years ago he'd started watching reruns of that show *The Closer* because a teammate once commented how Gracie resembled the main actress with her long blonde hair and sass. No offense to Kyra Sedgwick, but Noah would choose Gracie any day of the week—even now, with all the sweating and crazed muttering.

"Sure you don't want help with that pillow?"

She blew a sweaty strand of hair out of her face and flopped back against the couch, having apparently given up on adjusting the pillow more than half an inch. "What I want is for you to tell me the real reason you're here. What do you want from me? You lose all your million bajillion baseball dollars in a bad investment or something? Because I've got news for you. You're not going to find any extra cash lying around here. Not with the medical bills Dad and I have been racking up lately."

She clutched her ribs and squeezed her eyes shut. "Pretty sure I'll be adding funeral expenses here in a minute."

Noah lowered the footrest and grabbed her hand before she had time to toss out another *Don't!* "Hey, listen to me. If you need money—"

She yanked free. "I don't. Not from you. Unless we're talking about the rent. I do need that. But no. Not even that. What I need is for you to . . ." For the first time, her hazel eyes met his. And held. And he was reminded of the first time they met. When he'd slammed the locker shut his first day of starting a new high school, and a girl with a giant ponytail and an armload of books appeared next to him.

"You're new" is what she'd said back then.

"Go away" is what she said now. But she was looking at him with the same pair of eyes. Eyes that always contained a mixture of green, gold, and brown. But more importantly—interest.

Of course, mixed in with those swirls of interest, her eyes had always contained plenty of stubborn too.

The clock above the mantel ticked off several seconds as they stared each other down, waiting for the other to blink first. Well, guess what. It wasn't going to be him.

"Hate to break it to you, babe, but you're not getting rid of me. Not this time. I'm back and I'm staying. For as long as it takes. I'm not leaving until we figure things out."

Then before she could stop him, he leaned forward and adjusted the pillow further behind her shoulders because good grief, nobody's neck should be at an angle like that.

He no sooner had the pillow positioned than she flung it to the floor.

"We're divorced. We're long past the point of figuring things out. Besides, we both know your 'as long as it takes' only means until next season rolls around. Now grab me a tissue—and don't call me *babe*."

Until next season rolls around? Did she really not get it? Noah grabbed the pillow from the floor and propped her feet on it, then grabbed a tissue from a Kleenex box on the trunk and handed it to her. "Gracie, I'm done. For good. My arm finally hit its expiration date. I was lucky to last as long as I did."

Gracie dabbed her forehead. "Please. How many times have I heard you tell me you were done pitching? You never meant it before. You sure don't mean it now."

"Have you forgotten how old I am? I'm ancient."

"Have you forgotten I'm older than you? Watch your mouth."

"You know I'm talking baseball years. I'm the Crypt Keeper."

"So? That still doesn't mean you're done with baseball. You can be a coach, a manager, a hot dog vendor, *something*. Mark my words, you're not done. You'll never be done. So stop pretending this time is different, and leave. We both know it's coming."

Gracie fisted her sweaty tissue in a white-knuckled grip. "Besides, I imagine you'd rather go hang out with that little Joanna Gaines–wannabe girlfriend of yours instead of playing nursemaid to me. Pippy? Peppy? She's cute, whatever her name is. Of course, everyone's cute when they're twenty. Or is she over the legal drinking age by now?"

"If you're going to keep tabs on my social life, you might want to try a little harder at getting it right. Her name is Piper Green. And I have no idea how old she is because she's obviously not my girlfriend. You should know better than anyone that I would never even consider dating a woman who is—"

"Half your age?"

"I was going to say a Mets fan, but yeah, that too." Noah smirked at Gracie's attempt to bean him with her wadded-up tissue. He retrieved it from the floor and tossed it on the trunk. "You know there's never been anyone but you. Ever. And if you don't know that, then you at least ought to know you can't believe everything you see online."

"I know you two looked awful cozy in that picture I saw from whatever hospital fundraiser you attended last winter. I believe that."

"And what exactly were we doing in this picture? Standing next to each other and talking? Because if that's your idea of cozy, then you must've been really jealous all those times my catcher ran out to talk to me on the mound. Did you think Rooster and I were whispering sweet nothings to each other behind our gloves?"

"Wouldn't put it past you." Gracie tugged at the blue-and-gray quilt hanging over the back of the couch. "Look, this has been a real slice of heaven catching up with you and all, but it's time for you to go. For real. Forget whatever Matt told you, because I don't need you here. After a quick catnap, I'm going to work on my manuscript the rest of the day. I'm on a super-tight deadline and the last thing I need is any distractions, so . . ." She motioned him to shoo.

"Uh-huh. Back to the issue of the bathroom. Not sure we figured that one out yet. Whenever you need to go, you'll . . . pee on the couch?"

"It's a very absorbent fabric. Look, seriously, Mona will be back any minute to check on me. You're dismissed. Get back to the cottage. Better yet, get back to your precious baseball. Get back to your precious charity events. Get back to your precious *whatever*. Just. Go."

She spent the next two minutes trying to spread the afghan over her body without actually moving because any sort of movement clearly sent her into a breathless, sweaty tangle of pain. He had half a mind to let her struggle the rest of the afternoon. Would serve her right.

But then again, struggling the past five years since their divorce sure hadn't done him any good, had it?

He reached for his shoulder. Massaged the tightness. Times like this he wished he were a writer. Maybe then he could find the right words to get through to her. He sure hadn't found them five years ago. What made him think he could find them today?

"What's wrong with you?" Gracie's breathless voice cut into his thoughts. "What are you doing?"

Noah glanced down, then back to Gracie. "Standing here, massaging my shoulder? What's it looking like I'm doing?"

"You looked like you were about to cry."

"You know I don't cry."

"Oh trust me, I know your heart of stone better than anyone. Which is why I can't believe you were about to cry."

He knew what she was doing. And it wasn't going to work. Noah whipped his baseball cap onto the trunk, then marched to the door, calling over his shoulder. "Try picking a fight all you want, babe, but I'm not going anywhere."

Noah slammed the door shut behind him. Then swung it open again. "Except to the cabin to grab my phone."

"For the last time, don't call me *babe*, and hey—hey!"

"What?" He opened the door again.

"It's a cottage. And fix that porch railing while you're out there."

"Oh, I'll fix it all right." Easier than fixing their marriage—especially when he yelled, "Babe!" right before he slammed the door shut again.

4

Gracie woke up with drool crusting her chin. *Ugh.* How long had she been asleep with her head jammed in the corner of the couch? She used the collar of her shirt to scrub off her chin. Then froze. Why was Elvis Presley singing in her kitchen?

Another voice joined in with Elvis.

"Argh," Gracie groaned, sounding half-pirate. No wonder her brain felt muddled. Her ex-husband was here, singing off-key to "Don't Be Cruel"—and making some sort of stir-fry if her nose was to be trusted.

"Need more pain medicine?"

"Huh?" Gracie gingerly rolled her head to stretch her neck, stopping when her gaze landed on Noah standing between the kitchen and living room, a white dish towel draped over one of his shoulders. Goodness, she'd forgotten how much space Noah could fill with those shoulders. Her gaze drifted down to his white shirtsleeves stretched taut over his muscular biceps.

She covered her eyes and massaged her forehead. Not muscular. Average. Completely average. Well, Major-League-pitcher average. Some might place that in the category of muscular.

"Gracie?"

She spread her fingers to peek at him and his average-Major-League-pitcher-muscular biceps. "What? No. I don't take pain medicine. Makes me feel terrible. Makes me feel—" *Like this.* "Wait. *More* pain medicine? Did you give me pain medicine?"

He scratched the side of his overgrown beard. Seriously, someone get the man a razor. She'd always hated how he let his beard grow out like that every baseball season, all unruly and gnarly by the time October arrived. Though it did always sort of fascinate her to see how light and tawny his beard looked compared to the much darker shade of brown in his hair. Looked like some gray was sneaking its way into both.

He stopped scratching his beard long enough to hike a thumb over his shoulder. "I found a prescription bottle for pain meds in your patient belongings bag. You were kind of whimpering and your face was all scrunched up, so I figured it would help. You know I can't stand seeing you in pain."

"I've been sleeping the past"—she glanced beyond him to the clock on the kitchen wall—"five hours."

She did a double take. *Five hours?* She let out another groan, this time one hundred percent pirate. So much for a quick catnap.

"Here." He took the pillow out from beneath her feet and shoved it behind her shoulders.

"Oh, would you knock it off with the pillow already? How did you even give me those pills?"

He shrugged. "I crushed them up and mixed them with water, then used an eyedropper syringe-looking thing I found in the bathroom cabinet to pour it drop by drop into your mouth. What?" He adjusted the dish towel back over his shoulder. "That's what nurses do."

"That's what psychotic killers do." Gracie grabbed her forehead. No wonder she felt groggy. "I need some water. *Narcotic-free water.* I see now I need to specify."

The front door burst open and slammed shut.

"Sorry it took me so long to get back." Mona kicked off her high heels, talking a mile a minute into her purse. "I take it Matt got you inside okay. You need anything? Water? Tea? Sandwich?" Her nose crinkled. "Did someone drop off Chinese?"

When Mona finally looked up, her red lips froze in a circle as her eyes swiveled back and forth between Noah and Gracie, finally landing on Gracie. "What is he doing here?"

"Nice to see you too, Mona," Noah said in a low, sexy drawl.

Sexy? *No.* Gracie clutched the sides of her head tighter. See? This was exactly why she didn't take pain medicine. Not only did it affect her ability to operate heavy machinery, it clearly affected her ability to think rational thoughts around her husband.

Ex-husband!

How was she supposed to fix the ending of her story in this condition?

Mona stomped to the couch, her rosemary scent arriving a beat before she did. "Is this why you won't get serious with Luke? Because you've been planning to let this *buster* move back in with you?"

"Hey. Someone needs to take care of her," Noah said. "Who's Luke?"

"He's not moving back in with me. I can take care of myself."

"Well, listen here, little missy." Mona blinked rapidly, which she tended to do when she was flustered. Along with using terms like *buster* and *little missy*. "You can't take care of yourself, not really. But obviously we have things under control here, so as for you, *Jack*"— She blinked and pointed a finger at Noah—"you can hit the road."

"Right. You have things so under control you would have left her alone to die if it hadn't been for me," Noah said. "Who's Luke?"

"You would've left her alone to die five years ago if it hadn't been for me," Mona shot back.

"Nobody's dying here. Would you both knock it off?" Gracie shifted on the couch and winced. Before she could stop them, both Mona and Noah were in front of her, attacking the pillow and clawing her hair.

"You need that pillow adjusted?" Noah asked.

"Is your hair caught on your shirt?" Mona's talons snagged several long strands.

"Stop. *Stop.*" The pain medicine was not only making Gracie fuzzy, it was making her sick to her stomach.

"See?" Mona took over fluffing the pillow behind Gracie's back with enough vigor to bruise another rib. "She wants you to leave."

Now Noah's hands were on the pillow, whacking and tugging. "No. She said she wants you to stop."

"I want both of you to stop. Good grief, I'd be better off with Kathy Bates's character straight out of the movie *Misery* taking care of me instead of you two." Gracie fanned her face. "I don't feel so good."

"What do you need?" Mona and Noah spoke at the same time, jockeying in front of her for positioning. At least they'd stopped playing tug-of-war with the pillow. "Water? Ice? Fan? Water?"

"You already said *water*." Mona elbowed Noah's side.

"I know I already said *water*." He elbowed her elbow.

The two of them elbowed each other, arguing back and forth about what had been said and not said.

"Can one of you just grab me a trash can before I puke?" Gracie interrupted.

Noah spun in circles. "Trash can . . . trash can . . ."

"Are you sure you don't need to have a bowel movement?"

"Mona, you did not just ask me that."

"Why not? The nurses were always asking you that."

"Here." Noah raced back from the kitchen. He shoved a brown paper grocery sack into her face.

It must be the one she kept under the sink for trash. Gracie pushed it away. "*Ugh*, that smells awful."

"What do you mean?" Mona yanked it from Noah's hands and sniffed. "Smells like tuna. I brought some cans with me the other day to make a tuna salad sandwich while I was waiting to meet a client. You don't like tuna salad? Because I left a bowl of it in your fridge."

"She hates tuna salad," Noah said, grabbing back the sack and crumpling it shut. "How did you not know that?"

Gracie was kind of wondering the same thing.

"I did know that," Mona snapped. "I just figured it was a phase she would have grown out of by now."

Noah grunted and tossed the closed sack into the kitchen. "Maybe you need some more pain medicine. I read somewhere that too much uncontrolled pain can make you nauseous."

"More pain medicine? *More?*" Now Mona grunted. "Well, no wonder she's nauseous. She's never been able to keep pain medicine down. How did you not know that?"

"Maybe she never needed pain medicine when we were married," Noah responded. "Did you ever think of that?"

"Or maybe you were just never around enough to see all the times she was in pain. Did you ever think of that?"

"Or maybe—"

"Enough. You want to know what's causing me pain right now? You two. Acting like children." Gracie warned them both off with each of her hands in the shape of a gun. "If one of you even thinks about fluffing this pillow again, there will be blood. Now leave. Both of you."

"What about dinner?" Noah said.

"What about your bowels?" Mona said.

"Get out!"

Noah and Mona glared at each other. "Well," Mona said, waving Noah toward the door. "You heard her. After you."

"Please. Ladies first. After you."

"Oh, but I insist."

"I insist more."

"I insist you stop insisting."

Noah and Mona elbowed each other all the way to the door, both squeezing out at the same time due to their equal amounts of insistence. When the door finally slammed shut on their bickering, Gracie sank against the pillow in peace.

Well, in peace except for the terrible realization that supper was burning and she needed to go to the bathroom.

5

Why did hospitals always have to smell like pureed meatloaf slathered in sanitizer? Matt stepped off the elevator behind one of the hospital kitchen workers pushing a food cart and wrinkled his nose. No wonder his grandpa never had an appetite.

The wheels of the cart rumbled down the hallway the same direction Matt headed—the long-term care floor where his grandpa resided.

Matt hated that they hadn't been able to find Buck a better location after his physical therapy ended and insurance stopped paying for the inpatient rehab facility. At least somewhere outside the walls of a hospital.

But between Buck's continued weakening state, worsening COPD, and ongoing dialysis sessions three days a week, Mom and Aunt Gracie's choices had been limited when it came to finding him a place that could provide him with the level of care he needed without taking him too far from home.

So Haviland-Harrison Hospital it was. The building wasn't much to look at, but the hospital had been plugging away for more than a century on the outskirts of Alda, providing healthcare to all the surrounding communities in their rural area.

Not exactly the homiest of places for Buck to spend his final days. But it was the best option they had. The only option they had.

Sort of like when Matt called Noah the other day.

So maybe that wasn't the smartest move, going behind Aunt Gracie's back like that, offering her rental to Noah. But somebody had to do *something*. And not just in regard to helping Aunt Gracie get back on her feet. Something about Gracie and Noah's crumbled marriage. Matt wasn't sure what had happened between them, but he'd never stopped believing that they belonged together.

The way Matt saw it, there were only two ways this forced reunion of theirs could end—a passionate reconciliation that led to the renewal of their vows . . . or a double homicide.

Matt prayed for reconciliation.

Matt slipped into his grandpa's room, stepping past his grandpa's roommate, Shorty, with a wave before he caught himself. "Sorry," he said, then wanted to smack himself. Shorty was blind. He felt doubly stupid for waving, then apologizing.

Shorty grinned and waved back—somehow aware Matt did this every time he visited—before adjusting his radio, which was always on sports, whether it be high school, college, or professional. This evening it sounded like the local high school football game.

"You don't need to turn it down," Matt said.

Shorty shrugged and offered his typical response. "Nothing too exciting happening right now anyway." Shorty sat on the side of the bed with his hands clasped in his lap, dressed in a pair of clean but worn blue jeans, the left pant leg rolled up to accommodate his below-the-knee amputation. The blue-and-gray plaid button-up shirt looked big on his slender frame.

"Matt, that you?" Buck's groggy voice carried past the plastic curtain separating the two beds. He must've just woken up from a nap. "You're just in time to finish my sponge bath."

Shorty shook his head. "You need some new jokes, old man."

"Who you calling old, Shorty?"

"Who you calling short, Oldie?"

"Break it up, you two," Matt said, pointing a finger at each of them as he pushed back the curtain all the way to the wall, "before I call Nurse Ratched in here."

Both men pretended to shiver. "No need to get all nasty," Shorty murmured.

"The only nurse I know who gives a sponge bath without wetting the sponge," Buck said with another dramatic shiver.

The old-school nurse who never came to work without her white-skirted uniform, white hose, and white shoes was one of their favorite topics of conversation. Mostly because each of them knew beneath all that starch and antiseptic, the woman had a heart of gold. Maybe. Matt hadn't actually witnessed it yet.

"Hello, boys." And here she stood now. Both his grandpa and Shorty turned rigid. Matt straightened like a soldier at attention.

"Matthew," her cold voice sliced through the room.

"Nurse Ratch—uh . . .Wanda. Nurse Wanda. Just Wanda. Not Nurse Wanda. I don't know why I said Nurse Wanda even though you are a nurse so why not say Nurse Wanda?"

"Nobody calls me Nurse Wanda."

"And neither will I."

Wearing her white uniform that fell beneath her knees and shoes that squeaked with each step, Wanda clutched her ever-present clipboard against her chest and glared through her narrow spectacles. "I trust you boys are all behaving yourselves."

"Yes, ma'am," all three replied in unison.

"Shorty, did you remember to drink your prune juice this evening? We all know what happens when you forget to drink your prune juice."

Shorty fumbled with the tray next to his bed and rattled an empty juice can back and forth. "All of it."

Wanda nodded once. The scent of rubbing alcohol wafted off her as she stepped past Matt. He wondered if she dabbed it behind her ears like perfume every morning.

"And you, Buck?"

Buck smiled like a student trying to please his teacher. "I finished my prune juice first thing this morning, ma'am."

Her left brow slanted upward. "And you?"

It took Matt a moment to realize she was talking to him. He pointed at his chest. "Me? Drink prune juice?"

She hit him with a frosty glare, waiting for some sort of response. "I uh . . . no. I mean, I don't need . . . Do I? I don't think I do. Maybe I do? I mean, sure. I guess I could drink some."

Her lips twitched, her frosty glare thawing, the same moment Buck and Shorty burst into laughter. Matt's face flushed with heat. "Okay. I see what's going on here. Wow. Funny. You guys are a bunch of Jerry Seinfelds, aren't you?"

The smile on Wanda's face transitioned all the hard angles out of it. "We have to have some sort of fun, don't we, boys?" She winked and left the room with a promise to check back in an hour.

When all the chuckles had died down, Buck told Matt to take a seat. As expected, he asked about Gracie. Even though Gracie called Buck every day and assured him she was healing and would be back to visiting soon, Buck wanted a full scouting report on her reaction to Noah's arrival.

When Matt told Buck yesterday that Noah was moving into the rental on Gracie's property, Buck had gone into such a coughing fit, Matt thought for a moment he'd killed him with the news. Turns out, he was just laughing. "So how did it go? Did she look happy at all to see him?"

"Happy? Uh, well . . ." Matt tugged on the brim of his baseball hat. "You know, I think maybe beneath all the sweat and anguish, there was a glimmer of happiness, yeah."

"And you?" Buck asked when they'd finished talking about Gracie and Noah. "What's going on with you?"

"Oh, you know. Not much now that mowing season's over. Doing some odd jobs here and there. Volunteering at the animal shelter. Just trying to stay busy until snow removal season kicks in."

"Uh-huh. And what about your love life?"

Matt almost wished for a mouthful of prune juice right now so he could spray it all over his grandpa for asking such a silly question. Would've been more fun than merely raising his eyebrows and saying, "Excuse me?"

"Have to say I was mighty surprised when Mona let the cat out of the bag that you were engaged. The girl only moved back to town, what? A week or two ago?"

"I keep telling Mom we're not . . . Wait. Moved back to town? What are you talking about? *Who* are you talking about?" Matt removed the worn baseball cap Noah had given him in high school, rotating the brim of it around in his hands. Surely he wasn't talking about—

"Rachel. Who else?"

Matt jumped to his feet. Too bad there was nowhere to move in a tiny patient room with two beds. So he sat back down. "Rachel? Rachel's not . . . Why would you think . . . She doesn't live . . . No. Is she?" Matt cleared his throat. "Are you saying Rachel's back in town?"

Buck was coughing and laughing and coughing some more, clearly amused at Matt's rambling.

Was it too late to find that can of prune juice?

Buck finally settled down enough after several more coughing laughs to say, "She took some sort of temporary position upstairs on the dialysis unit since half of the department is out on maternity leave. Who'd you think I was talking about?"

"Aimee."

"Aimee." This time his laugh was more wheeze than cough. "Why would I be talking about Aimee? I thought you broke up with Aimee."

"I did break up with Aimee."

"Then why are we talking about Aimee?" Buck made a face like he'd just bitten into that pureed meatloaf slathered in sanitizer. "Good night, I saw more spark between a dead fish and a limp worm than I ever saw between you and *Aimee*."

"Aw c'mon, that's not true. Aimee's a sweet girl. Besides . . ." Matt stood, really wishing he could do more than march in place to burn off some energy. He sat back down. "Sometimes too much spark can lead to an explosion. Look at Noah and Aunt Gracie. Sometimes it's smarter to date a dead fish. Not that Aimee was a dead fish. Or I'm a limp worm. That's not—" He shoved his hat on his head. "Just because Aimee and I broke up doesn't mean something's going to happen between me and Rachel."

"Really? As I recall, you two used to be awful chummy. Some might even say . . . *sparky.*"

Time to go. Matt stood. "You got it all wrong, old man. I mean yeah, we were friends. Good friends." Some might even say best friends. "But not sparky. Nowhere even close to sparky. And that was a long time ago. That was, you know, back in high school."

"Ah. Well then. Practically a lifetime ago," Buck said. "What's it been? Three, four years?"

"Closer to five."

"Oh my. Who can even remember that far back?" Shorty said with a chuckle.

Matt tugged on his hat, forcing a tight smile. "Not me, that's for sure." Especially when it came to one of his biggest regrets.

6

Gracie clutched her knees together beneath her robe and stared at the buttery rays of morning sunlight melting onto the living room floor as she mentally calculated the number of steps to the bathroom. Fifteen. Twenty, tops. "Pick up, Mona. Pick up."

The walking wasn't actually too bad. She could almost nearly completely handle that part somewhat entirely independently on her own. Sort of.

But the whole transitioning from a sitting position to a standing position and vice versa? Gracie couldn't even attempt to come up with enough adverbs to fool herself about accomplishing that feat on her own. She needed help. Lots of help.

Which is why she really needed her sister to pick up the phone.

"Oh, thank goodness," Gracie said, starting to rock back and forth by the time Mona answered. "My bladder is two minutes away from bursting, so please tell me you're less than two minutes away from the house. Otherwise there's going to be a serious crisis situation involving my favorite undies."

"Final boarding all passengers. Final boarding all passengers."

"What was that?" Gracie pressed the phone hard against her ear. Her sister, not one to ever be at a loss for words, breathed into the phone like a woman at a loss for words.

"Mona, say something."

"I'm not sure what to say. Other than I'll be back sometime by the end of next week, and I really hope you get that undie crisis resolved by then."

"What? You didn't cancel your flight? You're still going to that conference? I'm your sister. How can you leave me like this? I'm completely helpless." Something she would never admit to anyone but Mona.

"You're not completely helpless. Matt promised to stop by. Noah's right next door. That FedEx lady that dropped off a package last week will probably be around again at some point too."

"And none of them need to be pulling down my underwear and helping me sit on the toilet."

"Gracie, listen. I know you don't want to hear it, but this is exactly why I tried telling you to go into that rehab facility. The workers there love helping people pull down their underwear to sit on toilets."

"I don't need a rehab facility. I need my sister."

"And I need this conversation to end. People are giving me strange looks. Grab some scissors and cut them off. I'll be back in a few days. Love you."

"Love you too. But for the record, I'm only saying that in case your plane crashes. I'm actually really mad at you."

"Duly noted." Mona gasped. "Oh, I know. Call the boys at the firehouse. I'm sure they'd—"

Gracie ended the call. She lifted her gaze to the ceiling, the pressure in her bladder filling. *Gah.* Was she seriously thinking about asking Noah to help her?

No. Absolutely not. Not when she'd decided her only means of survival around that man was to play the role of an ice queen.

And everybody knew the golden rule of playing an ice queen. Thou shall not let thy ex-husband anywhere near thine underwear even if a small part of thee still finds thou stupidly attractive. Or something like that.

The phone rang. Without looking, she tapped the screen. "Please tell me you changed your mind."

"Not completely, but I might soon."

Gracie gripped the edge of the couch. Not her sister. Simone. Her agent. "Did you get a chance to read my manuscript? I know it's a little rough and the ending needs some work."

"Oh, I read it all right."

Gracie held her breath, her nails digging into the soft fabric of the couch. *Please say it's better than you expected. Please say it's brilliant. Please say you love it. Please say anything but—*

"It's a disaster."

—that.

She glanced at the window and caught a glimpse of Noah stepping out of the cottage. Perfect. Get the timing just right and her agent could drop her the same moment she peed all over the floor in front of her ex-husband.

She started to take a steadying breath, then stopped when it hurt her ribs too much. She clutched her knees together, then realized that hurt too. Why did everything hurt? Including this conversation?

"Where do you see room for improvement?" Gracie asked as diplomatically as she could.

"Where do I see—?" Gracie heard her agent suck in a deep breath as a rapid *click-click-click* sounded in the background. Not a good sign. Gracie knew from first-hand experience that her agent squeezed the stapler on her desk like a stress relief ball whenever she was working hard to rein in her snark.

"Room for improvement. Okay, well, for starters, the first fifty pages are all about a woman shooting a horse and then justifying why she doesn't feel guilty for shooting the horse. We don't even meet the hero of the story until page ninety-eight, and by the end the only thing that would have made him a hero was if he shot your heroine. She isn't likable at all. Which I guess is why they don't end up together?"

"She's an independent woman. She's better off without him *or* the horse."

"Right. Well, I'm all for independence. But I'm also for humor and zing. Remember the conversation we had in the spring? Humor? Zing? Rom-com readers don't want cads and cadavers."

"Maybe it's time I branched out and tried something else."

The clicking stopped. "Gracie, once this project is over, you can branch out to whatever you want. Independently publish a collection of inspirational stories for geriatrics who love wearing matching pajama outfits with their cats if you want. I don't care. But in order to fulfill your *current* contract—the one I went to bat for you on, the one you've already received half of your advance payment for—you need to write what you promised your publishing house you would write. Which is romance. Humor. *Zing*. Something like the baseball series you wrote. The series that sold really well. Remember those stories?"

"Of course." Those were her only books people wanted to talk about. The books she'd love nothing more than to forget. "I'm trying, Simone."

"Try harder. Your editor wants to see the entire story in less than two weeks. We have to show her something better than dead horses and nonsensical soliloquies. Are you having writer's block or something? I thought you went to a dude ranch earlier this year for inspiration."

"I did. Back in the spring. The owner was rude, the accommodations were lousy, and the only horse I met kept trying to bite me. It was a complete waste of time. I suppose I might've been a little bitter when I came home and wrote the story."

"Gracie. I say this with all the love in my heart, really I do, but you've been bitter for years. And now your stories all stink. You really need to get over it, whatever the *it* is."

"I'm trying." Didn't Simone know she was trying? Why else would she have climbed up on that old, broken-down, coin-operated machine horse that had always sat outside the Alda grocery store for as long as Gracie could remember? Because she was *trying*, that's why.

Trying to be fun. Trying to be silly. Trying to get a photo so she could post it on social media and show that crotchety old rancher how she'd finally made it on top of a horse—*ha ha, look at how fun and silly I am, readers*—before the horse got carted away in the back of a pickup truck to a dumpster pile.

Sort of lost the amusement factor when her foot got caught in the tiny stirrup and she toppled over the side of the truck, bounced off a parked riding lawn mower, then slammed against the hard pavement.

A bunch of bruised ribs and a hairline fracture in her pelvis. That's what she got for *trying*.

Simone sighed into the phone. "I'll talk to your editor. See if I can push back the deadline another week. Think that will give you enough time to make the revisions?"

No. "Absolutely."

"Good. Now get back on that horse immediately. Not the biter in Texas. The one in your story. The one you absolutely can't kill. Got it? Oh, and hey, if you still need inspiration, there's a hilarious video going around right now of some lady falling off one of those mechanical toy horses from the back of a truck. I'll see if I can find it, so I can send it to you."

"No, no. That's quite all right. I'm plenty familiar with it."

"Isn't it a hoot?"

"Oh, it certainly made me hoot." And holler. And howl. Along with a whole manner of other sounds. So much for nobody capturing it on video. "Poor lady," Gracie murmured.

"I'm sure she's fine. Okay, enough of this. You need to get back to your story. Can't wait to see those revisions."

After the phone call ended, Gracie pressed a finger between her eyebrows where a sharp headache pierced her skull. That poor lady was a far cry from fine. What she'd give to hide under a blanket the rest of the day. The rest of the week.

With a short sigh, she dropped her hand from her headache to her sore ribs. She was just going to have to grit her teeth and write through the pain. No more wallowing. No more distractions. Only writing.

Which was why when Noah walked through the door she said, "Get me some scissors and don't ask any questions."

7

Matt tried going to sleep, but ever since his visit with Buck the other evening, he couldn't shut his mind off from one thought on repeat.

Rachel was back.

Rachel. His friend Rachel. Not his girlfriend Rachel. Nope. Because Matt had never worked up the courage to ask if she'd mind placing that one little word—*girl*—in front of their friendship.

Hey guys, this is Rachel. My girlfriend.

How many times had he dreamed of saying that? A hundred? A thousand? Didn't matter he never exactly figured out who he was saying that sentence to in a town where everybody already knew everybody.

But it was the same dream Matt fell asleep to throughout all of high school. Until the night of their senior prom. The night when everything had gone wrong, and Matt realized it was time to stop dreaming.

But now she was back. Maybe the dream wasn't dead. Maybe their friendship could finally develop into something more.

Or maybe he should cool his jets and make sure the *friend* aspect was still in play first, considering they hadn't spoken directly in five years other than texting the occasional GIF or meme to each other. Last thing he wanted to do was make a fool of himself the first time he saw her by assuming they could pick up right where they'd left off.

Somewhere in his thinking and dreaming, he must've finally fallen asleep. Because now a ringing sound was waking him up.

He snatched his phone from next to his pillow, praying it wasn't a call about his grandpa—the only reason he kept his phone so close to his head every night.

He squinted one eye open at the caller ID. Wombat? Why on earth would he be calling at quarter to one in the morning?

"Hello?" Matt answered.

"Hey, I'm out on Route 20. Rachel hit a deer on the curve. She's dead. You want the meat?"

Matt, only half awake before, sat straight up. "What?"

"You want the meat?"

"No." Obviously Matt wasn't asking about the meat. He was asking about—

"Okay, bye."

"Hey, no. Wombat?" Did Wombat seriously just hang up on him? Matt glared at the screen. He seriously just hung up on him. What was wrong with that guy?

Matt dialed Wombat back. No answer. He tried again. No answer. A text came through before Matt could tap the call button again. Can't take

Matt stared at the screen, trying to make sense of it. "Can't take? Can't take what?"

Another text pinged. *talk

"You can't talk, but you have time to correct your autocorrect words?" Matt muttered as he texted Wombat back. Is Rachel ok?

He waited for a response. Preferably something along the lines of a yep or thumbs-up emoji.

When nothing appeared after several seconds, not even three little dots to let him know Wombat was typing, he swung his legs over the side of the bed.

Surely Rachel was fine. Wombat had to have been talking about the deer. But why did he mention Route 20 on the curve? The curve everyone thought of as Dead Man's Curve because of its long history of fatalities. Who had died on that curve tonight?

Better have been Bambi.

Matt jumped from bed, reaching for the lamp on his bedside table. He needed light. And pants. He knocked over the lamp, so he moved on to the pants. Grabbed the first pair he tripped over next to his bed. Shoved on his running shoes. Snatched his truck keys from the kitchen table. Ran out the door.

At the edge of town, he realized he'd forgotten to put on a shirt. Twelve miles outside of town, he realized he'd forgotten to put on the pants. They were still clutched in his right hand against the steering wheel.

But apparently he'd also forgotten his plan to play it cool the first time he saw Rachel. Because another mile later, the moment he saw her standing on the side of the road and recognized her wild dark curls, he couldn't get out of his truck fast enough.

"Rachel!" he shouted, nearly forgetting to put his truck in park.

She shielded her eyes from the flashing yellow lights of Wombat's tow truck gathering her mangled car. "Matt?"

"You're alive." Matt slammed into her, wrapping both arms around her. "You're alive, I'm so glad you're alive."

"Thank you," she said, stumbling a step back to keep them both on their feet. "And I'm glad you're, um . . ." Her soft hands patted up and down the bare skin of his back. "Very scantily clad?"

"Yeah dude, where's your clothes?" Wombat sauntered over and gave a fleshy smack to Matt's shoulder.

"Where's my clothes? How about where's your phone?" Matt dropped his arms from Rachel, so he could punch Wombat's shoulder. "You can't just tell me Rachel's dead, then refuse to answer my calls."

"You told Matt I was dead?" Rachel punched Wombat's other shoulder.

"I said the deer was dead," Wombat said, smacking the back of his hands against Rachel's and Matt's arms.

"No, you said *She's dead.*" Matt punched Wombat again, this time with a lot more oomph as he relived the panic those two words had brought him.

"Well, she's a she, ain't she?" Wombat pointed to the shadowed form of a deer on the side of the road.

"So is *she*," Matt yelled, waving at Rachel before landing another punch on Wombat's upper arm.

"Hey," Wombat said, lifting his hands to block further punches. "Do you really want to get into a debate with me right now when you're the one standing out here in your underwear?"

"He makes a good point." Rachel's shoulders hunched as she dug her hands into the pockets of her puffy jacket. "You couldn't have taken five seconds to at least put on some pants?"

Matt hadn't noticed how cold the October night was until this moment. Or how naked he felt. Goose pimples rippled over his skin as he spun for his truck. "I thought you might be dead," he said over his shoulder. "So no. Forgive me for not taking five seconds to put on my pants."

He yanked his jeans from where he'd dropped them on the driver's seat, slammed the door shut, then began shoving one leg inside before realizing he still had his shoes on. This endeavor was obviously going to take longer than five seconds.

"Honestly, that's kind of sweet," Rachel said as he toed off one of his shoes.

"It is kind of sweet." Wombat, apparently immune to the cold in his short-sleeved T-shirt, looped his thumbs behind his suspenders. "Would you not put on pants for me if you thought I was dead?"

Matt threw his shoe at Wombat.

"I'll take that as a yes. Well, since you're so sweet, you mind giving Rachel a ride?" He handed Matt's shoe off to Rachel and motioned to his tow truck, the lights still flashing yellow. "I'll handle all this and get a hold of you later, okay?"

"Thanks, Wombat. Anybody mention you're kind of sweet too?" Rachel called after him as he walked away. He waved in reply.

"You know what would've been sweet?" Matt began hopping on

one foot as he attempted to get his other foot in the pants leg. "A five-second text to let me know you were moving back to town."

"I was going to text you. Eventually."

"When? After you were dead?"

"Immediately after. Promise."

"Well, I reckon that makes about as much sense as driving around Dead Man's Curve in the middle of the night. What were you doing out here? Are you crazy?"

"Says the man who still doesn't have his pants on."

"I'm working on it, okay?" Still hopping, Matt finally managed to jam both legs into his jeans. Jeez Louise, no wonder Aunt Gracie said she was giving up on wearing pants. He could hardly do it with two good legs and an intact pelvis.

Rachel handed back his shoe. "Look, I'm sorry. I seriously was going to text you. Things just . . . well, sort of fell apart in Florida. This whole coming back here happened kind of fast. Life's been a little crazy lately. I mean, obviously, it's settling down now," Rachel said, waving her hands at the smashed-in car now getting towed away by Wombat.

"What happened in Florida?"

He heard the fatigue in her sigh. "Nothing I want to get into tonight."

Fair enough. Matt worked his shoes back on and folded his arms over his chest, wishing again he'd brought a shirt. Or jacket. Maybe a parka. Now that the adrenaline had worn off, he was starting to shiver.

"I'm just glad you're okay." He'd find out what happened in Florida later. "Think your car will be salvageable?" he asked, hoping to distract her from the fact he was having his first face-to-face conversation with her in over five years completely shirtless after hopping around in a pair of Hello Kitty boxer shorts that he'd received as a gag gift last Christmas.

Hopefully she'd failed to notice that last bit in the dark.

"Hard to tell in the dark." Oh good. She hadn't noticed. Wait, no. She was talking about her car.

"To be honest," she continued, "the car wasn't in great shape to begin with. I'll probably need a new fender. New headlights. New windshield. New windshield wipers. New gas tank."

"Are you just naming car parts?" He breathed on his clasped hands, trying to warm them.

"New engine. New radio."

"Okay." Matt grabbed her by the elbow and guided her to the passenger's side door of his truck. "How about we continue this conversation somewhere a little warmer?"

"New seat belt. New coat hanger-hooky thing."

He opened the door for her. "If nothing else, I'm sure your insurance will cover the coat hanger-hooky thing."

She climbed into the seat. "But will it cover a rental car? Because otherwise I have no idea how I'm supposed to make it to my next shift."

"When is it?"

"Monday afternoon."

Matt lifted a finger, motioning they'd continue this conversation in a moment. He closed her door, then jogged around to the driver's side.

"I might just happen to know a guy who'd be willing to give you a lift to the hospital, considering he goes out that way every day anyway to visit his grandpa," Matt said as soon as he climbed in and started cranking up the heat.

"Yeah?" She tugged her seat belt into place. "Does this happen to be the same guy who runs around half naked at night in pink Hello Kitty underpants?"

Matt shot her a glance. "So you did notice that."

"I absolutely noticed that."

"Can we at least call them boxers and not underpants?"

"Because that somehow makes it more manly?"

"And possibly even admirable."

Rachel's laugh came out as a snort, and Matt couldn't hold back a grin. No doubt about it. His friend was back.

For now, a little voice whispered in the back of his mind. *She may pick up and leave as quickly as she did the last time.* Hadn't Buck mentioned something about her position only being temporary? And what exactly did she mean that things had fallen apart for her in Florida?

There was a lot about Rachel that Matt didn't know, including her plans for the future.

But for now, she was back.

And if he ever hoped to turn their friendship into something more, picking up right where they'd left off was the perfect place to start.

8

Noah's running shoes slapped against the pavement. He was going to stay in pretty good shape if Gracie kept ordering him out of the house every morning like she had the past three mornings.

Of course, he noticed she'd waited until after he assisted her from the couch to the bathroom—Saturday bringing her a pair of scissors that he wasn't supposed to ask any questions about—then assisted her from the bathroom back to the couch, fixed her breakfast, retrieved her laptop, and made sure it was plugged into the charger, before she ordered him out of the house because she was completely capable of taking care of herself, *thank you very much*.

At least she hadn't entirely given him the boot, thanks to Mona leaving town. He never did understand what Mona's job entailed, other than yelling at people over the phone about houses, but for some reason people thought she was good at it. Seemed like she was always traveling to conferences all over the country just to tell other Realtors how to yell at people over the phone about houses.

Dried cornstalks rustled next to the country road. Noah slowed his pace and tugged his earbuds out of his ears, not having heard a word of the podcast he'd been listening to on his smartphone. Some sort of true crime.

His fingers hovered over his phone screen, itching to check the latest baseball updates. But why torture himself? As much as he hoped his team made it all the way to the World Series, part of him couldn't help hoping they fell flat on their face without him. Not that any of his outings lately had exactly kept them on their feet.

He reached for his left shoulder, stretching and rotating his arm against an ache that had been bugging him since the start of the season. An ache he'd spent months trying to ignore. An ache he should have let heal. Which was no doubt why he found himself kicked off the roster instead of standing on the mound.

His phone rang with a FaceTime call, and Noah welcomed the distraction. He shoved his earbuds back in place and tapped the screen. Smiled. "Keeping my dog alive?"

His neighbor's son returned his greeting with a gap-toothed grin. "I don't know. What do you think?" Sammy climbed onto Cory's lap, his dark fur blocking the screen. Cory groaned and laughed. "Dude, your dog needs to go on a diet."

He certainly would after his time with Cory. Noah knew the old adage about a dog being man's best friend, and he would have loved to have brought Sammy with him, but he didn't have the heart to separate Sammy and Cory for too long. Cory's military dad had recently died overseas, and Cory had formed a strong attachment to Sammy from all the times he'd dog sat while Noah was on the road. "You're not feeding him too many snacks, are you?"

"Hey, Noah," Cory's mom popped her face down long enough to wave. "Don't think I didn't tell Cory to stop spoiling him with all those treats."

"Don't even, Mom. I caught you sharing your popcorn with him last night after you thought I went to bed." Cory shoved Sam's rear end out of his face and peered at the screen. "She did. I saw her. And two nights ago she picked him up a doggy cone from The Moo Shack."

"Stop sharing my secrets," his mom scolded, hitting her son with a dish towel.

Noah cracked his back side to side, smiling. "He's never going to want to come back to me." He noticed neither of them argued against that. Another FaceTime call flashed on Noah's screen. "Uh-oh. My agent's calling."

"Yeah, wanted to tell you he came by our house yesterday looking for you," Cory's mom said, crouching down again. "He rang the buzzer so long, I thought Sammy was going to bark himself silly."

Noah had been a little afraid of that. Scotty Jones might be great at his job, but sometimes he had a hard time accepting the word *no*. Probably why he was so great at his job. "All right, give Sammy a pat for me. I'll check in later. Thanks again."

Noah switched over to his agent's call.

"I think I've got the answer," Scotty said without any greeting. "Now, you're not going to like it. In fact, you're going to hate it. You're not going to even want to consider it."

"Sounds promising."

"Hey, where are you? Your neighbors said you left town." Scotty leaned closer to the screen. Noah could see the windows of his office behind him, as well as every one of his nose hairs. "Is that a scarecrow? Like a *Wizard of Oz* scarecrow?"

Noah twisted and held his phone up to give his agent a better view of the fall decor one of the neighbors a few miles down the road had propped up near the mailbox. "And those orange things are called pumpkins."

"I love it. This is the kind of stuff we need."

Noah turned the phone back to his face. "For what?"

"Your memoir. We've got to strike now while the iron is blazing."

Noah rolled his eyes and started walking back toward Gracie's house. "I already told you. I'm not doing—"

"No, no, no. Hear me out. Eventually you're going to like this. A buddy of mine in the publishing industry says memoirs are flying off the shelves right now. Especially memoirs about unsung heroes. Everyday people."

"So?"

"*So?* Your pitching career is over, right? Dead? Buried? Decomposing? Pushing up daisies?"

"Have we gotten to the part I'm supposed to like yet?"

"Don't you hear what I'm saying?"

"Unfortunately, every word."

"We need to get your memoir out there ASAP while you're a nobody, so we can remind everybody that you're a somebody. We need to remind them of that game."

Noah scraped his knuckles over his beard. He didn't need to ask which game his agent referred to. There was only one game when it came to Noah's baseball career. "Why does it matter?"

"*Why?* Because people love somebodies. They love heroes. They love legends. And you know what they do with those somebodies, heroes, and legends they love? They hire them to manage baseball teams."

"Sure. At the minor league level. You know how hard I worked to get out of the minors? No way I'm going back to that life. Forget it."

"No, no, no. Think about it. You've had a long run as a pitcher, longer than most. Yeah, as a whole, your career wasn't all that amazing. Most people won't remember it at all."

Noah grunted. "You ever moonlight as a motivational speaker? You're really inspiring."

"That's what I'm talking about."

"What on earth are you talking about?"

"You. That game. Inspiration. Listen to me. You pitched one of the most amazing games anyone could ever dream of. It's the stuff Disney movies are made of. A dying boy's last wish. A ho-hum, no-name pitcher."

"There you go, inflating my ego again."

"And a *perfect* game. Honestly, it was a miracle when you think about it. That's the type of story people love. The type of story that needs to get written. Because that's the exact type of story people are gobbling up right now."

Noah squinted up at the cloudless sky, shaking his head.

"I see you shaking your head, and I don't think you're following the vision here. Think about it, Noah. What else are you going to do the rest of your life? You're what? Thirty-eight? Thirty-nine?"

"Forty."

"Jeez Louise, I can't believe you're that old. But here's the thing. You're not that old. Get what I'm saying?"

"Please remind me why I ever let you handle my contracts."

"Because you love me. The same way you love baseball. We're both in your blood. Okay, I'm not. That's weird. But baseball is. And guys like you don't walk away from what you love."

The sweat from his run chilled against his skin. Hadn't Gracie said something along the same lines?

"Listen," Scotty continued, talking a mile a minute. "I know it sounds like I'm thinking about me. And I'll be honest, this all has a little to do with me because I like to eat expensive food off expensive tables. But really, this is about you. I've been in this business a long time. You've got longevity. Not just as a player. As a manager. Why? Because you're likable. Who doesn't like a likable guy?"

Must've been a rhetorical question. Scotty prattled on without missing a beat. "And listen, I know you don't want to get stuck managing a team in the minors forever. Nobody does. That's why we do this memoir. Get your story out there. Remind people how much they like you. You didn't hear it from me, but word on the street is Dusty may not be back for another season. You could be a strong contender, Noah. You could. Your teammates already love you. We just need to get the rest of the higher-ups to realize they love you too. A memoir could do that."

"I can't."

"Yes, you can. Listen—"

"I have. And I can't. What you're saying makes sense, kind of, but I can't do it. Not if I want to save my marriage. That game . . . No. I have to leave it in the past."

Because Noah had read sports memoirs before. It was never about the one game or the one season or even the one career. It was always about the life. And there were parts of Noah's life he wasn't sharing with anyone. Ever. Which was why he'd built a reputation for being tight-lipped during interviews, eventually not giving any at all.

Noah sniffed, the cold air starting to make his nose run. "Hey, I appreciate what you're trying to do, but—"

"I'm not accepting *no*. Think it over. We'll talk more later." His agent ended the call before Noah could say anything. Especially *no*.

Simone: How are the revisions coming? Did you make any headway this weekend?

Grace: Yep. Making headway. Really happy with the revisions I've made so far.

No need to tell Simone the entirety of those revisions was spent on tweaking the opening sentence all weekend long. But surely anyone would agree that Gracie's new first sentence—*Heather hated horses*—was far superior to her original first sentence—*Heather had never been all that fond of horses.*

The alliteration alone ought to hook readers.

Simone: Glad to hear it! Especially since you're not getting an extension on your deadline. Just heard back from your editor . . .

No extension. Okay. No need to panic. Gracie's got gumption. See? Look at that. Another alliteration. She was on top of her writing game.

Grace: Won't be a problem. Thanks for the update.

Simone: Go get 'em, Cowboy!

A GIF pinged through a second later. Gracie adjusted her reading glasses, but it didn't help. She still saw the same image of herself climbing onto the coin-operated horse in the back of a pickup truck and falling off the side a moment later. On repeat.

Thankfully the video was shot from behind, so nobody could see her face. But still. She was a GIF now. A GIF on a deadline. *Yee-haw.*

10

Monday afternoon Matt balanced a cardboard drink carrier in one hand as he reached for Rachel's doorbell with the other. If it could even be called a doorbell. More like a cracked fixture that promised electrocution.

Yeah, maybe not.

He opted to rap his knuckles on the door instead. A very gentle rap, since it looked like one solid pound could very well knock the warped door off its hinges.

"Rachel," he called out. Shoot, the sound of his voice alone might knock the door off its hinges.

He glanced toward the windows, searching for signs of life. Every curtain remained closed. Not that he would've been able to see any-thing past the condensation fogging up the panes.

"Wow, Rach," he muttered under his breath. "Lovely place you've got here."

His gaze wandered down to the gaping holes in the porch. The rotting floorboards. The uneven stairs.

Man. If he thought the house had looked run-down when he dropped her off late Saturday night—or early Sunday morning, rather—seeing it now in the full light of day made him half-tempted to call Wombat and ask him to tow it off to wherever he'd taken Rachel's mangled car.

What in the world had Rachel been thinking, moving into a dump like this? She mentioned getting it for a steal. Well, no wonder. Reminded him a little of how Aunt Gracie described her and Noah's house when they'd first moved in. Except without all the charm and potential.

Mindful of the holes in the rotting porch, Matt stepped down the stairs and set the drink carrier on the front hood of his truck. How long should he wait before he busted the door down to make sure she hadn't been murdered in her sleep? Because if ever there was a place a person got murdered in their sleep, this was it. On a lonely country lane that gave off vibes of *Deliverance*.

He glanced at his watch. Sent her a text. She *had* asked him for a ride to work this afternoon, right?

Since this time of year was his downtime in between mowing season and snow removal season, he'd assured her that he could chauffeur her around for the next few weeks or however long it took to fix her mangled-car situation. Surely he hadn't dreamed that entire conversation up.

He checked his watch again. All right. It'd been long enough. She wasn't answering his texts. Time to do something. But since he didn't actually want to bust down the door, he'd try the back.

After a quick tromp through tall overgrown grass that was definitely in need of his lawncare services, he found two cellar doors in the back. Two creepy-looking cellar doors. The kind that descended down to creepy basements with creepy skeletal remains chained to creepy walls.

His mom never should have let him watch so many horror movies growing up.

Yeah—no, thanks. He'd try a different door.

Climbing up the back porch stairs to the only other door available, he peeked in through a little window that must be above the kitchen sink. Because what he saw was an actually not too terribly creepy kitchen. A little glass mason jar of flowers sat on a small round table, proof that Rachel was at least trying to brighten up her decrepit little homestead.

He knocked on the door. "Rachel?" Tried turning the handle. "Rachel." Started pounding with his fist. "Rachel!"

Okay, really. She should've answered the door by now. Or texted him back. She didn't have a car. They were at least four miles outside of Alda. Not like she could've gone anywhere.

An uneasy feeling settled into his chest like that time he had pneumonia in middle school, making it hard to breathe. Had something happened to her? "Come on, Rachel, it's me—Matt. Answer the door!"

When he couldn't hear anything for several seconds other than the hollow plunk-plunk sound of her wind chimes, he gave in to the panic. Something was wrong. Way too quiet. Time to bust in.

He shouldered the door with all his might. It splintered. He rammed into it again. This time it cracked. Once more, and it snapped off the hinges.

After nearly falling onto the floor, he regained his balance and rushed through the kitchen, down the short hallway to the living room. Checked inside a small bathroom. Then headed up the staircase.

"Rachel!" he shouted, taking the stairs two at a time.

He rounded the top of the banister just as he heard a scream.

Which made him scream.

Rachel jumped out of a room, holding a baseball bat. They both screamed again.

It took Matt several seconds to realize nothing bad was happening, except maybe to their eardrums, as he and Rachel continued to stand at the top of the stairs, screaming.

Matt recovered first. "What is wrong with you?"

Rachel dropped the baseball bat and collapsed against the wall, clutching her heart. "Me? What is wrong with *you*?"

"I thought you were dead."

"What's with you always thinking I'm dead?"

"You didn't answer the door."

"I overslept."

"Overslept? Rachel—" Matt yanked his phone from his back pocket and held it right in front of her face. "Do you see what time it is?"

"Not when you hold it that close."

"It's the middle of the afternoon," he said, sliding the phone back into his pocket. "That's what time it is."

"I haven't been sleeping that well at night. I thought I'd take a little nap. Guess I fell asleep harder than I expected." She picked up the baseball bat from where it'd rolled next to Matt's feet.

"Guess you did. It's almost two-thirty. Don't you have to be to work by quarter to three?" The hospital was on the other side of Alda.

She must've done the math. Her eyes widened. She spun away from him, only to spin back and give another jab with the bat. "Did you break my kitchen door? I heard lots of noise."

"Just get dressed." *Please.* She was wearing tiny little gray draw-string sweat shorts and a form-fitting pink tank top. He was fairly certain that wasn't Florence Nightingale-approved nursing wear. Plus, he didn't know how much longer he could keep his gaze focused above her neck. The sooner she got dressed, the better for both of them.

"I'll wait for you downstairs. And yes, I completely demolished your kitchen door. Sorry about that. Get dressed," he said again when it looked like she was going to start arguing about the kitchen door.

The wooden floorboards groaned beneath his weight with each step he took down the stairs. "Overslept," he muttered.

"I heard that."

"You hear that, but you don't hear me pounding down the door and screaming your name," Matt muttered as he entered the kitchen and set about fixing the door.

"Yes," she called down to him.

He lowered his voice to a whisper. "What about this? You hear this? Yeah, didn't think so."

"Are you still saying something?"

"Just get dressed," he shouted.

After getting her door back on the hinges best he could—he'd swing back and fix it better later—he retrieved their coffees from the hood of his truck and returned to the kitchen.

Her creaky steps bounded down the stairs. "Kind of grumpy early in the afternoon, aren't you? Ready to go?" Rachel entered the kitchen in a pair of dark blue scrub pants and a white sweatshirt with a pink stethoscope in the shape of a heart on the front. Her gaze dropped to the coffee he was holding as she tightened her mass of dark curls in a ponytail.

"For me? Thanks." She grabbed it before he had time to respond and took a sip. "Ooh." She wrinkled her nose. "I take mine with extra sugar for future reference."

"And I don't typically share mine for future reference." Matt took the cup back from her hand and switched it out with the other cup in the carrier.

"Oh. Sorry." She giggle-snorted. Between that and her ponytail, she was just as adorable as she'd always been in high school. And apparently just as scatterbrained. Because when he asked if she was ready, she merely took a sip of her coffee and said, "For what?"

"*Work.*"

"Ah! Why haven't we left yet?" She started opening cupboard doors and banging them shut.

"What are you doing?"

"Getting more sugar for my coffee. They never put in enough. This'll only take a second." Another bang. "Where'd I put the sugar?"

"Rachel, we don't have time for more sugar."

"There's always time for more sugar. Here it is." She tugged a bag of sugar from the cupboard. A giant hole on the bottom corner leaked granules all over the counter.

"Now why is there a—" Her scream erupted the same moment Matt saw it.

Brown fur. Long whiskers. Pink tail. Rachel continued screaming as the mouse dashed from the sugar bag across the counter and onto the floor. Then it ran into the living room and disappeared through a sliver of space in the wall. But apparently that wasn't far enough away for Rachel. She had swung herself up onto Matt's back, circling her hands around his neck in a death grip.

"Rachel." Matt tapped her hands. "Can't really breathe when you grip my throat like that."

"Sorry." Her hands loosened and dropped to his shoulders. "I hate mice. Really hate mice. Hate 'em, hate 'em, hate 'em. Did you see that tail? I'm never sleeping again. All I'm going to see is that tail every time I close my eyes. Oh, I hate mice. Why aren't all mice dead? God never should've created such detestable little beings."

Matt didn't know where to put his hands while Rachel continued to rant over the inhumanity of mice. On her legs? They were completely wrapped around his waist. Pretty sure that made them fair game. He reached for his coffee. That seemed the safest place to direct his hands at the moment. "Think you're ready to get down now?"

"You kidding? I'm never setting foot on this floor again."

Matt nodded. "Reasonable. I mean, you bought a creepy, foreclosed house in the country. One that probably sat abandoned for months before you moved in. Why would you expect for a mouse to show up? That mouse should have known better."

Her hands moved back to his throat. "Keep up the jokes, pal. Not like I had a lot of options with a bank account of zero. Now get moving."

"When I said I'd give you a lift to the hospital, this really wasn't what I had in mind."

Her grip tightened.

"You do realize if you make me pass out, you'll be on the floor with the mouse."

Her hands dropped to his shoulders. "Don't even joke about such horror."

Matt downed another gulp of coffee and stopped worrying about what to do with his hands since she clearly had no inhibitions about plastering herself to his back. Grabbing beneath her thighs, he hoisted her further up his back for better leverage. "Got everything you need?"

"Can you put it in reverse a little?"

He took a step back. Rachel leaned down enough to grab a bag and stethoscope off the kitchen table. "Now I'm ready."

Matt shook his head. "You're lucky my grandpa likes you."

"How lucky?"

"Lucky enough I'll fix your door. Not lucky enough that I'm carrying you all the way to my truck."

"What about lucky enough to set two thousand mousetraps and get rid of all the dirty carcasses for me?"

"Depends."

"On what?" She hopped down from his back after they stepped out of the house.

"I get it that you don't like mice, but . . ." He touched her lower back and guided her to his truck. "How do you feel about cats and dogs? Because I know for a fact the animal shelter could always use some extra hands."

And maybe while they were volunteering together, she could tell him what happened in Florida and why her bank account was sitting at zero.

11

Scotty: Hey buddy! Given any more thought to doing the memoir?

Noah: I'm not doing the memoir.

Scotty: Still thinking it over? No problem.

Noah: I'm NEVER doing the memoir.

Scotty: Okay. Glad you're at least considering it. We'll talk more later.

12

Tuesday morning Gracie opened the bathroom door, feeling way too overtaxed for a woman who'd done nothing more than simply pee in a toilet on her own. Oh, the things she'd always taken for granted.

"Wow, this lady really hates that horse, doesn't she?"

One of those things she'd taken for granted was never living next door to her husband.

Ex-husband!

She cinched her robe tighter around her waist. "What are you doing here? You can't just pop in and out of the house all willy-nilly."

Noah stood in the hallway, one shoulder casually pressed against the wall, as he licked his finger and flipped a page in the pile of papers he was holding. "I can if I'm fixing breakfast so you don't starve to death."

The scent of maple syrup and bacon wafting from the kitchen punctuated his words and made her stomach growl. He must've heard, because one of his brows lifted.

"Fine. Maybe a quick breakfast. Hey, is that my story?" She peered closer at the papers.

"You tell me." He scratched his gnarled beard. "I thought your story was supposed to be a romance."

"It *is* a romance." Or it would be. Once she fixed everything.

"Between who? The lady and the horse? Because I actually

wouldn't mind seeing them reach some sort of happy reconciliation by the end. Not so sure about the guy."

Well, Gracie wasn't so sure she was going to make it another step if Noah didn't offer her any help soon. "Noah," she bit out.

"Huh? Oh." The papers flopped to the ground as he angled in front of her, offering both of his forearms so she could grip them like a walker the remaining steps to the kitchen.

"I thought the physical therapist said I'd recover quickly," Gracie said once they finally made it to the kitchen table.

"Considering you've only been home a few days and you're already using the bathroom on your own, I'd say you're recovering at lightning speed. More than I can say for the horse. Did she really have to shoot him?"

"It was an accident. He'll be fine. Everyone needs to stop worrying about that evil horse already." Noah helped lower her onto the kitchen chair, then retrieved the pile of papers off the hallway floor and straightened them into a tidy stack on the table.

"Hey, your dad tried calling while you were in the bathroom. Hope you don't mind I answered."

"Is he okay? Do I need to go see him?"

"Buck's fine. He specifically said you shouldn't visit him, that you should focus on getting stronger and finishing your story first."

"Oh, Dad." They talked all the time, so he knew more than anyone how hard Gracie had been struggling to write this story. How hard she'd been struggling in general.

She'd give him a call later this afternoon. Hopefully she could catch him between his dialysis session and his late afternoon nap.

Gracie ran her finger over the pile of papers that contained her mess of a story as Noah started grabbing plates from the cupboard. "Where did you even get a copy of this?"

"I printed it off last night from your computer after you fell asleep on the couch. Which reminds me, you're out of ink now." He opened the fridge and pulled out a carton of orange juice.

"Why?"

"Pretty sure the ink cartridge was low to begin with."

"No. Why are you reading my story?"

"Figured you needed the help. Didn't you say you were on a tight deadline?"

"Yeah, but I've got it under control. Thank you," she added when he set a glass of orange juice next to her plate.

He scratched the briar patch growing all over his jawline, making an *mmm* sound. She knew that sound.

"What? I *do* have it under control. This isn't even the right draft." She motioned to the stack. "This is from a much earlier draft." Like from a whole twenty-four hours ago. "I've made a lot of revisions since then." In her mind. Not exactly on paper. "The story is taking on a whole new shape now." A big sort of blobby shape.

He leaned against the counter, continuing to run his knuckles over his jaw, which Gracie knew from their years of marriage meant the same thing as his little *mmm* sound. "So you've fixed that whole scene in the middle then?"

"Of course. Probably. What scene in the middle?" If this were anybody but her ex-husband, she'd be opening a notebook and uncapping a pen, ready to scribble down any scrap of advice she could get on this story. Because good golly, she needed help. So much help.

"The scene where the guy, whom I can only assume is supposed to be the hero of the story since he has broad shoulders and smells like sandalwood, accomplishes a physically impossible feat that no reader in their right mind would ever buy?"

And see, this is exactly why she hadn't pulled out a real notebook to take advice from her ex-husband. She'd already be slamming the notebook shut and recapping her pen. "What's wrong with sandalwood?" She'd get to the supposedly impossible feat in a minute.

"Nothing's wrong with sandalwood. I just don't understand why every guy in every romance novel always has to smell like it."

"Because you've read every romance novel, have you?"

"I've read every one of yours."

Gracie opened her mouth, ready to toss out a retort. Then closed her mouth, not sure she had one to make. "My men all smell like sandalwood?"

"Every last one."

That wasn't true, was it? It might be true. "Fine. I'll make him smell like . . . I don't know. Lemons. But back to the issue of the scene. Are you thinking a guy can't lift a woman up onto a huge horse that easily?" Because honestly, Gracie had a few doubts about it as well.

"Now that you mention it, yeah, probably not. But that wasn't the scene I was talking about. I'm talking about the scene right after that one. Where they're back at the house looking at the stars."

"Back at the house . . . You mean the porch step scene? When they kiss? What's wrong with that scene?" That was probably the only scene in her entire book she wouldn't have to fix. The one scene that held anything remotely close to zing.

"There's no way they would kiss like that," Noah said. "It's not believable."

"Because they don't like each other? They actually do. That's how the whole enemies-to-lovers trope works. Plus these characters in particular have tons of history together, because this is also a second-chance romance story." Or it would be. Once she fixed everything. "I know it seems like they've just met, but really—"

"I'm not talking about the motivation behind their kiss." Noah grabbed the maple syrup off the counter and plopped it in front of her. "Good grief, they can kiss the first time they meet as far as I'm concerned."

"Then what's the problem? They've certainly got chemistry." Or they certainly would. Once she fixed everything.

"The chemistry isn't the problem either."

"Then what's the problem?" she asked, her voice raising as she leaned forward over her plate.

"The problem," he said, his voice matching hers in volume as he palmed the table and leaned toward her, "is logistics."

"Logistics?" She might be shouting.

"Logistics." He was definitely shouting.

Gracie took a deep breath. Noah did as well. Perhaps because they both realized certain words don't require being said at top volume. Words like *logistics*.

As soon as Gracie believed she was ready to speak at normal conversation level again, she said, "I'm sorry, but what does logistics have to do with a kiss?"

The way he stared at her, she may as well have said, *I'm sorry, but what does pitching have to do with baseball?*

"Everything, babe. Everything." Before she could scold him for calling her *babe*, he rushed on. "Think about it. If Mr. Broad Shoulders is sitting two entire porch steps above Miss Horse Hater, how's he able to kiss her with all the . . . you know." He moved his hands around as if he were locking someone in a passionate embrace. "*Logistics.*"

"He lifts her onto his lap. That's not logistics. That's common sense."

"I thought she'd lost the use of her legs at this point. Like in that whatever movie you kept referencing at the beginning of the story. Something about an affair?"

"*An Affair to Remember.* Yes. My heroine gets injured after she first knew the hero, and now she can't use her legs. So what?"

"So I don't understand how he does it. How does he scoop her onto his lap so easily if he's sitting on the top step and she's two steps below?"

"He was able to lift her onto a horse earlier that afternoon, wasn't he?"

"Which I thought we already established is rather questionable."

"He's Mr. Broad Shoulders, okay? He's strong. He can lift her onto his lap."

Noah raised his hands in surrender. "Hey, it's your story. If you want to insult your readers' intelligence, go ahead."

"Insult my readers'—" With a pirate growl—she was getting rather good at those—Gracie swiveled in her chair and motioned for Noah to help her up. "Fine. Let's go. Front porch. Right now. I'll prove it to you."

"Prove what?"

"That I can drag you up those porch steps, that's what."

"Oh, so you're going to play the role of Mr. Broad Shoulders, are you? Miss I-Can't-Even-Sit-On-The-Toilet-Without-Sounding-Like-A-Deranged-Bird? That's right. I hear the noises you make inside that bathroom."

"Well, you're about to be the one making deranged noises when I prove it can be done." She reached for her phone. "I'm calling Matt."

"Because he's going to drag me up the porch steps and onto his lap with a passionate embrace?"

"That's exactly what he's going to do."

"Put down the phone. You're not calling Matt."

"Oh, but I am. And he's answering right now. Matt?" Gracie said before her nephew could even offer a hello. "Don't ask questions. Just get here as fast as you can. It's an emergency."

13

"So just to be clear," Matt said roughly nine minutes after getting Aunt Gracie's call and breaking the speed limit to get to her house as he imagined every worst-case scenario possible, which made him grateful for Rachel's company since the majority of his worst-case scenarios involved copious amounts of blood, and she was a nurse, so she probably had a better chance of not passing out, unlike him—especially if his greatest fear had come true and Aunt Gracie had murdered Noah. "When you said there was an emergency . . ."

"She meant that she needed you and me to pretend to make out on the front porch," Noah answered. "Now please, ignore your crazy aunt and have some pancakes."

Rachel giggled as she took a seat at the kitchen table, and Matt allowed his heart rate to return somewhere to normal levels as he took a seat across from her.

So, *not* an emergency then. He and Rachel could have gone out to breakfast like he'd planned once they finished buying every last mousetrap in a fifty-mile radius like Rachel had planned. But at least Noah and Gracie were feeding them breakfast. And he was spending time with Rachel on her day off. He supposed things were sort of working out as planned.

He shoveled a bite of pancake into his mouth.

"Why do you need Noah and Matt to pretend to make out on the front porch?" Rachel asked, sounding way too amused. Matt shook his head at her. She really shouldn't encourage his aunt.

"Something for a story I'm working on," Gracie said. "But honestly, it wouldn't work with Noah and Matt. I need a girl, of course."

"Oh. Well, can Matt and I do it then?"

Matt froze with his fork halfway to his mouth. Maybe Rachel *should* encourage his aunt.

"Can we just enjoy a nice breakfast, please?" Noah asked.

"He's stalling because he knows I'm going to prove him wrong," Gracie said from the side of her mouth to Rachel.

"Oh, you don't have to tell me," Rachel said out of the side of her mouth to Gracie. "I recognize a good stall from a mile away."

Well, apparently Matt and Rachel weren't the only two picking right back up where they'd left off. But then, Gracie did always love Rachel. Unlike his mom, who'd only ever had eyes for Aimee.

"I'm just trying to prevent you from eating crow and cold pancakes all at the same time," Noah finally retorted when he finished swallowing a giant bite of pancakes. "Coffee? Orange juice?" Noah asked, pointing his finger at Rachel.

"Orange juice, please," Rachel said.

While Noah poured her a glass, Rachel dug into another pancake. "So what's the issue? The characters forget where each other's lips are or something?"

"Oh, they know where their lips are," Noah said, handing the glass to Rachel. "They're just going to need to take a road trip to get there. Matt? Coffee? Orange juice? Milk?"

"I don't understand," Rachel said to Gracie.

"Maybe some milk," Matt said to Noah. "But I'll get it."

Gracie started explaining the scene to Rachel—something about an old Cary Grant movie, leg issues, and a bunch of porch steps—as Matt went to the fridge for the milk.

After more explanation, Rachel said, "Why can't you put the girl on the top step and have him pull her down onto his lap? Might be easier?"

Gracie clunked her orange juice to the table. "You too? Really?"

"Told you," Noah said with a satisfied air.

Before Matt could return to the table with his milk, Gracie was making pirate sounds and directing everyone out to the front porch. "Put down the pancakes. We're doing this."

"Can I at least finish my milk?"

"Nope." Rachel took his glass away and started shoving him toward the front door. "Didn't you hear? Your aunt's on a tight deadline."

"She's been on a tight deadline for years."

"I heard that," Gracie shouted from the kitchen where Noah was still assisting her to her feet.

A few minutes later, Matt found himself seated on the top porch step, Rachel two steps below him, while Gracie watched on like a movie director from the kitchen chair Noah had brought out to the front yard for her.

"Okay, so you're talking, right?" Gracie said, making talky motions with her hands. "Act like you're talking."

"Cut," Noah immediately responded. "I don't think our porch steps are average height. Are the steps in your story average height?"

"I don't know. What's the average height of a porch step?"

"See? These are the logistics I'm talking about."

Meanwhile Rachel hadn't stopped opening and shutting her mouth without making a sound. "We're not background actors in a movie, you know," Matt said.

"She said to *act* like we were talking."

"Well, *act* like you're not a lunatic while you're at it, please."

She giggled. "But I don't know what my character's supposed to be saying."

"Hey, what's the dialogue in this scene?" Matt asked Gracie, but she was still too busy arguing over the average height of a porch step with Noah.

"If Mr. Broad Shoulders built his own house, can't he make the steps any size he wants?" Gracie said.

"Fine, but I still say he can't deadlift Ms. Horse Hater up two of them. Not without throwing his back out."

Rachel frowned at Matt. "Lifting me wouldn't throw your back out, would it?"

Matt wagged his head side to side in a *maybe-maybe not* gesture. She smacked his leg.

"They're kissing," Gracie shouted at Noah. "Why is it so hard to believe he pulls her onto his lap?"

"Because you said he was cupping her face," Noah shouted back. "What does he do? Drag her by the jowls?"

Rachel belted out a laugh.

"So what if he does?" Gracie shot back. "Sometimes romance readers just want a sexy jowl-grabbing scene. Nothing wrong with that."

"Where exactly are your jowls anyway?" Matt said, leaning down to poke Rachel's cheek.

She slapped his finger away. "Don't you ever go searching for my jowls again."

"You know, I actually kind of hope that is dialogue straight out of Aunt Gracie's story."

Rachel massaged her cheeks, unable to stop giggling. "My jowls are getting sore."

"Yeah, well I reckon my back's about to get sore, because there's only one way to end this if we ever want to get back to those pancakes." Especially now that Noah and Gracie had gotten into a debate about whether a tape measure or a yard stick would be more accurate to measure the height of the porch steps.

"Rachel," Matt shouted loud enough to be heard over Gracie and Noah's bickering. Loud enough to get their attention. He cupped Rachel's face, squishing her cheeks so hard that her lips puckered up like a fish. "My little horse-hater darling, I can't deny it any longer. I love you. I've always loved you. And even though I don't know where our future will take us, hopefully back to the kitchen where we can finish our pancakes, I'll be happy. So long as I'm with you."

"Oh Matt, or Mr. Broad Shoulders, or whatever your name is," Rachel replied with her face still smooshed together in his hands. "You're the only man who's ever looked past my jowls to see me for the woman I really am."

"Oh brother," Noah muttered.

"Quiet," Gracie scolded. "See how easy he lifts her now."

Easy? Yeah, Matt wasn't so sure about that. Not if he was supposed to drag her up by her face. "Um . . ." He moved his hands to the top of her head, then the back of her head. Patted her hair.

"What are you doing? Checking me for lice?" Rachel said.

"I'm not sure where to grab."

"Wow, this is really romantic," Noah said.

"They're supposed to be kissing right now. There'd be a lot more embracing. Why aren't you guys embracing?" Gracie said.

Because Matt didn't know what to embrace in order to lift her. Her rump would be helpful. But her rump was still currently situated two steps below him. Plus he didn't imagine grabbing her by the rump would go over any better than grabbing her by the jowls.

"Come on, we've got this." Rachel began tugging the front of his flannel shirt like he was their gym rope in P.E.

Matt's nose banged into her forehead. "Ow."

"No using your legs," Noah said.

"She's not using her legs," Gracie said.

"You're going to need to use your legs," Matt whispered into a mouthful of her hair. "And you're going to need to buy me a new flannel shirt." At least three buttons had popped off. He reached for the belt loops on the back of her jeans.

"You're giving me a wedgie."

"Can't help it. I'm caught up in the throes of passion, baby." He tugged harder, getting enough leverage to slide his hand under her rump. No way around it. Had to be done if he was going to lift her. He squeezed his eyes shut, channeling all his strength into this feat. *"Aaarrr,"* he groaned, now sounding like the one who'd turned into a pirate as he slowly lifted her.

"Stop acting like you're lifting a Buick," Rachel said, still clutching his shirt.

"Wow," Matt heard Gracie murmur. "His face looks worse than yours did when you carried the steamer trunk up those stairs."

"Yeah, well that steamer trunk weighed a ton," Noah said.

"What are you saying?" Rachel shouted.

Matt was pretty sure spittle had started flying from his lips at this point.

With a yell worthy of a bodybuilder setting a new world record in some sort of dead lift competition, Matt heaved Rachel the rest of the way onto his lap. Then released another guttural yell of victory. Followed by a whimpering, "Sweet mercy, I really may have to call my chiropractor."

"My hero," Rachel deadpanned, giving him a hearty pinch on the jowls.

"See? Told you it could be done," Gracie said.

Noah started a slow clap. "And *booy* was it sexy."

14

Noah had hoped by now to find some time to talk to Gracie about . . . well, their future. Mainly, did they still have a chance for one or not?

But after all the jowl-grabbing on the porch yesterday morning, Gracie kept brushing him off whenever he approached her, declaring she couldn't afford to waste another single minute on anything but her story. She spent the rest of the day on the couch, pecking away at her laptop, and said she planned to do the exact same thing today until her entire manuscript was fixed.

Well, pecking away and finding sustenance on nothing more than toast and tea might work for Gracie, but Noah was in dire need of some real food and conversation this morning. Which is why he now found himself climbing out of his Jeep on Main Street in Alda, getting heckled by Bobby the Barber.

"You know," Bobby said, sweeping the sidewalk in front of his barbershop the same way he had since the first time Noah rolled into town some twenty-plus years ago, "if you're still looking for those five strikes, the men's bowling league starts up on Tuesday. They might even let you finish out the season," he added with a guffaw.

What was it Jesus had said about a prophet without honor? Well, this might not be Noah's hometown, but it still rang pretty true. Not that Noah minded. Sometimes it felt nice just being known as plain old Noah Parker, Gracie's fella.

"I'll keep that in mind, Bobby," Noah said, reaching for the door to Lyla's Diner just as Mert Adley pushed it open.

"Well, howdy do there, Noah." Mert Adley, wearing a green mesh John Deere cap and bib overalls, held the door open for him. "Good pitching earlier this season. Not sure what happened there toward the end."

"I think I got old."

"Ha!" Mert slapped him on the back. "Happens to the best of us, doesn't it? But hey, there's always next year, right?"

The door clanged shut with a ding. "Not always," Noah muttered, not wanting to give any thought to what next year might look like for him. Not before he poured some coffee down his throat at least.

The scent of freshly brewed coffee, maple syrup, and greasy bacon welcomed Noah further inside. Conversations and silverware clattering on plates sounded along with the song "A Teenager in Love" by Dion and the Belmonts. Place hadn't changed a bit since Noah was a teenager. Shoot, probably hadn't changed a bit since Dion was a teenager.

No, he hadn't grown up in this sleepy little town. But he'd spent plenty of time here winning Gracie over. And somehow this town had wormed its way into his heart. Probably because the people here had allowed him to worm his way into theirs.

The tension Noah put on every day like a T-shirt loosened from his shoulders. Felt good to be home.

"Ooop. Everybody sit up a little straighter now," a deep feminine voice boomed. "We have us here a see-leb-er-tee. Yes, we do." Lyla hoisted her tray with a coffee pot and mugs up over her fleshy shoulder and sashayed over to Noah. "Well, hello sir. I do believe we have your special booth ready and waiting. Right this way."

"Thank you, server." Noah replied in a snooty tone. "And do you still have my usual drink, the triple non-fat sow-cow macchiato with an extra shot of caffeine-free espresso, two spoons, one straw?"

"Oh, but of course." She motioned to a booth covered in wet streaks. A dishrag was still perched on the edge of the table.

When he sat, she plunked a mug in front of him and poured dark coffee from her pot. "Does it meet your standards?"

Noah tasted a small sip of the plain black coffee, strong enough to put as much hair on his chest as what was currently covering his face, and made a show of working it around in his mouth before swallowing. "It will do quite well, thank you."

Her stoic features finally broke loose into a toothy smile, and she cackled. "Stand up and give me a real hello."

Noah slid out from the booth and wrapped the short, hearty woman in his arms. She squealed when he lifted her off her feet. "Silly boy."

"I've missed you," Noah said, setting her back down and grinning into her round face.

"Of course you have. Nobody makes breakfast like me. I tried telling you that." She waved her fingers at another customer who'd just stepped inside. "Figure out what you want. I'll be back in a few."

No sooner had Noah settled back in the booth, than his old friend Abe slid into the seat across from him. "You dirty dog. Why didn't you tell me you were coming back? I would have lined up a parade. Organized a bake-off. Put together a talent show. A kissing booth. Something."

"I think you just covered all the reasons I didn't tell you." Noah emptied creamer into his coffee, then flung the empty container at Abe. A few years older than Noah, Abe was one of the guys who had tried staking a claim on Gracie before he realized he had no chance once Noah started dating her.

Abe caught the missile and grinned. "See that. Lightning-fast reflexes. I should have gone pro."

"Really missed your chance."

Abe hunched his shoulders, a what-do-you-do expression on his face. "Too bad this town would've fallen apart without me as their mayor."

"Such a shame."

"Don't I know it. I could've been making the big bucks, living the good life, but no. I chose to fight the good fight. Put this little town on the map."

"You're a good man, Abe McKinley."

"They don't make them like me anymore."

"So humble."

"So *handsome*."

"So . . . so . . . full of it." Noah shook his head, smiling. "How you been?"

Abe shrugged. "Living the dream, I guess." He pointed to his ring finger. "Least that's what Lizzy keeps telling me."

"How're the kids?"

"Good. Got another one on the way."

Noah paused with his coffee halfway to his mouth. "No kidding?"

"Lizzy had to pick me up from the floor when she told me." Abe shrugged. "But I guess you know what they say about making God laugh. He must've laughed pretty good when I had my vasectomy fourteen years ago because we planned to be done."

"Wow."

"Yeah. Wow. That's pretty much the same thing my urologist said when I told him last week."

Noah rested his elbows on the table and lifted his coffee mug up as a toast. "Well, congratulations."

Abe grunted, but Noah could see the spark of joy in Abe's eyes. "Diapers. Strollers. Man, who would've thought. Just hope I've got another season left in me." His eyes narrowed on Noah. "Got any more seasons left in you?"

Noah scratched his beard. "Guess it all depends on Gracie."

Lyla returned, saving him from having to elaborate. "Know what you want, honey?"

"Pancakes. Lots of them," Abe answered.

She frowned. "Not you, honey. Him-honey."

"Pancakes," Noah said. "Lots of them."

She grabbed the giant menus off the table and pretended to bop Noah and Abe on their heads. "You two are just as much trouble now as when you were fighting over Miss Gracie."

Noah and Abe feigned innocent looks. This time she bopped them for real, then sauntered away.

"Speaking of Miss Gracie." Abe leaned forward and lowered his voice. "Is that why you're back? Came close to calling you a dozen times or better, but then Lizzy would tell me it wasn't my business. Plus, I was pretty sure Gracie would kill me."

"I get it. No worries. Matt called me."

Abe fiddled with a sugar packet. "So what are you planning to do about it? I hate to say this, but honestly, you know . . . he's not a bad guy. He and Gracie seem to get along real well even if he is a bit older. Part of me keeps expecting to hear she'll be walking down the aisle again—"

"Whoa." Noah lifted his hands as if Abe were suddenly pointing a gun at him. "What are you talking about? Who are you talking about? Is Gracie . . ." His voice grew hoarse as he lowered his hands to the table and leaned forward. "Is Gracie . . ." He didn't even want to finish the sentence.

"Getting friendly with Luke? Yeah. Thought you knew." Now Abe leaned forward, his voice all weird and raspy. "Something tells me you didn't know."

"Who's Luke? And what do you mean my wife's *getting friendly* with him?"

Abe dropped his crumpled sugar packet on the table and reached for another one. "Ex-wife. And honestly, he's a good guy. I doubt you know him though. He only moved to the area a few months ago."

"And they're already getting friendly?"

"She's not a teenager."

"She's my wife."

"Ex-wife."

"Stop saying that."

"He's a good guy."

"Stop saying *that*." Noah massaged his temples. First chance he got, he was stringing Matt up to a telephone pole. He couldn't have mentioned Mr. Friendly? Given Noah a heads-up?

"Here you go, sugar." Lyla plopped down two plates of pancakes stacked high with melting butter. "Need anything else?"

A barf bag. Noah grabbed his stomach.

"We're good. Thanks." Abe pulled his plate closer and began slathering butter all over his pancakes. "You really didn't know?"

"How would I know? Gracie hasn't said a word." Noah stabbed his knife into his pancakes. "And why isn't this bozo helping her out if he's so *friendly* and great?" Not that Noah wanted this bozo anywhere near Gracie.

"He had to leave town this week," Abe said around a mouthful of pancakes. He wiped syrup off his lips with a napkin, then continued. "He's a business owner. Runs some construction companies. Does a lot of traveling, I guess, to get the new projects up and running. At least that's what Lizzy says. She knows a nurse at the hospital who's good friends with the lady who plays organ every third Sunday at church. Personally, I think there's more to him than meets the eye."

Noah stopped hacking at his pancakes long enough to aim his knife at Abe. "What do you mean?"

Abe eyed the knife. "Can you at least put some butter on that utensil so this doesn't feel quite as threatening?"

Noah dipped the knife to his plate, scooped up a glob of melting butter, then flung it at Abe's face. "Better?"

"Much." He cleaned off his buttery chin with a napkin. "I don't know. Luke just has this look about him. A swagger. Like he's a gunslinger with a mysterious past. You know, like that one movie about that one guy. Oh, what's it called? Classic Western. The kid keeps yelling his name at the end. Shawn! Shawn! Come back!"

"You know why he didn't come back? Because his name was Shane."

"Ha!" Abe snapped his fingers with a laugh. "That's right. *Shane.* Anyway, Luke reminds me a little of him. Only super nice. The women here all love him. Even Mona, and you know that's saying a lot."

That was saying a lot. Noah fiddled with his fork.

"But you want to know the real kicker? He's rich. Yeah, apparently his business is doing great and he's made quite a fortune for himself. But here's the *real* real kicker—"

"How many kickers does one guy get?"

"He's handsome too. At least that's what the women say. I wouldn't know. Just looks like a mysterious cowboy to me. But Lizzy claims he's like our very own Sam Elliott. Without the mustache though. Which I really don't get. How can he be Sam Elliott without the mustache?"

"No idea." Noah didn't even know who Sam Elliott was. But right now he was more concerned about Bozo Luke. "So will he be moving again because of his job?" Noah certainly hoped so.

"Good question. I'm guessing it depends on how friendly things get between him and Gracie—or if he needs to defend any homesteads from getting overtaken by bandits. What? I've been watching a lot of Westerns lately. I can't help it."

"Define *friendly*."

"Oh, you know. Getting coffee. Going to movies. Chatting after church. Friendly stuff."

Despite the nausea still swirling inside his gut, Noah dug into his pancakes. Forced a bite down. "Okay, fine. Friendly. But friendly doesn't mean Gracie's about to walk down the aisle again, does it?"

"For Buck, I think it does."

"What's Buck got to do with this?"

"Everything. You know how much she adores her dad. And he's not doing so well."

"What do you mean? I just talked to him the other day on the phone, and he sounded great."

"Well sure, he has his good days. But a lot of bad days too. From what Lizzy says that the dietician at the hospital says, which she heard from one of the phlebotomists who hired Mona to sell her house last winter, his days are really getting numbered."

A bite of pancakes lodged in Noah's throat. He shoved it down with lukewarm coffee. Cleared his throat. He really needed to go visit that guy. Should've already. "Hate hearing that. He's a good guy."

"One of the best. In some ways Luke sort of puts me in mind of Buck. Which is why we all think Buck wouldn't mind seeing Gracie end up with him. And why Gracie might be ready to walk down the aisle again soon if she thinks it'll make her dad happy before he goes."

Well, it sure wouldn't make Noah happy. And he had a hard time believing it would make Buck happy. Or Gracie. Nobody should be happy about this.

Noah slid out from the booth and dropped some cash on the table. "Good seeing you, Abe. Give my best to Lizzy. And congratulations again."

Abe pushed his empty plate away. "Thanks. I hope what I told you didn't run you off."

"Nah." Noah scratched his scruffy cheek. "You know I don't give up that easily."

Abe grunted. "True enough. I've seen you fight for Gracie before. Just thought you should know you're going to have a little stiffer competition this time. My heart wasn't really in it back when we were competing."

"Yeah, well . . ." Noah glanced around the diner. Not a whole lot had changed during his absence. Which gave him hope. If he won Gracie's heart before, he ought to be able to figure out how to do it again. "Think I'll go pay me a visit to Bobby."

"Good thinking," Abe said. "Gracie never did go for the facial hair as I recall. Pretty sure that's what swayed her from me to you."

Noah rolled his eyes. "I don't think I'd call what you were growing facial hair. Maybe more like peach fuzz."

"Do you want me on your side or not?"

Noah smirked and tapped Abe's shoulder with his fist. "See you around, buddy." Time for Noah to up his game. Which for now meant a shave and a haircut—and a whole lot of prayer.

15

Gracie stared at the cursor blinking on the computer screen. All day, ever since Noah left for breakfast, she'd been typing word after word. Then deleting word after word. Words that held zero zing. Words that made zero sense. Words she'd clearly forgotten how to string together in anything that might be construed as a story.

Maybe she should call her dad again.

No. They'd already talked once today, and he was adamant about her not visiting until after she met her deadline next week. He was right. The only thing she should be focused on right now was her story.

Five minutes later she still couldn't focus on her story. "What is wrong with me?"

"Well, for starters you're not supposed to be up here."

Gracie flinched at Noah's voice, then closed her eyes and took as deep a breath as she could with ribs that still hurt like the dickens. "What are you doing up here?"

"What are *you* doing up here? Hello, stairs? Not supposed to be climbing them alone? That whole falling and plummeting to your death scenario? Any of that ring a bell?"

Gracie gave up on her deep breathing exercise and flapped a hand

Noah's direction without looking away from her screen. "Thank you for the concern, but I climbed them just fine."

Okay, that might be the most liberal use of the words *just fine* in the history of mankind, but the important part was she had climbed them.

"Why are you even up here?" Noah asked. "Why aren't you writing on the couch?"

She tutted as if the answer was obvious. "How am I supposed to add zing to my story if I'm not sitting at my special writing desk?"

Never mind that roughly two hours ago was the first time in her life she decided the monstrous old desk in the spare bedroom should be her special writing desk. And never mind that her special writing desk had yet to add one iota of zing to her story.

"How did you get up the stairs?"

She slammed the lid of her laptop shut, Noah's nagging not helping in the zing department either. She started to suck in a deep breath, then remembered that deep breaths were overrated and painful. But so was meeting his gaze. So she settled for staring at the thinning tree branches tapping against the glass window panes above her special writing desk.

"Well, if you must know, I scaled the maple tree, swung branch to branch, then somersaulted through the window. Nailed the landing too. Should've gotten all tens, but the Russian judge only gave me an eight."

From her peripheral vision, she saw Noah fold his arms as he crept closer into her central vision, nailing his own perfect landing with a prop of his rear end on the corner of her special writing desk.

Surely she'd called it her special writing desk enough times in her mind by now to truly make it her special writing desk.

"My my," Noah drawled. "I'd say someone's wearing their sassy pants today, but considering you've given up wearing pants all together, I'll just assume you're wearing your sassy undies." He leaned down and whispered, "Which, as I recall, is the red pair."

Gracie clutched her robe tight at her neck and swung her gaze to meet his. "Don't you dare"—her breath rushed out of her, which didn't take long since she'd lost all capacity for deep breaths ever since her accident—"shave."

His palm scraped across his smooth cheek, over his mouth. Like a magician's trick, a devastating smile appeared beneath his fingers. "I think I already did."

Oh, he certainly had. Shaved. His face. His stupid handsome face. No beard. No scruff. No . . . Oh my. Goodness. Oh . . . everything.

Gracie forced her gaze back to her laptop. Lifted the lid. Tried typing something. A sentence. A word. A punctuation mark. *Something.*

Ajdskfsa;lkdfjdka!

Well, that was something.

She closed the lid again. Why did he have to be so stinking hot? She didn't need that. No ex-wife needed that.

What she needed was for him to go. Away. Far away. Far enough away she wouldn't have to look into his eyes and be reminded of everything she'd ever felt for this man. Especially not the good parts. She refused to think about the good parts with this man. Not when the bad parts had nearly destroyed her.

Clearing her throat, Gracie shifted in her seat and opened her laptop. "I need to . . . You should really. . ." She angled her head sideways toward the door without taking her eyes off the computer screen where the cursor blinked, taunting her as much as the scent of Noah's aftershave.

Because, oh no, it couldn't be enough for him to look wonderful. *Of course* he had to smell delicious too. She tried not to inhale any more of whatever scrumptious scent he was wearing. A scent that was definitely not sandalwood. From now on all her heroes would smell like that—whatever *that* was. Not that Noah should be setting the bar for her heroes.

She was going back to sandalwood.

"So which part of the story are you working on now?" He slid from the desk, then grabbed the back of her chair and leaned down to look at her computer screen.

"Nothing." She slammed the lid shut again. "You know I can't work with you—" *Smelling like that.* "Hovering next to my nose." *What?*

"Nice picture. Did you draw this?" He reached around her shoulders and picked up a flyer lying next to her computer.

Oh, how that smooth-shaven, delectable face was crowding her space. Seriously though, what aftershave had Bobby put on him? It took all her willpower not to bury her nose into Noah's neck.

"Gracie?"

"Huh?" She blinked. He'd asked a question, hadn't he? "Uh, yes. Doodles. Those are my doodles." Is that what he'd asked? "Matt, um, asked me to design something to help promote the animal shelter. He wants to pass those out at the Alda Pumpkin Festival this Saturday."

She grabbed the brochure, then started to fan herself with it. When had this room turned into a sauna?

Noah perched back on her desk. "You've gotten better, you know that? You were always talented, but that—" He pointed at the flyer. "That's really clever."

Gracie tried not to let his praise seep past her defenses. "Yes, well, doesn't exactly pay the bills, though, does it? Now are we done playing fifty questions? I'm sure you've got better things to do than grill me over my animal doodles." She waved the brochure toward the doorway. "Time to go." *And take that glorious yummy-scented face with you.*

"How long do you think you'll be up here?"

"Hours. Days. Long time."

From the corner of her eye she caught him rubbing the bare spot around his left ring finger. How long had it taken before he'd removed his wedding band?

"Promise you won't take the stairs again without me?"

Where did he put it? Sock drawer? Desk drawer? Snack drawer?

Did he ever lose sleep in the middle of the night wondering when she'd taken her wedding ring off? Or where she'd put it?

"Gracie?"

"What?" She lifted her gaze from his bare finger. At some point she'd gone from side-eyeing to full-on staring.

"The stairs?"

"What about them? Oh. The stairs." She shook her head. *Focus, Gracie.* "Right. Yes. I mean, no. I'm okay. I won't need you. I made it up them without any issue."

If *without any issue* meant taking a good twenty minutes to clear three steps, then probably never making it any further if the FedEx delivery woman hadn't just happened to see her through the window while dropping off a package and assumed—rightly so—that Gracie was going to fall, and rushed through the front door to help drag her up the remaining steps while swearing she'd never report anything she had seen in exchange for an advance reader copy of Gracie's next book.

"I'm good, Noah." Or at least hopefully she would be. One day. When her ex-husband stopped living right next door to her. Which reminded her . . . "Don't you think it's about time for you to move out of the cottage and head back to Seattle?"

"Why? Want me out of the way before Luke gets back to town?"

Gracie couldn't help it. She snorted. "Sounds like you got more than a shave and haircut from Bobby."

He gripped the edge of her special writing desk. "Can't help wondering why you didn't tell me."

"Because there's nothing to tell. Besides, you didn't exactly consult me when you started playing patty-cake with Piper Green, you know."

"Patty-cake? Really?"

"Well, when she looks like a little girl playing dress-up, what else would you call it?"

"Not patty-cake. And I already told you, she was never my girlfriend. We were photographed at one event together. One. That's it."

"So that's why she was wearing your jersey on her little YouTube channel last month? Because nothing's going on between you?"

"I'm not in charge of her wardrobe. It's not like I gave it to her. What do you think this is? High school? You think I gave her my class ring, too? Wrapped it in that argyle string you girls always used?"

"Angora. Not argyle."

"You're acting just as jealous as you did back when you thought I was taking Patti Sinclair to prom."

"You *were* taking Patti Sinclair to prom."

"Because you broke up with me after I'd already rented a tux and paid for the flowers. I had to take *somebody* to prom that night just to get my money's worth."

"I didn't break up with you. I just said I didn't feel like we were on the same page since I was off at college and you were still a senior in high school. You were the one who made it into something it didn't have to be. All I wanted was for you to talk to me."

"We talked all the time."

"But never about anything important. Never about you."

"Are you kidding? We talked all the time about me."

"We talked about baseball. That's not the same."

"Baseball is me, Gracie. I don't know why you never got that."

"Because maybe you never got me." Gracie pressed the headache building in the space between her eyebrows. Trying to be an ice queen around Noah was giving her a brain freeze. "Look. I don't want to fight. We've both moved on. Let's just leave it at that."

"When does Luke get back? I'd like to meet him."

Gracie focused her gaze out the window, Noah obviously not ready to leave it at that—or anything else. The maple tree in the front yard waved, its branches growing thinner each day. "There is absolutely no reason for you two to meet."

"Why not? Is he too busy being rich and handsome? I just want to have a chat with the guy."

"Let's not do this." Gracie would rather go outside and rake leaves in her robe the rest of the day than continue this conversation.

Noah braced his hands on the desk, stretching his back like a cat. Then he peered out the window, the lines around his eyes more prominent in the sunlight. "Why the rush to move on, Grace? What's this really about?"

"First off, I wouldn't call five years after our divorce a 'rush to move on.' Secondly, Luke's a good guy. He's a *really* good guy. Any woman would be lucky to have a guy like him to move on with after—" *Going crazy losing a guy like you.* "I just like who I am with him, okay? He's . . . He's . . ."

"What? Mysterious?"

"Safe."

Noah's chin jutted back as if that was the last word he expected. Honestly, it was kind of the last word Gracie expected. But now that she'd said it, the word rang true. Luke *was* safe.

"I can take care of you, Gracie," Noah said.

Gracie knew he wasn't boasting. Just stating a fact. She didn't know the exact sum of his income anymore, but she knew it had to be hefty. And just like when they divorced, she didn't want a single penny of it. "This isn't about money."

"Who says I'm talking about money?"

She couldn't hold his gaze. Couldn't continue this conversation. Where it might lead scared her too much. Some days she didn't have the strength to keep pushing Noah away.

But if she'd learned anything, she'd learned that Noah was the complete opposite of safe. With him, she risked everything.

She'd paid that price once already. She wouldn't pay it again.

"I really need to get back to work."

"Fine." Noah straightened, running his knuckles over his smooth cheeks. "But don't think about taking those stairs again without me. I'll be in the living room when you need me."

"I won't need you." If she said it enough times, maybe someday she'd believe it. "For a while." She added the last bit solely for his benefit. Otherwise he might never leave the room.

Noah retreated to the doorway. She almost allowed herself to breathe easy. But his soft voice carried back to her. "I would, you know. Take care of you. If only you'd let me."

She closed her eyes as his footsteps disappeared down the stairs. She didn't even attempt to take a full breath. So long as Noah remained in her life, there was no such thing as breathing easy.

16

A clamor of barks echoed off the walls. Matt hunched his shoulders to block some of the noise as he scooped food into a dish for the new mutt that'd arrived earlier this morning.

He gave her a quick scratch behind the ears while Snarls, a Chihuahua mix in the cage next to them, jumped without bending his legs in a rat-a-tat motion. Matt squatted, holding the Chihuahua's buggy-eyed gaze through the chain links. "You watch your mouth, pal. There's ladies present."

"I don't think he cares," a soft voice said behind Matt. So soft he almost missed it with all the barking.

Matt jumped to his feet. "Aimee. Hi. Hello. Hey." Good grief, should he throw in an *Hola* while he was at it? He forced a smile that probably looked about as natural as a ventriloquist dummy's grin. "What brings you by?"

He hadn't seen her since they shared one of the world's most awkward breakups a little over a month ago. Which in a way brought things full circle. Their entire relationship had been awkward. Probably because it had such an awkward beginning.

"I found this in my car." She held up a coupon for a free two-liter soda with the purchase of a large Casey's pizza. "It's yours. Thought I should give it back to you. Since we're not together anymore. And it's yours."

"Oh." Matt took the coupon from her. "Thanks."

"Do you have anything of mine?"

"What?" A cacophony of barks continued ricocheting off the concrete walls.

"I thought I might've left behind a sweater or something at your place?"

"Uh . . . no. Sorry. I can't think of anything. Unless you want the cactus?" It was technically his cactus and technically a dead cactus—he shouldn't have watered it so much—but after five years of dating he felt kind of bad they didn't have a single thing to return to each other besides a coffee-stained coupon that had likely already expired.

"Can I ask you a question?" Aimee took a step back, bumping into the cage behind her. A shepherd mix jumped up to eye level and let out several deep barks. She flinched and plugged her ears.

"Jonesy," Matt said, snapping his fingers. "Down. And you—*enough*." He pointed his finger at the mouthy Chihuahua. "Sorry about that," he said to Aimee once the dogs finally quieted down enough for them to talk again.

She unplugged her ears, shooting all the dogs a wary look. "Did you break up with me because of Rachel?"

"What?" Except he heard her just fine. "No, I—"

"People have been saying she moved back recently. And I just wondered if that was the reason why—"

"No. No." And just because it truly wasn't the reason he broke up with her, since he hadn't even known Rachel was back at the time, he added another "No" for good measure.

"Okay." Aimee nodded and started for the exit. "It's just that I remember how close you two were in high school," she said, spinning back to face him as she hovered in the doorway. "And when Rachel offered to set us up on that date for prom, she assured me you guys were nothing more than friends. But I've always wondered if there was something more. Was there something more? You can tell me. I can handle it. I just really, really need to know if there was something more."

She stared, obviously waiting for some sort of confession. But all he could tell her was "No. There was never anything more between us."

Aimee nodded, not looking all that convinced before she disappeared out the door. But it was the truth.

Matt shook his head, remembering how stupid he felt thinking there *was* more between them. Thinking Rachel was going to be his date for prom. Thinking the girl she talked about—the one who'd had a secret crush on him for years, the girl who was too embarrassed to say anything, the girl who'd never gone to a dance before, the girl who thought it'd be fun to be his blind date for prom—was *her*.

But all along she'd been setting him up with Aimee.

"You don't know how close I came to telling you so many times," Rachel gushed later, after prom, when Matt swung by her house to confront her. "But I didn't want to spoil the surprise."

Well, Matt had certainly been surprised. "It was Aimee," he kept saying with a wooden grin. "You set me up with Aimee."

"I know. Didn't I tell you that once you saw who it was, you'd realize she was the perfect match for you?"

"You did say that. I remember." And he'd been one hundred percent certain that Rachel had been talking about herself at the time. "It was Aimee."

"I know. Isn't she so sweet and gorgeous?"

She *was* so sweet and gorgeous. That was the problem. His mom loved the match. Aimee loved the match. Rachel *clearly* loved the match. Everybody loved the match.

So when Rachel told him a week later that she and her older sister were moving to Florida as soon as the school year ended to get away from her sister's slimeball of a boyfriend, Matt wondered if Aimee was the best match he was ever going to get. He decided to make a go of it.

Took him five years to realize what his grandpa knew from the start. Their relationship never had any spark—as evidenced by the coupon in his grip. He shoved it into his back pocket. Hopefully that was the last of their awkward interactions.

By the time Matt finished feeding all the dogs, everyone had gone home except Gloria, the office manager. "We had another drop-off," she told him as soon as he closed the door between the back kennels and the front office.

"Please tell me it's not another mastiff."

"It's not another mastiff."

Matt's shoulders sagged with relief.

"It's a St. Bernard."

"What?" Matt squeezed the bill of his ball cap as Gloria's lips spread into a mischievous grin.

"Gotcha." She slid off her stool and bent over. "It's only this little guy. How could I say no?" She hoisted a caged guinea pig in the air and plopped it on the counter.

"A guinea pig? Gloria, this isn't a pet store. We're here to find homes for stray dogs and cats. We can't start taking in every Tom, Dick, and Harry that comes wandering through our doors. What next? Birds? Giraffes? This place can barely make ends meet as it is."

He didn't mean to harp at Gloria. She was here on a volunteer basis just as much as he was. The woman was a godsend, considering she manned the front desk twenty hours a week.

"I don't mind answering the phones or doing the clerical work, just so long as I don't have to do more than pet the occasional cat. My pooper-scooper days are behind me," she'd informed Thad, the man who ran the animal shelter, straight from the get-go.

"I'm sorry, Gloria. I don't mean to—"

"Don't say another word. After being married to Stan the last forty-five years, I've developed a pretty thick skin when it comes to taking a man's griping." She grabbed her purse and keys from a drawer in the desk. Patted Matt's arm on the way past. "I know finding good homes for these animals means a lot to you. Which reminds me. Is it true Noah's back in town?"

"He's been helping out with my Aunt Gracie, yeah."

"Interesting. Interesting. Well, maybe Mr. Baseball wouldn't mind helping the town dig a little deeper into their pockets to support this animal shelter while he's back."

"What did you have in mind?"

Swinging open the front door, Gloria made a show of shrugging her shoulders. "Honey, do I have to be both the looks and the brains of this outfit? I don't know. Think of something. And while you're at it, watch the wet floor. I just mopped. Mind putting the bucket away for me? Thanks, doll. See you Saturday at the Pumpkin Festival." She tossed a wave over her shoulder.

Matt caught a glimpse through the window of Gloria tossing another wave at someone before she pulled out of the parking lot.

Matt stepped closer to the window to see who she'd been waving to. The shelter sat a few miles outside of town. People didn't usually swing by unless they were dropping off or picking up animals.

He didn't see anybody. Which was good because the shelter was already filled to the brim. If somebody came in with another stray, he had no earthly idea where to put them. Matt couldn't wait for Thad to get back from vacation, so he could stop pretending to be in charge of this place and hand the reins back over.

"What're you looking at?"

Matt jerked backwards, spun, slipped on the wet floor, and caught himself with his elbows against the windowsill. "Good night, woman. You trying to give me a heart attack?"

Rachel smiled triumphantly. "Ha. Now you know how I felt when you snuck into my house the other day. At least I didn't come in breaking down the door and screaming like a fool."

"Hey, there's no fool to be seen here." Matt stepped forward, kicking Gloria's bucket. A gush of soapy water flooded the floor.

"My shoes!" Rachel squealed and jumped onto the reception desk. "Mouse!" She squealed a second later, jumping off the reception desk when she noticed the guinea pig.

"Careful." Matt caught her by the elbows before she slipped and fell, then hefted her back onto the desk. "This floor's going to be a skating rink until it dries. You're safer on the desk."

"With the rodent? I don't think so." Rachel peered into the cage. "Though I guess he's not completely horrible to look at once you get past the whole mousey aspect of him."

"Make you a deal."

"What sort of deal?"

"Pick out a cat and a dog, and I'll throw in the guinea pig for free." He scooted onto the desk next to Rachel and patted the cage.

"And where exactly is the deal in that?"

"You get a mouse catcher, a security guard, and a cute little cuddle-bug all for free."

Rachel wrinkled her nose. "I thought I was just here to clean litter boxes and take dogs for walks in exchange for you fixing doors, setting mousetraps, and giving me a ride to work this past week."

"True. But if you want me to keep doing all those things, these are my new terms."

"Well, seeing as my insurance finally coughed up a rental until my car is finished getting repaired, I actually don't need any more rides from you. So if we're going to be throwing out new terms, then my new terms include helping me replace my entire front porch and ridding the house of every species of arachnid and varmint. Deal?"

He jutted a thumb over his shoulder. "No deal until I see you start cleaning out some litter boxes first."

"Watch me."

"Watch me watch you."

Without thinking, they both hopped off the desk. Then immediately smacked against the wet tile floor the very next moment. Well, Rachel hit the floor. Matt mostly hit Rachel.

"Ow," Rachel groaned.

"I am so sorry. Are you okay?" Matt asked. His right arm was somehow pinned beneath her back while his left hand was caught in her curls. "You didn't hit your head, did you?"

"My head is fine. My rib cage, however—" She wheezed dramatically.

"I'm crushing you, aren't I? I'm so sorry. I don't know why Gloria insists on mopping every day she works. It's not like the floors get that dirty. I think she just likes to mop." The more he attempted to free his right arm, the more tangled her hair became with the watch on his left wrist.

"Ouch."

"Sorry. If I just get my other arm—"

"Nope. Worse. And why is my sweater unraveling now?" Matt followed her gaze down to his waist. "Because your sweater is putting the moves on my belt."

She gasped. "Don't talk about my sweater like that. If anything, your belt is seducing my sweater." She winced. "Okay, my hair. Can we get back to focusing on that? Although I really do like this sweater. Okay, forget the hair. Save the sweater." She began to unclasp his belt.

"Hey now, tiger." He chuckled uncomfortably and tried shifting away from her. "Let's keep our hands off my belt and get back to worrying about your hair. Our new terms can include me buying you a new sweater, okay?"

When Rachel giggled, Matt made the mistake of meeting her eyes. Of smiling back. Leaning in just a little bit closer. Close enough to kiss her if he wanted. But was that what Rachel wanted? *She assured me you guys were nothing more than friends.*

He could hear Aimee's voice as if she were standing right in the room.

It took Matt a second to realize she *was* standing right in the room. With possibly more coupons in her hands. He couldn't tell for sure. "So you breaking up with me had nothing to do with Rachel?"

"This isn't what it looks like." He and Rachel started speaking over one another.

"My belt's caught in her sweater and—"

"Can't get my hair free and—"

"Such a slippery floor and—"

"I was just on my way to clean the litter boxes!"

Aimee flung the pile of papers in the air—yep, they were more coupons—and slammed the door shut on their words, leaving Matt and Rachel in an awkward tangle of unclasped belt buckles, unraveled sweaters, and now, fluttering coupons.

"Well, glad we got that straightened out," Rachel deadpanned.

17

Grace: Hey, this is Gracie. Hope you don't mind that I asked Matt for your number.

Rachel: Of course I don't mind! What's up?

Grace: Wondering if I could ask you some random questions for my story.

Rachel: Fire away! (Unless it has to do with jowls)

Grace: Ha! You wish! First question—what's your favorite scent on a man?

Rachel: Does laundry soap count? Not sure what brand Matt uses, but he always smells good.

Grace: Interesting. Next question—do you think it's plausible for a woman to recognize a man just by his kiss?

Rachel: Maybe. Does the guy kiss especially weird?

Grace: No. He's not slobbery or anything. They just have a history of lots of kissing. And now years have gone by, so the woman doesn't recognize him at first. Maybe she's blind. Or blindfolded. Or not wearing her glasses. I don't know why she can't see him. I don't even know why they're kissing in this scene! The question is do you think she'd recognize him just by his kiss?

Rachel: I suppose. Do you think you'd recognize Noah just by his kiss?

Grace: Yes. But only because he's slobbery.

Rachel: Ha! Somehow I doubt that.

Grace: Is it strange kissing a different guy at first?

Rachel: How would I know? Do I look like some jowl-grabbing serial kisser to you?

Grace: Sorry. Just figured you've probably kissed more guys than me. My track record is one.

Rachel: Really? That's so romantic!

Grace: How is it romantic that the only man I've ever kissed is my EX-HUSBAND?!

Rachel: You're the romance writer. You figure it out.

Grace: If I could figure it out, I wouldn't be stuck right now.

Rachel: Are we talking about your story or Noah?

Grace: Hey, I'm supposed to be the one asking the questions.

Rachel: Sorry! Got any more?

Grace: Just one. Do you think it ever makes sense for a woman to choose safety over love?

Rachel: Absolutely! But I also think it would make for a dreadfully boring story. (We're still talking about Noah, aren't we?)

Grace: SO . . . Laundry detergent, you say?

18

Okay, time for Noah to up his game. If he wanted another shot with Gracie, he needed to make a move and somehow get her to talk about a possible future between them. Which had been the plan earlier today until he'd gotten distracted by all that Luke nonsense.

Well, Gracie might want to play it safe, but Noah couldn't afford to. Not if he wanted to win her back. He'd waited long enough. Time for them to talk—whether she was ready to take a break or not.

Something told him she was not.

Noah shook his head at her from the doorway. Good grief, she'd been pecking away at that keyboard the past eight hours with nothing more to sustain her than one measly piece of toast. She didn't even doctor it up with jam. She couldn't go on like this. Nobody could go on like this. Not even a writer on a deadline.

"Gracie—"

"Just some tea, thanks. You can leave it on the desk." *Peck, peck, peck.*

He braced both hands on the doorframe of the spare bedroom. The room they'd both assumed would get converted into a nursery someday. It took them several years to learn the hard truth that sometimes, *someday* never arrives.

"It's time to give it a rest, babe." Other than one bathroom break—the woman must have the bladder of a tank engine—she

97

hadn't vacated that seat in hours. "There's something I need to talk to you about."

"Sure. Just need to finish this section first." She reached her fingers beneath her reading glasses to rub her eyes, then went back to pecking at the keyboard. Another pair of glasses peeked out from the rat's nest growing on top of her head. He didn't have to search her robe pockets to know he'd find another pair there, easy. She collected reading glasses the same way she collected ChapStick. One of every color. One in every room. Because goodness knew she couldn't keep track of any of them.

"You're going to develop one of those pressure sores on your butt if you don't get up."

She flapped a hand in his direction, then went back to peck-peck-pecking. "I just took a break not that long ago."

"Gracie, the last time you took a break from that computer, New Kids on the Block were new."

Her lips twitched. Not much, but he saw it. And it was enough to encourage him. "Last time you took a break, *ALF* was on prime time."

"Knock it off." Her lips swiped to the side in an attempt not to smile.

"There were only three *Star Wars* movies."

"Get out of here."

"I could dance the Running Man." Noah pumped his arms and legs, dancing in place. "Still got the moves." His left shoulder twinged in protest. "Okay, maybe not." He stopped and massaged his shoulder.

But her laughter had already bubbled out—even if she immediately did press her lips together afterward and act like it didn't happen. "I'll let you know when I'm hungry, okay?"

No. Not okay. Noah leaned his shoulder against the doorframe, folding his arms across his chest. "You're sort of forcing my hand here."

Gracie's brow furrowed, her eyes never leaving the computer screen. *Peck peck peck.* "Just eat lunch without me. I'll snack on something later."

"Lunch? Babe, lunch was years ago. I can't even remember lunch at this point."

"Fine. Supper. I'll eat something in a bit," she said, starting to raise her voice.

Which, doggone it, always tended to make him raise his. "This isn't about food. Would you just stop for a minute and listen to me? I've got something important to tell you."

"So then say it already."

Well, he couldn't very well bring up his hopes for a future between them like this. Her, not even sparing him a glance. Him, already annoyed. So, he brought up the other little matter that needed addressing. "You want me to say it? Fine, I'll say it. You stink."

Well, looky there. Her undivided attention. Not a single peck as she lifted her hands off the keyboard to grip the top of her robe together and face him. "Excuse me?"

"You stink." They'd just have to talk about their future later. "And I'm not talking figuratively in case you're wondering. I mean your body literally stinks. Bad."

Gracie's mouth gaped open.

"Hey," he said, stepping further into the room. "I'm not judging. I wouldn't smell good either if I stopped practicing regular hygiene."

"I practice regular hygiene."

"You think that *this*"—Noah grabbed her left wrist and lifted her arm over her head—"is the smell of regular hygiene?"

Gracie jerked her face away from her armpit and tugged her arm down. "Fine. Maybe I'm not a garden of roses at the moment. What do you want me to do about it?"

"Take a shower. That's what I want you to do about it."

"And how am I supposed to do that?" Gracie fisted the top of her robe as her cheeks flushed dark pink.

"Well, you start by turning on the water."

"Later. After I finish this scene."

"That scene's not going anywhere. And once again, I do mean

literally. I read it over your shoulder a while ago, and there is like, nothing happening at all in that scene."

"Which is exactly why I need to work on it."

"You are getting in the shower."

"Not until Mona gets back."

He took a moment to just breathe so they didn't go back to shouting again. "Excuse me, Mona? Mona who ditched you the second you got home from the hospital? Mona who won't be getting back for who knows how long? That Mona?"

"That Mona." Her fingers strangled her robe with a white-knuckled grip.

He lifted a dismissive hand and turned for the doorway. "Well, I'm sure as heck not waiting for *that* Mona. I'm starting the shower right now, and you better believe you're getting in it. So get ready." She could get mad all she wanted, but good grief, this was happening. "You stink," he shouted over his shoulder as he started down the hallway.

"So do you," she shouted back. "And I *do* mean figuratively."

He paused outside the upstairs guest bathroom. Nah, what was he thinking? A quick shower wouldn't do. This woman needed the full treatment. He hustled into the master bathroom, straight to the giant claw-foot bathtub Gracie just had to have even though it had meant nearly disassembling the house to get the cast-iron monstrosity through the front door and up the stairs ten years ago.

Talk about a major headache.

Well, talk about a major headache until they took their first bubble bath together. From that point on, it was more like one of the best ideas Gracie had ever had in her life.

Lot of good memories in this tub, that was for sure. But something told him this evening wasn't going to be one of them.

Noah spun the dials and tested the temperature. Dumped in some bath salts. Couldn't hurt. Then rushed out of the bathroom to get back to Gracie, who was no doubt trying to escape out a window at this point.

Close. She was trying to escape down the stairs. She'd made it as far as the top step, snorting and frothing worse than a manager yelling at an umpire for making a bad call. "You can't do this to me. I have rights."

"Well, I have the right to inhale a breath of air without gagging whenever I'm in the same room as you."

She bumped into the wall as he reached for her. "It is not that bad."

"It's darn close." Trying to be both firm and gentle, he tugged her away from the wall and scooped her into his arms.

"Noah, please."

"Please, what? Stop trying to help you?" Woman weighed less than a sack of laundry. "You're not taking care of yourself, Grace. That's the truth. So whether you like it or not, I'm going to help you. And right now that means getting you squeaky clean."

Noah glided down the narrow hallway, making extra effort not to jostle her. He knew her bruised ribs still had to ache. He'd taken enough line drives on the pitcher's mound to have a taste of what that felt like.

"Okay," she said once they reached the bathroom, panting as if she'd been the one doing the carrying. "You win. I'll do it. I'll take a bath. Just put me down. I can handle it from here."

Noah started to kick the bathroom door shut behind him, then thought better of it. Why bother? Nobody else was in the house. He used his foot instead to knock the toilet seat lid down so he could set Gracie on top of it.

Her clenched jaw jutted out. "Did you hear me? I've got this. You can go. I'm completely capable of taking a bath on my own."

"Is that why you've been wearing the same stinky robe days on end with nothing but your skivvies on underneath? Because you're so darn capable?"

Her face blushed a deep shade of crimson and she fisted her robe together tightly against her throat.

"Or hold up. Wait a second now." A thought struck him. One

he'd probably be smart not to voice out loud. But since when had anyone ever accused him of being smart? "You're not wearing any skivvies, are you?"

"Would you stop saying the word *skivvies*?"

"You've been going commando. That's what was up with the scissors a few days ago. Okay. Makes sense. Oh, but please tell me you didn't destroy the red pair."

"Leave."

"Not until you're covered in bubbles, my dear."

"I'm serious."

"Me too." Noah squeezed soap into the tub, the scent of lavender quickly flooding the room. Bubbles frothed and lifted as the water level rose. "Just about there."

She shook her head, clutching her robe together at her neck. "I'm not getting in until you leave."

"You know there's nothing under that robe I haven't seen before."

"I know there's nothing under here that you're ever going to see again."

"Would it even out the playing field if I got naked too?"

"*Noah—*"

"I'm kidding. Oh my goodness, calm down. I'm not trying to have my way with you. I'm merely trying to give you a bath and make you smell better. Would it kill you to let somebody help you out just once in your life?"

"If there's nudity involved, yes."

Noah twisted off the jets. "I'll keep my eyes closed."

Gracie gripped her robe, staring him down as bad as the batter he'd beamed on the hip a few weeks ago with a wild pitch. He'd thought for a moment they were going to clear the benches.

"Come on, Gracie. You know you can't climb in and out of that tub on your own. And you know you're going to feel a thousand times better when you're done. Just let me help you. Because right now, whether you like it or not, I'm all you've got. I'm the one who showed up for you."

"You showed up for me because you had nothing left to keep you away. I call that playing second fiddle."

"Well, I don't care what you want to call it, because right now I'm calling the shots. And you, little lady, are getting into that tub."

"Don't call me *little lady*. And I'm keeping my robe on."

"Fine." He lifted her from the toilet and stepped toward the tub. "But only until you're beneath the bubbles, then I'm taking that robe and burning it."

She started to squirm. "Absolutely not."

"Keep that up, babe, I'm going to drop you."

"Don't call me *babe*."

"I'm about to call you *wet*."

"You're not taking my robe away."

"At least let me wash it."

"That'll take too long. Deal's off. I'm not getting in the tub. Put me down." She started hitting his shoulder. His bad shoulder.

"I wouldn't do that."

"I mean it, put me down this instant."

"Fine." He couldn't hold on to her squirming like that anyway. He dropped her into the tub.

She screamed. A gush of soapy water splashed over the edge of the tub. One of her hands latched onto his shirt just as his foot slipped on the tile floor. He fell forward. His face dove in the water. Then his shoulders. Next thing he knew, he was in the tub on top of Gracie.

"What are you doing?" Gracie shrieked inches away from his face.

"You pulled me in." He spit out a soap bubble.

"Well, get out."

"I'm trying." His hands kept connecting with her robe and her skin and lots of things that his hands probably shouldn't be connecting with, because now his hands were giving him all sorts of ideas. So he opted to stop moving all together.

She must have reached the same conclusion. She stopped splashing. Stopped moving. Definitely stopped shrieking.

They stared at each other for seconds. Minutes. Honestly, he wasn't sure.

Her lashes, spiked with water, blinked several times. "What are you doing?" she whispered. Calm. Gentle. Almost like she wasn't mad at him. Almost like she might be thinking the same thing he was thinking. Especially when her hazel-eyed gaze lowered to his mouth.

"What are you doing?" she asked again.

What was he doing? Trying to stay afloat in dangerous waters, that's what he was doing. His body shook with restraint. He needed to get out of this tub. Right now.

But he also needed to kiss her with every fiber of his being.

"Gracie, I—"

A deep throat cleared.

Noah barely had time to glimpse a tall man standing in the doorway before Gracie's sudsy palm smacked his face. "Luke," Gracie sputtered. "I didn't expect you."

"I can see that."

"That's Luke?" Noah asked right before she dunked his head in the water with all her flailing.

"Didn't mean to interrupt," he heard Luke say when his head came out of the water.

"No, wait." Gracie writhed and another rush of soapy water flooded Noah's face. "I can explain."

"Just thought I heard screaming. Wanted to make sure you were okay. Obviously you are."

"This isn't what it looks like."

Noah wasn't sure what *anything* looked like, the way Gracie kept shoving soapy water into his eyes. But he heard the bathroom door click shut.

"He's just giving me a bath," Gracie shouted as footsteps jogged down the stairs. "He's just trying to help me get clean."

Noah wiped the soap from his eyes in time to see Gracie scrunch her eyes shut and whimper, "Oh man, I stink," right before she sank beneath the bubbles.

19

Simone: Not trying to pressure you, but . . . tick-tock. We're almost to the deadline. How's the story coming along? Keeping that horse alive?

Grace: The horse is alive and well.

Which was more than Gracie could say for the rest of the story. Or herself.

After the bathtub incident, when it became clear hours later that sleep wasn't an option—since any time she closed her eyes she either saw Luke's stony expression or Noah's up-close lips—she spent the entire night *click-clacking* on the old typewriter she'd made Noah dig out of the closet before he left.

Obviously her special writing desk hadn't been cutting it on its own. So obviously she needed the special typewriter she'd never used before. Because obviously her special typewriter would give her story that missing zing.

And at three in the morning, it had. Oh, it had!

Funny, though, how ideas that sound positively zingy at three in the morning feel positively stupid hours later in the bright light of day.

Simone: Great! Knew you could do this!

Gracie stared at her phone screen, tempted to text back, *I lied. I can't do this. The horse has a terminal illness and I can't save him. I can't save the story. I can't save anyone. Sorry sorry sorry.*

But after a tired sigh, she searched for a GIF of a horse giving a big toothy grin up close to a camera. Then hit send.

20

Saturday afternoon Matt's truck bumped over the grassy field being used as the parking lot for the town's annual Pumpkin Festival. A high school girl, looking cold with her hooded sweatshirt tugged tight over her head, waved a flag to a parking spot at the end of a long row.

Temperatures had dropped the past few days. The cloud cover today added a wicked bite to the air. Didn't seem to be affecting the crowds though. Kids climbed all over the tower of hay bales. Families entered and exited a corn maze. A steady crowd gathered beneath the food tent.

Matt checked his watch. Hopefully Gloria wasn't upset with him for running a little late. When he swung by Aunt Gracie's to grab those brochures she'd made, she asked if he'd help Noah move some sort of special writing desk from the upstairs to the downstairs.

That part hadn't taken long. It was the argument afterward between Aunt Gracie and Noah about where to put the desk downstairs that had caused the delay.

Matt hustled past a carousel, ignoring the enticing scent of fried bliss each time he passed a food stand. He'd grab a bite later. His eyes wandered from face to face in search of a pair of brown eyes he hadn't seen since the coupon incident at the shelter. At least that's what he was calling it. Better than calling it the belt buckle incident. That just made him feel dirty. Like he and Rachel really had been fooling around on the floor.

They hadn't.

But even if they had, why should he feel dirty?

Well, other than the fact they'd been rolling around on a humane society floor, even if it had just been mopped. But he shouldn't feel *dirty* dirty. Like, *guilty* dirty. He and Aimee were over. Finished. They were never a good fit to begin with. Why didn't she get that?

And how long would it take Rachel to get that she and Matt would be a perfect fit?

Maybe they'd get a chance to talk about it later this evening when he went over to help her paint her living room walls. Yesterday he'd squeezed in a few hours to replace some of the rotting wood on her front porch. Slowly but surely her place was starting to look more like a home and less like ground zero.

"Hey Gloria, sorry I'm late. I brought the brochures . . ." Matt slowed to a stop, his eyes taking in the scene playing out next to the animal shelter booth. "What's going on?"

Wombat, shirtless beneath his suspenders, was holding a kitten. Leo, also shirtless, was posing with an axe propped over his shoulder. And half a dozen other firefighters, not shirtless but striking different model poses, pretended to walk a runway as people snapped pictures from their phones.

"Isn't it great?" Gloria pointed to the gaggle of women, all probably around Gloria's age. "I'm thinking next year we sell calendars. Who doesn't love a fireman with a kitten?"

"What's going on?" Matt asked again.

"Well, we weren't seeing a lot of action this morning, so Wombat and I came up with an idea to drum up some business. People donate to the firehouse, and they get a ticket to enter a drawing for a date with a fireman. People donate to the animal shelter, and they get a cat. So far nobody's gone for the cat option. Which is why next year I think we sell calendars and split the profits with the firehouse."

"Gloria, are you telling me it's been three hours, and we haven't made a single penny for the shelter?" Thad was going to kill him.

"Of course not. I found a penny next to the fried onion stand and donated it to our cause straight away." When Matt slouched, she swatted his arm. "I'm kidding. A few people have stopped by to donate. Emphasis on *few*," she added with a murmur.

"Hey Matt," Wombat hollered over to him. "Why haven't you ditched your shirt to come over here and pose with a kitty? Are you not man enough? Ouch, her little claws," Wombat said in a voice an octave higher as he detached the black kitten from his shoulder with a wince.

"Well, you certainly look manly right now," Matt said with a laugh.

Wombat smirked. "More manly than you in your Hello Kitty undies the other night."

Well, that got everyone's attention. "Hello Kitty what now?" Gus, the department's fire chief, asked Sasha, the lone female firefighter of the group. She lifted her hands like she wanted nothing to do with this conversation.

Neither did Matt. "Let's just move on," he said.

"To the dunk tank," Gloria shouted, pointing to the pool of water behind them. "Come on, boys. You know Mayor Abe always donates five hundred dollars to the cause of one's choosing if they're the first to try out the tank. Nobody's done it yet."

Of course nobody had. Not on a freezing day like today. A person would have to be nutso to even consider it.

And apparently Gloria thought he and Wombat were nutso. Her eyebrows bounced up and down. "Wombat? Matt? What do you say? We could find out right now which of you is man enough."

As much as Matt appreciated Gloria diverting the conversation from his Hello Kitty underwear, he really didn't want to spend the rest of the day recovering from hypothermia. The sight of the dunk tank alone dropped his body temperature at least five degrees.

"Go ahead, Wombat." Matt nodded toward the tank. "Prove to everyone how manly you are."

"Me? I ain't got nothing to prove when it comes to my manliness. Besides, I don't have time. I promised my grandma I'd meet her at bridge club this afternoon since they need a fourth player." He handed the black kitten off to Gus as he scratched behind the kitten's ears and said, "Bye-bye, sweet little angel baby face," in a singsong voice.

"You sure you don't need a dunk in the tank?" Gus muttered.

"Tell you what." Wombat rubbed his finger down the kitten's nose. "If Matt gets in the dunk tank right now wearing nothing but his undies—which may or may not be Hello Kitty, I guess we'll see—I'll adopt this sweet little angel baby face and tack on an extra hundred bucks to Abe's donation."

Gloria's eyebrows nearly hit her hairline. "Six hundred dollars *and* one of our kittens gets adopted? Thad will be over the moon. What do you say, Matt?"

What *did* he say? He'd say this was crazy. Ludicrous. Insane.

But he'd also say it might just be impressive enough that Thad would consider giving Matt an actual paying job at the shelter. A little extra income would certainly help hold him over during the downtime between mowing and snow removal season.

Matt reached for his belt buckle. Looked like he was about to go pant-less in public again.

†
†

Thirty minutes later, Matt was really regretting his decision to take off his pants. His jacket. His shirt. His socks and shoes. Everything but his boxers—which were *not* Hello Kitty, thank you—for the sake of six hundred dollars and one single cat adoption.

Why did he think that was enough to impress Thad? Thad wouldn't care. Nobody would care. Not even the animals at the shelter would care. He never should have agreed to this.

Because now look at him. He was freezing. Shivering. Possibly dying.

And nobody in this town could hit the broad side of a barn, let alone the bull's-eye that would drop him into the tank and end this torture. Talk about terrible aiming. Where was Noah when he needed him?

One hit, people. That's all. Then he could submerge into the glacial waters, lose all remaining feeling in his body, and be done.

Abe's deal every year was that in order to get the donation, the person sitting on the platform had to remain there until they got dunked—whether it took a single throw or a hundred. By Matt's count, they'd reached over two hundred fifty million.

The next person in line stepped up. He had a dog next to him, wearing one of those service-dog vests. Wonderful. Probably a seeing-eye dog.

The man attempted his three shots, none of them any closer than when the four-year-old girl before him had tried. Matt was about to open his mouth and yell for mercy when the man stepped aside, and Matt saw the next person in line.

"Aim-m-mee." His teeth couldn't stop chattering.

She stared at him, a determined look on her face. He prayed all that focus and determination was geared toward dunking him in the tank. She reached down into the basket of balls. "Why did you lie to me?"

Oh please. Not now. Just hit the bull's-eye. Or his head. He'd take anything at this point. But she clutched the ball, not lifting her arm. She obviously wasn't going to throw until he gave an answer. "I—didn't." There. An answer. Now please throw the ball.

"You told me nothing was going on between you and Rachel."

"J-just—th-throw . . ." They could talk later. Hopefully when he could feel his lips and form words again.

"How long have you loved her? Tell me."

"Sh-sh-sh-sh." He pressed a shivering finger to his lips. She needed to stop talking. Now. Because Rachel had just appeared next to the animal shelter booth. And any second she was going to spot him. In his undies. On the platform. With his ex-girlfriend hurling questions instead of balls.

"Why can't you just tell me?" Aimee, whom he'd never once heard raise her voice in all their time together, had started to shout.

Oh, please don't shout.

Too late. Rachel spotted him. Spotted Aimee.

"Because you've always loved her, haven't you?" Aimee whipped a ball over his head.

"Loved who?" a young boy holding a caramel apple asked.

Oh, please don't answer that.

"Rachel," Aimee shouted. And now a crowd was gathering.

Rachel's eyes widened. "Stop," he caught her lips saying.

Aimee wasn't stopping. "Through high school. The night of senior prom." A ball sailed past his left ear. "The entire time we were dating." A ball bounced off his knee. Maybe. He'd sort of lost feeling everywhere. "That's why you broke up with me. Admit it. You love Rachel. You've always loved Rachel. Just say it."

And now she was throwing every ball in the bucket, one after another. "Say it, say it, say it. You love her. You want her. *Just say it.*"

A ball hit his shoulder. Another his shin. Jeez Louise, how many balls were left in that bucket? He blocked two more with his forearms, then caught a glimpse of Rachel reaching into the bucket.

"Stop. He doesn't love me. We're just friends, okay? Just. Friends." Rachel's arm cocked back. Her words smacked him as hard as the ball hitting the target. He heard the thunk. Then dropped in the tank.

Bull's-eye.

21

"Sooooo . . ." Mona lifted her coffee mug toward her red pursed lips, pausing as she leveled her gaze at Gracie. "How exactly did you end up taking a bubble bath with your ex-husband?"

Outside the kitchen window, gray clouds gathered. Gracie spooned a heap of sugar into her tea. She should've known the only reason Mona dropped by this afternoon after finally getting back to town late last night was to give her a hard time. "Can we not talk about that right now?"

"Hey, I'm not judging." Mona blew on her coffee. "I mean, why would I judge? Noah's a handsome man, you two have a lot of history together, and let's face it—there's just some areas you cannot reach on your own. Now me, personally, I use one of those loofahs on a stick, but—"

"Enough." Gracie was stirring her tea into a whirlpool. "I don't need this. Not from you. *You* who's been gone the entire last week. *You* who didn't check on me once. *You* who has no idea what I'm up against right now. A deadline. A terminally ill father I haven't visited in over a week. An annoying husband I can't get away from. *Ex-husband!* I haven't slept in . . . I don't know. I can't even do the math anymore. Is today still Saturday?"

"Yes. And quick question. Does any of what you're talking about have to do with why there's a typewriter sitting on a desk next to the oven right now?"

"He shaved, Mona. *He shaved.* Do you have any idea how hard it is to concentrate on writing a funny, zingy story when your smooth-shaven ex-husband won't stop getting into your personal space and smelling like a warm, buttery cinnamon roll?"

Some of Gracie's tea had sloshed over the rim. She reached for a napkin to wipe off the kitchen table. "Which is probably why some-how in the past twelve hours my manuscript has turned into a time travel story. That's right. Instead of witty banter, my hero is now giv-ing a seven-page lecture in chapter eight about the theoretical physics that make time travel possible. Why, you ask?"

"I'm mostly just curious about why there's a desk next to the oven."

"So that he can go back and prevent the heroine from getting into that accident that caused her to lose function in her legs prior to chapter four, of course. But wait, Gracie. Won't that completely screw up your entire story that's due in a matter of days, you ask?"

Gracie waved her spoon at Mona. "Why yes, Mona, it will. It has. But I guess I'd rather destroy my story, possibly my entire writing career, by focusing on the quantum mechanics of time travel instead of how close my ex-husband came to kissing me in the bathtub, and more importantly, how close I came to kissing that stupid, handsome face back."

Mona, her mug frozen a few inches below her lips, stared back at Gracie. "Wow."

Yes. Wow. Because it would've been a great kiss too. Just like every other kiss she and Noah had ever shared in that giant ridiculous tub.

But apparently it wasn't thoughts of kissing Noah that had caused the *wow* factor for Mona. She lowered her mug to the table. "You stood. You're standing. Gracie, you're standing all on your own."

"I am?" Gracie looked down. "I am."

Her tea-sloshing monologue had somehow launched her onto her feet. Without help. Without thought. Without . . . pain?

She shifted her weight from foot to foot. Winced. Okay, a little bit of pain. Especially when she lowered herself back to the chair with an ungraceful plop, which rattled the table.

Mona dabbed at the splash of coffee running down the side of her mug. They were going to be out of clean napkins before a trace of beverage made it past their lips at the rate they were going.

"Listen." Mona finished cleaning off her mug and wadded her napkin. "One of the reasons I came over this afternoon was because I wanted to tell you I'm sorry."

"You are?" That was a new one from her sister.

Mona plunked her mug down, splattering more liquid onto the table. "Well, not really."

And there was the Mona she knew.

"How dare you not tell me you've been fooling around with your ex? I had to hear about it from Lizzy when I swung by the Pumpkin Festival to see Matt earlier, and she didn't even have the details right. She said you and Noah were fooling around in the shower."

"We weren't *fooling around* anywhere. How did Lizzy even know anything had happened at all?"

"Have you forgotten where we live? There are no secrets. Plus, I'm pretty sure that FedEx lady has a big mouth. She seems to know an awful lot just from delivering packages. Anyway"— Mona picked up her coffee mug and ran another napkin over the table—"you need to tell me these things. It really caught me off guard."

"How do you think I feel?"

Mona's red lips twitched as she slurped a drink, then quirked an eyebrow. "Clean?"

Not with the image of Luke standing in the doorway seared in her brain, she didn't. "I don't want to talk about this anymore. The whole thing's starting to feel like a love triangle, and you know how much I hate that trope."

If Gracie never included one in her fictional stories, she wasn't about to entertain one in real life.

"Did you at least try explaining things to him?" Mona asked.

"Who, Luke? Of course. He doesn't want to talk about it either."
Maybe. After never finding the courage to send him a text message
that night, Gracie had worked up the courage to call him the next
morning—then lost all courage to leave him a voicemail when he
didn't answer.

"So you two just aren't going to talk about it? Very adult-ish.
Worked out so well for your relationship with Noah five years ago."

"You do realize Luke and I are not in any sort of committed
relationship."

"Well, you're certainly not now."

"We're friends. That's all. I made it clear from the start that I
probably wasn't ready for anything serious."

"Not if you're still taking baths with your ex-husband, that's for
sure."

"Was there another reason you stopped by other than to tease me
about Noah? Because I've got a hero who accidentally time traveled
ten centuries back too far, and I really need to figure out how to break
him free from a dungeon before he dies of general malnutrition and
dehydration."

"Wow. You've really lost control of your story, haven't you?"

On the page and in real life.

Mona flapped her hands. "Fine. I'm leaving. But before I go, can
I just say one other thing? Something I can't even believe I'm saying?"

"Why do I already know I'm going to hate this?"

"Would it be so bad if you and Noah got back together?"

"Oh my word. Are *you* suffering from malnutrition and dehydration?"

"All I'm saying is Luke's perfect. You'd be crazy not to snatch up
a guy like him. And you're not crazy, Gracie. I mean, you're crazy."
Mona pointed to the desk next to the oven. "But you're not *crazy*
crazy. Which makes me think the reason you're not snatching Luke
up is because you've never gotten over Noah. And if you've never gotten over Noah, then maybe—"

"You want to know what I've never gotten over?" Gracie fisted her napkin. Rain began pelting the windows. "The number of times he put baseball first. Before me. Before the family we wanted to start. Before the future we dreamed of."

"Gracie—"

"No, listen. I get it. That's what the baseball life is. I knew going into it that there was going to be a lot of uncertainty, a lot of traveling, a lot of moving, a lot of separation. And all that was fine at the beginning. In our twenties. Even for the first half of our thirties. But eventually there came a time when I needed him, Mona. I needed him to be here. Not there. On the road. At another stupid game."

"I understand, but—"

"Just once I needed to be the priority." Now that she'd started, she wasn't stopping until she got it all out. "I needed him to drop everything and come hold me after I sat in an ultrasound room all by myself, listening to a doctor explain that she couldn't find a heartbeat and how sometimes these things just happen."

Mona didn't even try to interrupt this time. She pressed her lips together and clutched her soggy, coffee-stained napkin.

"All along everyone kept saying to just give it time. Just give it time. But I was running out of time. And we'd already tried everything. Spent so much money. So many tests. So many shots. And just when I thought it had finally happened . . . You have no idea . . ."

Mona darted glances around the kitchen, no doubt for escape. She'd never known how to handle Gracie's emotions. Which is why Gracie had stopped confiding in her years ago. If Mona had a theme song, it'd be Frank Sinatra's "That's Life."

But after five years of never confiding in anyone, Gracie just needed someone, anyone, to listen. And right now that someone, anyone, was Mona. *Sorry, Sis.*

"Did you know when I walked out of there, I couldn't even remember where I'd parked? Some nurse on a smoke break from one of the other clinics found me wandering around an hour after my appointment had ended. She asked if I needed to call someone. But I'd been so nervous before the appointment that I'd forgotten my phone at home. I was a wreck. An absolute wreck. Somehow I made it back to the house."

The rain pelting the window sounded heavier now. More like sleet.

"Want to guess what Noah said after I called him and told him the news? Think he was wrecked? No. He wasn't wrecked. He said, 'Guess it's not meant to be, babe,' then went on to pitch the best game of his life. Spent the rest of his night smiling. Celebrating. Getting a cooler dumped on his head. Worst day of my life, and he acted like it didn't matter at all."

"I . . ." Mona rose from her chair. "I think I should go."

Gracie nodded. *Sure. Thanks for stopping by. Sorry to slosh my feelings all over the table in front of you.* Gracie may as well have gone and spilled her guts to one of the dogs at Matt's animal shelter.

Mona escaped from the kitchen and out the front door. When nothing but the sound of the ice maker churning inside the freezer filled the silence, Gracie reached for the last napkin in the holder to dry off her face.

And that's when Noah's voice, hardly above a whisper, reached to her from behind.

"It mattered. I just didn't know how to deal with it. Maybe I still don't."

22

Noah: I need you to tell me everything you know about Luke.

Matt: Who's Luke?

Noah: You don't know Luke?

Matt: Do you mean the Sam Elliott guy?

Noah: You know who Sam Elliott is?

Matt: I just know everybody in town keeps saying Luke looks like him.

Noah: So what do you know about him?

Matt: Luke?

Noah: No! Sam Elliott!

Matt: Not much other than I'm guessing he must look a lot like Luke.

Noah: I'm starting to wish I'd been the one to drop you in the dunk tank this afternoon.

Matt: You heard about that?

Noah: Even Sam Elliott heard about that.

Matt: Did Sam Elliott hear about your little bathtub episode with Aunt Gracie?

Noah: Hey. We're supposed to be talking about Luke.

Matt: Right. What do you want to know?

Noah: Not sure. Guess I just want to know if I need to be worried about Luke and Gracie having any little bathtub episodes together.

Matt: Thanks for that disturbing mental image. And no, I don't think so.

Noah: What makes you say that?

Matt: Well, to steal a line from Grandpa, I've seen more spark between a limp worm and a dead fish than I've seen between Luke and Gracie.

Noah: I love Buck.

Matt: He's the best. Any other questions?

Noah: Guess not.

Matt: Can I ask what's going on with you and Aunt Gracie?

Noah: You can ask. Not sure I can answer. It's complicated.

Matt: I get it. I'm still trying to find a few answers myself.

Noah: About you and Rachel?

Matt: About Sam Elliott.

23

Later that evening, once Matt had finally warmed up from the dunk tank incident, he headed over to Rachel's house. No need to bust down any doors. She answered on the first knock.

"Matt. Hi. What are you doing here?" Rachel stood on the other side of the screen door, her hair piled high in a crazy bun with gray paint smudges all over her cheeks and chin.

How could anyone look so beautiful with paint smeared all over their face?

He cleared his throat. "I thought we were painting your living room tonight. I brought pizza." Matt lifted the carboard box for evidence. "We talked about this. Remember?"

She obviously remembered. She held a wet paintbrush that was dripping all over the floor.

"Right. I just wasn't sure if you were still coming since . . . you know, we hadn't talked about it since we first talked about it." She opened the screen door and waved him in, accidentally brushing his left arm with paint on his way past.

"We first talked about it yesterday." He examined the streak of paint on his arm, then noticed two giant drops on his shoe. Which led him to discovering a trail of gray-painted footprints all over her carpeted living room floor. Way things were looking, he'd be lucky to snag a piece of pizza that wasn't splattered in paint by the time he made it to her kitchen.

The screen door slammed shut as her footsteps creaked after him from the entryway. "Yeah, but a lot has happened since we first talked about it yesterday. I mean, for starters you were out in public wearing nothing but your undies again. Which I can't help thinking is starting to be a habit for you, one you should definitely kick before winter arrives."

"I'll work on it." He slid the jar of flowers on her kitchen table over so he could make room for the pizza and the real conversation they needed to have. The one about Aimee. And everything she said before he fell in the tank earlier this afternoon.

Admit it. You love Rachel. You've always loved Rachel. Just say it. Say it, say it, say it. You love her. You want her. Just say it.

Yeah, definitely something they needed to address. Would have earlier if it hadn't taken him so long to dry off and return to regular life-sustaining temperatures again. "So, hey. About earlier."

"Paper plates." Rachel snapped her fingers and spun for the cupboard. "Can't eat pizza without paper plates. I know I've got a few here somewhere."

"Right. So, the whole dunk tank thing."

"Oh my goodness, yes. Congratulations," she said, her voice much louder than it needed to be as she continued opening and slamming cabinet doors. "I heard you raised close to a thousand dollars between Abe and all those other donations. Even sold some cats. That's great."

"Well, we didn't technically sell any cats. They were free for adoption. And Wombat was the only one who took one. But anyway, that's not—"

"Eureka! Knew I had some. Shoot, they're on the top shelf. You mind grabbing them?" She must not have realized he had already stepped behind her. She spun and stabbed his chest with her paintbrush.

All he could do was look at his shirt. Look at her.

She grabbed a paper towel to clean off his shirt, and in the process somehow managed to swipe a streak of paint on his jeans. "I should probably just set the paintbrush down, shouldn't I?"

"What is your problem?" And he didn't just mean her uncanny ability to touch everything but the walls with her paintbrush. Why was she avoiding this conversation and yelling out words like *Eureka!* She held his gaze, her dark eyes pensive. Undecisive. As if she couldn't decide whether to call out the elephant in the room or just dump a bucket of paint over it instead. She took a step back and swallowed so loudly it could be labeled a gulp. "What do you mean?"

"I mean—" Matt lifted a shoulder, not at all liking the sudden tension permeating the air between them worse than paint fumes. Not at all liking how Rachel was looking at him like a student about to get her score back on a test she hadn't studied for. And trust him, he'd seen that look plenty enough times on her face throughout their four years of high school French to know it.

What was going on? This wasn't their relationship. Awkward. Strained. Stiff. No. Their relationship was fun. Relaxed. A breath of fresh air. That's why she'd always been his favorite friend. His best friend. That's why he loved her.

He inhaled a slow breath, afraid he was about to start making gulpy sounds if he wasn't careful.

Oh, wow. Aimee was right. He loved Rachel. Had for a long time.

Which is why he couldn't afford to rush things and lose her. Even if that meant staying in the friend zone a lot longer than he wanted.

He blew out his breath. "You have lit-er-ally"—he made a great show of enunciating the word as he circled his finger in the air around them—"left a crime scene of paint throughout this entire house. Don't act like you don't have a problem."

And just like that, it was as if the windows opened, clearing all the tension-filled fumes right out of the room.

Rachel's shoulders relaxed and her eyes took on their usual playful glint. "Um, excuse me, but I don't have to *act* like I don't have a problem because I *don't* have a problem."

She folded her arms over her chest, smearing her inner arm with paint since she was still holding the paintbrush. She slanted a look at her arm. "Okay, I might have a problem." One of her trademark giggle-snorts followed.

"You do understand the idea is to get the paint on the walls, right?"

"I was getting to that. I just had to get everything prepared first." She dropped the brush in the sink and started washing her hands.

He stepped next to her and scraped a finger over a crusted glob behind her left ear. "Is dunking your head in the paint can part of the preparation process?"

More giggles as she finished washing her hands. "There was a little bit of an issue when I poured paint into the roller cover thingy."

"Uh-huh, and did this little issue cause you to step in the roller cover thingy and leave gray-painted footprints all over the carpet?"

"I saw a mouse. I can't be held responsible for what my feet do in a moment of crisis."

"Really?" Matt opened the fridge and grabbed two of the root beer cans he'd left behind the other day when he started repairing her front porch. He handed her one. "I would've thought we set enough traps earlier this week to put mice on the endangered species list."

She sank into a kitchen chair and snapped back the tab. "All right, fine. It technically wasn't a mouse that I saw. It was the black hair scrunchie I flung in the air this morning when I freaked out over seeing a legit mouse."

He leaned against the counter and narrowed his gaze at her. "And by legit mouse, you mean . . ."

"The gray ankle sock I whipped on the floor two nights ago to kill a spider."

"And when you say spider . . ."

"I mean black sock fuzz." She opened the lid to the pizza and pulled out a slice, the cheese stretching all the way from the box to her plate. "Now can we be done with the interrogation and just enjoy a fun evening eating pizza and getting at least one streak of paint on the walls?"

Matt joined her at the table. Someday he really would like to have more with this woman. But for now, for tonight, he lifted his root beer. "To a fun evening eating pizza and getting at least one streak of paint on the walls."

She clinked her can against his, then lifted her pizza to her mouth. And Matt didn't know what he was going to do with this girl. Especially now that she had just as much tomato sauce on her chin as she did paint.

24

Gracie still hadn't talked to Luke since the bathtub incident.

And now two days had passed since the kitchen conversation incident—which probably shouldn't be labeled a conversation or an incident since she and Noah never made eye contact and he disappeared after saying a sum total of three sentences.

But neither of those incidents mattered at the moment.

No, the only incident concerning Gracie right now was the incident in her final chapter where her heroine finally figured out how to time travel from the past back to present day and move forward with the rest of her life.

An incident that appeared to be completely baffling Rachel, based on her furrowed brow.

Gracie leaned forward in the rocking chair Rachel had helped settle her into when they decided it was the perfect fall afternoon to enjoy out on the porch. "You've been staring at the last page for over five minutes, Rach. I'm dying here. What do you think?"

Seated on the porch swing with the three-ring binder containing Gracie's manuscript in her lap, Rachel finally lifted her gaze to Gracie. "I think I'm a little confused."

So was the weather. Their warm sunny afternoon had suddenly pivoted to cloudy and brisk. Gracie tugged the sleeves of her long cardigan sweater down over her hands. "Is it the time-travel-on-a-horse aspect? I know that's kind of out-there."

"That's certainly part of the confusion."

"What's the other part?"

Rachel wagged her head to the side. She looked down at the manuscript. Back to Gracie. "I guess I just thought romances were all supposed to end with a happily-ever-after."

Now Gracie was confused. Had she given Rachel the wrong draft? "Don't the heroine and the farmer ride off into the sunset on that silly horse at the end?"

When Rachel nodded, Gracie leaned back in her chair. "Well, what's more happily-ever-after than that?"

"Maybe riding off into the sunset with the man she actually loves? You left the hero of the story stuck in the past. Can you do that? I don't think you can do that."

"I didn't do that. The hero did that when he decided staying behind to try and rescue a lost boy from the forest was more important than chasing after her. And why can't the farmer be her new hero?"

"Because she doesn't love him like she loves the real hero. She thinks the farmer is fat and boring."

"She thinks he's portly and cautious."

"Well, who wants portly and cautious when you can have rugged and passionate?"

"My heroine, apparently. What? Stop looking at me like that. I don't make the rules."

Rachel slammed the binder shut. "What do you mean you don't make the rules? This is your story."

"Exactly! This is my story. So maybe trust that I actually know what's best for these characters, okay?"

Rachel lifted her hands in surrender. "Fine. The portly, cautious farmer it is. I'm sure romance readers everywhere will be swooning over his heart-throbbing jowls in no time."

"I'm sure they will. Speaking of jowls, why are yours speckled in paint?"

"What? Oh." Rachel scratched at her cheek, then examined her nail. "After I finished painting the living room the other day, I thought it'd be fun to remove all the popcorn-style ceilings in the house. And you know what? It's not. At all. In fact I'd say undoing popcorn ceilings is pretty much the portly farmer of fun."

Gracie couldn't help laughing. Then groaning. She scrubbed her face with her sweater-covered palms. "My story's a complete disaster, isn't it?"

"I wouldn't say that." The porch swing squeaked, then Gracie felt Rachel squeeze her shoulder as the weight of the manuscript settled onto her lap. "But I would say the ending could use another rewrite."

Gracie groaned again as she peeked through her fingers up at Rachel. "What if I don't know how to get the heroine together with the real hero of the story before time runs out? Wouldn't it just be easier to leave her with the farmer?"

"Sure. It'd also be easier to leave my ceilings popcorn-style, but since when do we ever do what's easy? Get back to work. Neither of us is out of time yet. You work on saving those characters and I'll do whatever it takes to rescue my ceilings."

25

Noah: Sam Elliott's a problem.

Matt: I take it you've met Luke.

Noah: I may have followed him to Lyla's Diner this morning.

Matt: You stalked him.

Noah: I stalked him.

Matt: And?

Noah: He's one of the most likable guys I've ever met! I can't stand him! Or Sam Elliott! Or you!

Matt: Likable guys are the worst.

Noah: He says he's a big fan of baseball!

Matt: The nerve of this guy.

Noah: He says he's a big fan of me!

Matt: Well, maybe you shouldn't be so likable either.

Noah: What am I going to do? I can't just let him go around being all likable around Gracie!

Matt: I wouldn't worry. Pretty sure I heard he's leaving soon for his next project.

Noah: Yeah? Well, what if another likable guy comes strutting into town after he's gone? I can't keep risking losing Gracie to likable guys. And you know she's not going to let me keep renting that cabin forever. I need to do something!

Matt: Like what?

Noah: Something drastic! Something I swore I'd never do.

Matt: Listen to me. You CANNOT kill Luke. Or Sam Elliott. Or anyone for that matter.

Noah: But I CAN force Gracie to talk to me.

Matt: Conversation? Oh my. Drastic indeed.

Noah: Kid, you have no idea. This might be the most drastic thing I've ever done.

26

Elevator doors pinged open. Matt held his arm out, allowing an elderly woman he recognized as a regular visitor to exit first. Her husband was one of the patients on the long-term care unit. They seemed like a sweet couple.

His favorite couple, though, was the husband and wife who both battled dementia and stayed in a room together at the end of the hall. Every night the wife would say, "Well, it's getting late. You reckon we should book a room for the night?" Like clockwork, her husband would return from inquiring at the nurses' station and say, "Don't worry. I got us all checked in." Then they'd shuffle off arm in arm down to room 222.

With hands stuffed in his pockets, Matt sauntered past the nurses' station, catching the unit secretary's eye. "How's my grandpa today?"

"Ornery as ever."

He smiled. That's what she always said. He feared the day she described his grandpa as docile. Buck would probably already have both feet in the grave the day she said that.

"Oh, hey." Matt snapped his finger as if just remembering, even though it was all he'd been thinking about. "Maybe you can help me out with a situation. One of the dialysis nurses and I have been play-ing phone tag." Kind of true. "About a, um, question." Not quite as true. "Regarding my grandpa's dialysis." Not true at all. "Could you by chance find out if she's working today?"

The phone rang and the clerk held up a finger so she could answer first.

Matt hadn't seen Rachel since they'd eaten pizza and painted her living room walls three nights ago like a couple of good friends. He'd offered to help again the past two nights, since she mentioned wanting to redo the popcorn-style ceilings, but she brushed him off. Said she had other plans.

Which was fine. Good friends are certainly allowed to have other plans, even if those plans are vague, and the good friend sees no need to elaborate on said vague plans.

But it was kind of weird she hadn't responded to any of his texts lately. The particularly hilarious meme he sent earlier this afternoon deserved an lol response at the very least.

The unit clerk finished her call and returned her attention to Matt. "If it's Rachel you're asking about, I can tell you right now that she's not here. Buck already asked me to request her for his dialysis session this afternoon, but she called in. Sick, I guess."

"Mono." Nurse Ratched-slash-Wanda popped her head out from behind a computer. "Heard it's going around bad on the fourth floor. At least that's what the X-ray tech told our dietician the other day. If that's the case, she won't be back for a while. Took me a month to get over it when I had it in high school. Of course that was back in the Middle Ages. People probably bounce back quicker these days without all the bloodletting."

"Nah," another nurse carrying a pile of linens on her way past said. "When I ran down to grab a drink from the cafeteria earlier, I'm pretty sure I overheard one of the dialysis nurses at the salad bar say something about being short-staffed today because one of their nurses was having real bad neck pain. I just hope it's not meningitis."

Meningitis? That sounded worse than the mono. Matt dug out his phone. "Has anyone checked on her?"

"She's okay." One of the techs, a young woman with pink-streaked hair and a tattoo sleeve on her right arm took the linens from the nurse. "She probably just got a little roughed up is all."

"What?" Matt whipped to face the tech, knocking a pen holder off the counter with his elbow. He scrambled to pick up the scattered pens.

"Yeah, one of the night shift phlebotomists who's good friends with the dialysis unit manager's daughter knows the guy who used to date Rachel's sister and works at that bar up in Rock Island."

Matt was going to need a corkboard with pictures and strings like they used on old detective shows to keep following this conversation. "Wait, are you talking about Ace?"

As he recalled, Rachel had never been impressed with any of her sister's boyfriends, but she seemed to especially detest Ace. Or rather, Stupid Face Ace, as she liked to call him.

The tech nodded. "That's the one. Guess he showed up out of the blue in Florida, begging Rachel's sister to take him back. She did. Then of course he started sweet-talking her for money. Before Rachel knew it, her sister somehow dipped into her account too. Ace pretty much wiped them both out, then hit the road. That's the whole reason Rachel moved back to this area. She's been wanting to track him down. Heard she finally did a few nights ago."

"What happened?" Matt was almost afraid to ask.

"Nothing happened," Wanda said. "That's one hundred percent gossip and all hearsay. Now stop spreading rumors and get back to work."

The tech offered a shrug on her way past Matt. "Just saying what I heard, that's all."

"I still vote it's meningitis," the other nurse muttered, heading the opposite direction.

"Well, I'm telling you it's mono," Wanda said from behind her computer. "Heard it straight from the on-call chaplain that the kissing disease was wreaking havoc once again. But whatever it is, I'm sure she'll bounce back. Nothing to worry about."

Too late for that. Matt shot Rachel a text. Hey, sort of worried you're dead again. Can you please respond with proof of life before I knock your door off its hinges?

A cafeteria worker pushing a dining cart rumbled past. Matt took that as his cue to go find his grandpa. He'd been making it a habit lately to visit him around suppertime in hopes of encouraging him to do more than just push food around on his plate.

"What's got you down in the dumps?" his grandpa asked a few minutes later in between bites.

"I'm not down in the dumps."

"You're definitely down in the dumps," Shorty said from the other side of the curtain. "Could hear it the moment your feet hit the tiles."

Matt's grandpa lifted his fork in a "there you have it" motion.

"I'm fine. I'm fine." Matt shrugged and opened his grandpa's milk carton for him. "I'm totally fine."

"Oh boy," his grandpa said, dropping his fork on the plate.

"Three 'fines' in three seconds." Shorty clucked his tongue. "It's worse than I thought."

"What happened? The animal shelter go belly-up or something?" This from his grandpa.

"Nah. Sounds worse than that," Shorty responded. "His woman must have gone belly-up."

"Nobody's gone belly-up." He hoped. "I told you, I'm—"

"Fine," all three of them said at the same time.

Matt squeezed the brim of his ball cap. "You guys are impossible."

"Better than being fine," his grandpa said with a wink. He picked up his fork again and dug into his food. "This doesn't have anything to do with a certain dialysis nurse not showing up for work today, does it? Because that's certainly not fine."

"Oh-oh," Shorty said. "I think you might be onto something there, Buck-o."

"Notice he's not protesting," Buck said around a mouthful of mashed potatoes.

"If I did, you'd only accuse me of protesting too much."

Buck shrugged. "If the shoe fits."

Matt stood. "Well, you two look like you have everything under control here."

"Always do," Shorty said.

Matt kissed his grandpa on the top of the head. "I'll see you tomorrow."

"Same bat-time," Shorty said.

"Same bat-channel," his grandpa finished.

Matt could hear his grandpa holler after him from halfway down the hallway. "And go check on our girl, will you?"

As if Matt needed to be told. He took the stairs, too impatient to wait for an elevator. Roughed up? Kissing disease? Meningitis?

He needed answers. Because right now it felt like his good friend was keeping a whole lot of secrets from him.

A text message pinged just as he hit the parking lot.

I'm alive. Don't bust down any doors. Not up for company. Talk to you later.

So much for getting any answers tonight.

27

Good grief. Noah knew plenty of baseball players with weird pregame rituals and crazy superstitions, but Gracie here just might surpass them all. "Tell me again why I'm moving your desk—"

"*Special* writing desk."

"Excuse me—*special* writing desk—into the dining room now?" He folded his arms and leaned back against the counter next to the kitchen sink.

"Because," Gracie said with a long-suffering sigh as if she couldn't believe she had to explain something so obvious. "I need my special writing desk to be in my special writing place so I can meet my special writing deadline."

"And where was all this special thinking when you told Matt and me to drag this beast of wood down the stairs and into the kitchen a few days ago?"

"So sue me if I forgot my special writing place was in the dining room and not the kitchen. I've had a lot on my mind lately."

"And the reason you can't just plop your special laptop and special typewriter and special notepad with all its special color-coordinated matching pens on top of the dining room table is because—"

"It's not my—"

"Special writing desk," he answered along with her. "Yeah, yeah. Got it. One question though."

"Make it quick. I promised my agent I'd send her my final revisions today, and I still need to rewrite the whole ending."

"How did you manage to write that entire baseball series years ago when you were nowhere near any special writing desks or special dining rooms?"

"That series wasn't my best writing. Now please move the desk."

That baseball series was definitely her best writing. But sure. If moving the desk from room to room kept her distracted for the rest of the afternoon, fine. He'd move it out to the front porch if that's what she wanted. Anything to buy him enough time to hear back from his agent and hopefully put his big plan into play.

"I'll move it. But for the record, I think you're nuts."

"Noted. Now try not to scratch up the floors."

Noah finagled the heavy oak desk down the hallway and into the dining room next to the westward-facing set of windows because they were apparently more *special* than the southward-facing windows. But he got it there. That should count for something. Even if he did scratch up the floors.

After spinning a chair from the dining room table to face the desk, he massaged his left shoulder. "Anything else?"

"Think I'm all set now. Thank you." She settled her laptop on the desk, then slid into the chair, tugging her long sweater out from where it'd gotten trapped beneath her thighs when she sat.

Midway through October now, the temperatures hovered in the low fifties most days, dipping to the thirties at night. Gracie was wearing thick socks, a pair of sweatpants, and a long gray open sweater over a white T-shirt.

Noah never thought he'd say this, but he missed the coffee-stained robe. She looked way too capable wearing real clothes again. Like she didn't need him at all. If it weren't for her deadline and her crazy-desk-moving-panic this morning, she probably wouldn't.

As if reading his mind, she said, "By the way, when were you thinking of leaving the cottage? I appreciate all the help you've given me this past week. Really, I do. But Wombat has a cousin moving to the area next month. He gave her my number and she's already reached out to see if the cabin would be available to rent. Probably time for you to head back to Seattle, don't you think?"

That was actually the complete opposite of what he thought. And the reason he needed to make his big move.

He dug his phone from his pocket, hoping to see a message or missed call from Scotty. The screen stared back at him, not a single notification.

Had his agent died? Scotty couldn't even go to the bathroom without his phone. Why hadn't he called back yet?

"Uh, not sure when I'll be ready to head back to Seattle. Soon maybe." *Hopefully never.* "There's a couple of things I still need to take care of here first."

"What sort of things?"

"Important things." *Like convincing you to forget about every other likable guy in the world except me.* "Haven't visited the apple orchard yet."

She quirked a brow. "Apple cider donuts are your definition of important?"

"They're everybody's definition of important. No way I can leave town without getting half a dozen. Figured while I was there I'd grab enough apples to whip up an apple pie for dessert later today." Gracie loved apple pie.

"Since when do you know how to whip up anything that involves using an oven?"

Since about five minutes from now, when he planned to google *easy apple pie recipes for beginners who don't know how to whip up anything that involves using an oven,* that's when.

"Don't you think you'll deserve special pie for meeting your special deadline?"

That did the trick. She stopped her terrible line of questioning and swiveled to her computer. "Deadline. Right."

"Right. I'll leave you to it."

She was already waving him off and digging out a pair of reading glasses from one of the desk drawers.

"Good luck with the ending," he said over his shoulder, making his way to the front door. "Try to work in some sort of passionate reconciliation between her and that horse, will ya?"

"Too obvious," she called back to him. "I need a surprise ending that will send my readers into a tizzy."

"Nothing like a good tizzy," he said, closing the door behind him. And he was about to be in one if Scotty didn't call him back soon.

28

Grace: I ended things with the portly farmer.

Mona: I don't know what that means. Have you been secretly dating Farmer Mac?

Grace: Whoops. Meant to send that to Rachel.

Mona: How'd Rachel know about you and Farmer Mac?

Grace: She doesn't. I was talking about my story . . . and maybe kinda sorta talking about Luke.

Mona: He's a farmer? I thought he owned a construction company.

Grace: He does. Just ignore everything I'm saying.

Mona: I can't now. You ended things with Luke? I thought you said you two weren't in a relationship.

Grace: We weren't, technically speaking.

Mona: So what did you technically end?

Grace: The friendly chats we occasionally had that hinted at the possibility of a potential future relationship if we ever decided to make a commitment.

Mona: You heartbreaker. Hope he took it well.

Grace: Annoyingly well. Probably because all he wanted to talk about was how he met Noah the other day and what a likable guy he was.

Mona: Portly farmers are the worst.

Grace: Complete backstabbers.

Mona: So what are you going to do now?

Grace: Focus on my story. I still haven't worked out a happily-ever-after for my heroine. If I don't come up with something good in the next couple hours, she may just have to ride off into the sunset alone.

Mona: We can't have that.

Grace: Really? I'd think you'd be all for that.

Mona: Maybe if this was my story. But I happen to believe the heroine in your story deserves a much happier ending.

29

Later that afternoon Noah adjusted the paper bag full of Jonathan apples and three dozen cider donuts—who was he kidding when he said half a dozen—in one arm while digging out his phone. Scotty. Finally.

"I'll do it. Make it happen," Noah said as soon as he answered Scotty's FaceTime call and saw his agent sitting in his office, the city skyline behind him past his office windows.

"Really? Great!" Scotty lifted his hands like a football referee right after a touchdown. "Love that. Yes. I'll make it happen. Right now. Emailing the general manager of the Riverton Rowdies as we speak."

"Who are the Riverton Rowdies?"

"Your new baseball club."

"Why are they my new baseball club?"

Scotty paused in pounding away at his computer keyboard. "You just said to make it happen."

"Make what happen?"

"Get you hired on as the new baseball manager for the Riverton Rowdies. They're that new farm league team in Oklahoma. The one I emailed you about a few days ago."

Noah hadn't checked his email in weeks. "I don't want you to make *that* happen."

"Then what am I making happen?"

"The memoir."

"The memoir?"

"The memoir."

"The memoir?"

Noah adjusted the sack of apples and donuts in his arms. "Are we doing some sort of shtick right now? Because I'm having a real hard time following this conversation."

"You're not the only one." Scotty leaned closer to the computer screen and frowned. "What is happening right now? Why are there a bunch of kids climbing onto a tractor trailer behind you? And why do they look so happy about it?"

Noah held up his phone to give Scotty a better view. "That's Farmer Mac. He always gives the kids hayrides with his tractor during harvest season. Now back to the memoir."

"Where are these kids' parents? Shouldn't they be supervising them or something?"

"The kids are all probably here on a field trip. They're fine. Now did you hear what I said?"

"The kids aren't even strapped in."

"Scotty."

"I heard you, I heard you. Now tell me again what you said."

"The book. The memoir. I'm ready to do it."

Scotty's office chair squeaked as he straightened in his seat and adjusted his tie. "The memoir. You're serious?"

"I'm serious."

"Serious serious?"

"Scotty."

"Okay. Got it. Serious serious. Wow. Just didn't . . . okay. I'm surprised. Didn't expect this. But this is . . . Oh, wow. This is great. Really great."

The way Scotty pounded his computer keyboard, Noah would think he was playing ragtime music on a piano. "I already know a couple of publishing houses who will eat this right up. Trust me. You won't regret this. Especially once I get Darren on board. He's the author who helped write the book for that blind soccer goalie. He's great at working with athletes. I'm sure he'll—"

"No. No Darren. I'm only working with Gracie. That's my one stipulation. Deal's off if Gracie doesn't write it."

"Gracie? Who's Gracie?"

"You know Gracie. My wife? Well, ex-wife."

Scotty stopped playing the keyboard and sprang forward in his seat, inches away from the camera on his computer. "You want your ex-wife to write your memoir? Noah, the point of this exercise is to make you look good and springboard you into a management position in the majors."

No, the point was to buy him some one-on-one time with his wife before she gave him the boot and started getting friendly with likable guys. "She's the only one I want writing my story. Take it or leave it. Also, I need this contract put into place now. Immediately. Today."

"Today?"

"Today."

"Today?"

"Is this parroting technique something you actually find productive?"

Scotty sank back in his seat and massaged his temples. "I'm starting to wish you'd take a ride on the back end of a tractor without supervision."

"You know you love me."

Scotty snorted. Then after a quick shake of his head, he straightened and began tapping away at the keyboard. "Fine. I don't know why I'm agreeing to this. But fine. Who's your wife's agent? You know what, never mind. I'll figure it out myself. I'm done with you. You annoy me."

"Love working with you too." Noah ended the call.

The high-pitched voices of children talking and laughing carried through the fields as he headed back to his truck.

No, he didn't relish the idea of opening a can of worms to his past, but what other option did he have? Noah had to do *something* that would keep him close to Gracie and make her start talking to him again.

He glanced at the sack of apples. Something other than baking a pie he had no idea how to bake.

30

Simone: Are you and Noah back together?

Grace: What? No! Absolutely not!

Simone: He's not living with you right now?

Grace: No! I mean, yes, he's living on my property at the moment, in the cottage next door. But not for much longer.

Simone: How much longer?

Grace: What is this about?

Simone: Did you send me the wrong story?

Grace: I don't think so.

Simone: This is the right draft?

Grace: What's going on?

Simone: Are you the lady who fell off that horse in the truck?

Grace: I'm about to lawyer up if you ask me any more questions.

Simone: Don't let Noah leave until you hear back from me.

Grace: Why?

Grace: Why?

Grace: Simone, answer me. Why?

Simone: BECAUSE I'M TRYING TO SAVE YOUR CAREER!

31

Matt turned off his truck and grabbed the paper sack filled with a container of chicken noodle soup and a gourmet grilled cheese sandwich. He hadn't texted Rachel that he was coming over. Mostly because he didn't want to give her the chance to stop him this time. Not until she at least answered the question *Do you have mono or meningitis?*

Matt climbed the porch stairs, much sturdier since he'd repaired them, and knocked. A flash of movement behind the living room window caught his eye. The curtain rustled back in place.

He waited for her to come to the door. After a minute, he took a deep breath, and waited another minute for her to come to the door. Another minute later, he knocked again. Louder.

Why wasn't she coming to the door? Was she avoiding him?

Too bad if she was. He wasn't leaving until he found out what was going on.

"Rachel." He pounded the door. "I know you're in there. I just . . . Are you okay? I heard you were sick, maybe." Or roughed up. But his brain preferred to go with the sickness theory. "I brought some food. Open up. Please."

Just when he didn't think she was going to answer and he might have to knock another door off its hinges, the door cracked open.

Rachel's head, nearly at a ninety-degree angle on her left shoulder, peered back at him.

"Hey," she said.

"Hey," he said back.

He peered through the sliver of space, not wanting to shove the door open, but . . . yeah. Really wanting to shove the door open. Was she going to let him inside? Offer an explanation as to why she wasn't letting him inside? Something?

He lifted the sack. "Are you hungry?"

"Sure. Just, um, leave it on the porch. Thanks."

"Rachel, what's going on?"

"Nothing. Just having a little bit of an issue."

"What sort of issue?" He slid his foot in the door opening to keep her from closing it.

"Neck issue. But it'll be fine. Thanks for the food." The pressure against his foot increased.

"Wait. What's wrong with your neck? Do you have meningitis? That's what some of your coworkers are saying."

She let out a soft laugh, then immediately winced and grabbed her neck. "No. Nothing like that. It's just a stiff neck. I'm seeing a chiropractor tomorrow. Thanks again for the food."

"Well, let me at least take it into the kitchen for you."

"I'm not really suitable for company."

"Rachel. It's me. You don't have to set out the fine china. Just let me in." He brought his palm up to the door.

"I can't."

"You're starting to freak me out. Are you sure you don't have meningitis?"

"Do you even know what meningitis is?"

"No, but it sounds terrible. Possibly contagious. Why else won't you let me inside?"

"Because I haven't showered in days and I can't straighten my head. I look terrible, I feel awful, and nobody should see me like this. Except for the chiropractor. I desperately want for him to see me like this."

She tried for a light laugh, but it quickly turned into a whimper. When her face scrunched up and a tear ran down her cheek, Matt couldn't stand still another second on the porch. "Hey," he said, stepping inside and setting the sack on the floor inside her entry.

"Hey, Rachel, hey . . ." He wasn't sure what else to say. He'd never seen Rachel cry before. Sure, cry from laughing too hard maybe. But never *cry* cry.

More tears dripped sideways off her cheek. She gripped her neck. "I thought it'd be better by now. It hurts so bad, I can't even move enough to change my clothes."

She was wearing paint-speckled leggings and one of his button-down flannel shirts over a T-shirt undoubtedly covered in more paint. The flannel shirt must be the one he wore the other day to work on her porch, then took off when the afternoon sun got too warm. He forgot he'd left it behind. But boy, was he glad he did. That shirt had never looked so amazing.

Probably would look even better if the person currently wearing it wasn't crying with her head stuck sideways on her shoulder.

He patted her arm. Seemed a safe place to touch her without causing more pain. "What happened?"

"It's probably from redoing the popcorn ceilings and having my head tilted back at a weird angle for hours, then sleeping with the window cracked open to let out some of the fumes. I think the cold air froze my neck like this."

"Why didn't you call me?"

"I really thought it'd be better by now. Plus I didn't want to bother you. I feel like all you do is help me."

"What's wrong with that? I'm your friend."

"Yeah, but this just seems above and beyond the average call of friendship duty."

"Well, who said anything about our friendship being average? Come on. You can't stay here alone like this. Why don't you at least stay the night at my place?" He gently grabbed her elbow. "I've got a heating pad that might help. Plus, I'll be able to give you a ride to the chiropractor first thing tomorrow morning."

"You really don't have to do all this."

"I know, but let me anyway." After helping her pack a few things, he was soon helping her into his truck.

"You weren't serious about the meningitis, were you," she said as he leaned over to buckle her in.

"One nurse was placing bets on mono."

"Where do they get this?"

"Oh, that's not all," Matt said, straightening and grabbing the edge of the truck door to close it. "Some girl with pink hair tried telling me you got beat up because you confronted your sister's ex-boyfriend Ace for stealing a bunch of money from you."

"*Pssh*. That's crazy."

"I know."

"He didn't even come close to beating me up."

"I know." Matt started to close the door, then opened it wide again. "Wait—what? Are you saying you did confront Ace?"

"If confronting means pouring a glass of beer over his head."

Matt gripped the door harder to keep his knees from buckling. "You did what? When?"

"Weeks ago. That night I was driving home late and hit the deer. I was on my way back from his bar."

"And you've just been living out here by yourself with zero security, broken-down doors, and . . . and . . . *mice?*"

"Can we save this discussion for a time when I can hold my head a little more perpendicular to my shoulders?"

"*Rachel.* I cannot believe you. If I hadn't already packed a bag to bring you home with me, I'd be packing a bag right now to bring you home with me. Are you nuts? You can't just go around dumping beer on people's heads."

"It wasn't people. It was Ace."

"That's even worse. You're coming home with me right now and I don't want another word about it."

"I'm in the truck, aren't I?"

"I said *not another word*. You practically have a hit out on you, do you realize that? Picking a fight with Ace," he muttered as he slammed the door shut. Good thing he was here to save her neck—in more ways than one.

32

"No. No way. Absolutely not. Never gonna happen."

"Gracie, you didn't even let me explain," Simone pleaded through the phone.

Gracie slammed the refrigerator door shut. "What's to explain? I'm a romance writer. I don't write memoirs. Certainly not my ex-husband's memoir. The answer is no. I can't believe you thought I'd even consider the idea."

"Hear me out."

Gracie pressed her lips together, wanting to scream. Wanting to vomit. Wanting to swear. It took all of her willpower not to end the phone call. She limped to the kitchen table and yanked out a chair. "I don't want to come across as ungrateful. Honestly, you've been incredibly patient with me and I'm so thankful for that. But—"

"Your rom-com's a bust. I looked it over right after you sent it, and I'm telling you, there's no way your editor is going to accept this story. Time travel? Really? You didn't even make it clear whether the hero and heroine actually end up together."

"I thought I'd leave it open for a sequel."

"What reader in their right mind is going to want a sequel to this?"

Gracie lowered herself into the chair, her legs as weak as they'd been right after her horse accident. "I know it still needs a little work. I'm sure my editor will—"

"—never offer you another contract again? Me too."

"Simone. Come on. Cut me some slack."

Gracie heard the sounds of a stapler clicking in the background. "I have zero slack left to give. Don't you get it? Your book sales have plummeted. You haven't written anything new in years. The last book you published was a complete dud. Not to mention that you're practically nonexistent on social media."

"I know, I know. I've just had so much going on lately."

"Listen, I get it. The divorce. Your dad's health. The recent horse accident you didn't tell me about, though I can sort of see why. But Gracie—this is life. Everybody goes through stuff. You still have to hit your deadlines. And you still have to deliver what your publishing house is paying you for."

"Right. Which I believed was a romantic comedy, not a baseball memoir."

"But you haven't written a romantic comedy. You've written a time-travel travesty. You hear what I'm saying? We have *nothing* to give them."

"I'm close. So close. A few more tweaks here and there. If I can just get a little more time—"

"There's none left, not if you don't do the memoir. Don't you get it? This is your last shot. Just write the stinking memoir."

"What about the stinking rom-com?"

"It's stinking dead. So unless you want to pay back your whole stinking advance, you will write the stinking memoir."

Gracie grabbed her forehead. "I stinking see."

Simone sighed and the clicking sound of the stapler stopped. "It's going to be fine. Really. Honestly, you should have heard how excited the editor for the nonfiction team was over the idea. For whatever reason, memoirs are selling like hotcakes right now, and one of their other deals recently fell through. Noah's memoir can fill a giant hole in their publishing schedule, so long as we jump on it right away. No messing around. They want a full outline and the first three chapters by the end of the month."

"The end of the month? That's—" Gracie looked at the wall calendar.

"Less than two weeks," Simone confirmed. "But it's just an outline and three chapters. I know you can do it. I mean, Noah is there, right? You both have the time. And who knows? Maybe this is what you need to get unstuck from whatever's blocking you in your romance story. You won't have to worry about making anything up. Just ask questions and weed out the boring stuff."

"Right. Which would be perfect except for three minor details. One—I don't want to work with my ex-husband. Two—all of baseball is boring. And three—I don't want to work with my ex-husband."

"Do you want to keep working as a writer?"

"You know I do."

"Then I suggest you find a way to deal with those three minor issues. Or at least one of them. That'll solve half the battle right there. If the editor likes what she sees in two weeks, they'll give the official green light for the rest of the story, and more importantly, you'll be off the hook for the rom-com. The publisher said they'll push back the timeline for that so you can focus on the memoir."

"All right." Gracie knew a lifeline when she saw one. She'd be a fool not to grab hold of it. "So an outline and the first three chapters?"

"If you can write more, that would be even better. But no worries if you can't."

Oh, Gracie had worries. Lots of worries. Chief among them was how she was going to survive another two weeks with Noah back in her life.

Maybe it wouldn't take that long. Maybe she could crank out all the information she needed from Noah in less than two weeks. Shoot, she should know most of his story already, shouldn't she? "All right, Simone. I'll do it. I'll get started right away."

Because the sooner she started, the sooner they finished, and the sooner Noah didn't have any reason to stay.

33

Grace: Cock-a-doodle-doo! Daylight's burning! Wakey-wakey!

Noah: Do you see what time it is?

Grace: Sure do! So you better get over here! We don't have a minute to waste!

Noah: It's not even six in the morning, babe. You think I can remember anything about my life before six in the morning?

Grace: If I can remember that you're an early bird, then I'm betting you can remember plenty. (Including the fact that I don't want you calling me babe!)

Noah: I'm supposed to meet up with Matt this morning.

Grace: What? Why?

Noah: Not sure. He says he has something important to talk about.

Grace: So do we!

Noah: I'll come over after I meet him for breakfast.

Grace: How long will that be?

Noah: I don't know.

Grace: Come over now. We can at least get started.

Noah: Can't. Already headed out the door for a run.

Grace: Thought 6 was too early for you.

Noah: Good thing you reminded me I'm an early bird. See you this afternoon, babe.

Grace: Afternoon?!

34

"You're writing Noah's what?"

"Don't laugh, Dad. It's not funny." Plus Gracie never liked how her dad's laughter often turned into wheezy coughing fits that led to increased oxygen requirements. She gave her scrambled eggs another stir in the frying pan just as her toast popped up warm and brown from the toaster. "C'mon, Dad. Take a breath. You okay?"

His coughing subsided enough on the other end of the phone that she could hear the gentle hiss of the oxygen flowing from his nasal cannula. "I'm fine, I'm fine. Oh, but that's rich. You of all people."

"Tell me about it." Gracie added a little cheese to her eggs.

He coughed a few more times. "So he's sticking around then? Noah?"

"Has to. For now. We're supposed to get started on it immediately."

"Well then, I better not keep you."

"You're fine. Noah's not even here. Apparently Matt needed to talk to him about something important, so they're meeting up for breakfast." She snapped off the burner. "Here we go again. Same old tune. I remember the lyrics to this song. *Hey Noah, I need you. Sorry, babe, gotta go.* Yeah, this project is going to work out oh so great."

"Aw c'mon. Cut him a little slack."

"You do remember that Noah is my ex-husband, right?"

"Trust me, honey. I remember exactly who Noah is." His tone

sounded way too forgiving to be talking about the man who broke her heart. "Uh-oh. Looks like they're bringing my breakfast tray in. Better go."

"Why are you eating breakfast in your room? Why aren't you going out to the dining hall?"

"You mean depressing hall," he muttered.

"Well . . ." Okay. It wasn't the cheeriest of places. But still. He shouldn't be eating his meals locked up in his room. "They're still getting you up into your wheelchair throughout the day, right? Do I need to come up there and talk to someone?"

"Honey, I'm fine. Sometimes Shorty and I just prefer keeping our own company in the morning."

"All right. But remember you've still got to get out and about. You can't just stare at those same four walls all day, every day."

"I know, I know. Don't you worry about me. You just focus on Noah for now. I'll talk to you later." He hung up before she could respond.

Focus on Noah. Right. She turned off the burner and stared at her eggs. This new project stole her appetite worse than her previous deadline.

35

Noah was starving. He dug into the Western omelet Lyla had just delivered. His left elbow banged into Matt's right elbow as they both attempted to lift a forkful of food to their mouths. "Tell me again why we're all sitting on the same side of the booth."

Abe, smashed between Noah's right shoulder and the wall, spoke around a mouthful of biscuits and gravy as The Everly Brothers belted out "Wake Up Little Susie" from a speaker system above their booth. "Yeah, kind of wondering that too."

"Because I don't want anyone overhearing what I say," Matt whispered.

"What did he say?" Abe said.

"He doesn't want anyone overhearing," Noah repeated.

"Shhh. Keep your voice down," Matt whispered. "Plus sitting like this keeps our backs to the entrance."

"What did he say?" Abe said.

"Oh shoot, I meant to ask for ketchup," Noah said.

"He wants ketchup?" Abe said. "I thought he ordered pancakes."

Noah lifted a finger to grab Lyla's attention. "Ketchup," he mouthed to her across the diner. "Okay, but why did we have to wait until our food arrived to talk about whatever it is you need to talk about?"

"Because I wanted to act natural," Matt said. "Like we had nothing more important to talk about than the weather."

"What? Weather? I already told you it's supposed to be sunny all week." A glob of gravy slid off Abe's fork and landed on his tie. "Aw, nuts. I promised Lizzy I'd keep this one clean."

"So what's this top secret conversation then?" Noah thanked Lyla for the ketchup and squeezed the bottle over his hash browns.

"Do you think water will get the stain out or just make it worse?" Abe dabbed a wet napkin at his tie.

"I'm scared Rachel's sister's ex-boyfriend is going to come after her."

"I should've worn a bib."

"Why?" Noah dug back into his omelet.

"She dumped a glass of beer over his head."

Abe leaned over his plate to look at Matt. "What's that about beer? Does it get rid of gravy stains?"

"Okay. Enough." Noah shooed Matt out of the booth. "I don't think anybody's going to hear us over The Everly Brothers, and I'll take my chances against any assassins attacking my back at Lyla's Diner."

Noah slid into the other side of the booth and tugged his plate in front of him. "There. Much better. Now what's going on with Rachel? Why'd she dump beer on some guy's head?"

"Because he stole money from her, and she was mad."

Noah shrugged. "As good a reason as any."

"I kind of wish Lizzy would just dump beer on my head whenever she was mad," Abe said, scrubbing his tie. "That way I'd know, you know? No guesswork. No silent treatment. Just lick the beer off my chin, say sorry, and try again with a clean tie."

"I don't think Ace is the type to just move on." Matt pushed away his plate of pancakes. "I'm worried about her. I'm really worried about her."

"Remind me again who Rachel is," Abe said.

"An old friend from high school. She moved back a few weeks ago. Now she's a temporary nurse on my grandpa's dialysis unit."

Abe stopped scrubbing his tie. Lifted his gaze to Matt. "Oh, wait.

Yeah. I heard about her. The dunk tank incident. Lizzy was telling me how she was the one Aimee caught you fooling around with on the shelter floor."

"It wasn't what it looked like," Matt said.

"Where have I heard that one before?" Abe's glance slid to Noah.

"It wasn't," both Noah and Matt said at the same time.

"Hey, what the two of you do behind closed doors is your own business. Think that looks clean?" Abe lifted his tie.

"Sure," Noah said. "Other than the giant gravy stain in the middle."

Abe scowled and jerked off his tie. Shoved it in his pocket. "Who wears ties anymore anyway?"

"Can we get back to Rachel?" Matt said. "I want to keep her safe. But I don't know what to do."

"Have you thought about asking Luke for help?" Abe asked. "Aw c'mon man," he said after Noah picked up a chunk of hash browns covered in ketchup and threw it on his white button-down shirt. "Was that really necessary?"

"Sometimes I wonder who has a bigger crush on that man, Lizzy or you?"

Abe dunked his napkin in his water glass and started dabbing his shirt. "I'm just saying he seems like the type of guy who knows how to handle beer and scary men. What's wrong with that?"

"Is this because you've gotten to know Luke or are you still basing everything you know about him off whatever Western series you're watching this week?"

"Definitely the latter. Now I'm picturing Luke more like Tommy Lee Jones's character from *Lonesome Dove*."

"Woodrow F. Call? You know, I can kind of see that," Matt said. "Commanding presence. Tight-lipped about his past."

"Oh, would you two knock it off?" Noah growled. "You guys can't see anything." Especially when it came to Luke. "Listen, Matt, you want some advice about what to do with Rachel? Tell her you love her, ask her to marry you, then promise to do whatever it takes to keep her safe and cherished for the rest of her life. That's what you do. Now let's finish our breakfast so I can get back to doing what I need to do."

Mainly, keeping Gracie's thoughts far away from the likes of anybody resembling Woodrow Call. Besides, he probably resembled this Woodrow Call character more than Luke did. Especially if the tight-lipped part was true.

He set his fork down, his appetite suddenly gone. Maybe he should've thought through this whole memoir idea a little better.

36

"Chattanooga?" Gracie squinted at Noah's handwriting. "Why does this say Chattanooga?" Noah never lived in Chattanooga. Did he? She didn't think so.

"Noah, did you ever live in—oh forget it." She tossed aside her reading glasses. Two days into this memoir project and it was going nowhere. Fast. On the "Chattanooga Choo Choo".

She pursed her lips, beginning to whistle the old Glenn Miller classic when a text chimed through on her phone.

> **Simone:** Making good progress?

Gracie stopped whistling. Good progress? Well, let's see. Yesterday after getting back from breakfast, Noah, with Matt's help, moved her special writing desk back to the spare bedroom on the second floor, then decided two questions into his memoir that he should take advantage of the nice weather and clean up some of the brush along the property. Then today, after scribbling down some indecipherable notes, Noah decided he should take advantage of the ongoing nice weather to burn the pile of brush, branches, and leaves he'd gathered up yesterday.

So . . . Yep! Making good progress! Her property looked better than it had in years.

> **Simone:** Glad Noah's giving you material to work with. He's got

that reputation for never wanting to give interviews, so I was a little worried. Sounds like you two are working well together. Imagine that!

Yeah, imagine that. Gracie glanced to the scrap paper covered in Noah's scrawl.

After their scant progress yesterday—*jeez Louise, Gracie, I feel like I'm getting interrogated on some Dateline special*—Gracie thought it might be easier for him to jot down notes about the key moments of his life. Something to help her at least start putting together an outline.

And so far the sum total of that outline was Chattanooga, whatever that meant.

But hey, the yard looked good.

Gracie tipped her head back. Oh, this project was doomed. Her career was doomed. Everything was doomed. Start the funeral dirge.

Her lips apparently preferred something livelier than a funeral dirge. They returned to whistling a Glenn Miller tune.

"Pennsylvania 6-5000."

Gracie jerked, whipping her gaze to find Noah standing in the doorway. "I thought you were still outside."

Noah stepped into the room, bringing the smell of fall and smoke along with him, as he set a cup of tea on the corner of her desk. "Needed a break. Thought you might be ready for one too. It's herbal."

"Thanks. And it was 'Chattanooga Choo Choo,' by the way. The song I was whistling."

Noah removed a gray stocking hat he must've dug out of the hall closet and shoved it into his back jeans pocket as he ran his fingers through his flattened hair, making it stick up in sweaty angles. "I promise you that wasn't 'Chattanooga Choo Choo.'"

"Because you're a Glenn Miller expert, are you?"

"Pretty much. *The Glenn Miller Story* was my grandma Rosie's favorite movie. Must've watched it at least a dozen times the one summer I lived with her. So trust me, if anybody knows Glenn Miller, it's this guy." He pointed his thumbs at his chest.

"Well, sounds like you need to watch it again. Because this girl"—Gracie jabbed her thumbs at her chest—"was whistling 'Chattanooga Choo Choo.'"

"I'm telling you, 'Pennsylvania 6-5000.'"

"If I'd been whistling 'Pennsylvania 6-5000,' it would have sounded like this—" Gracie began whistling.

Noah immediately started shaking his head. "That's 'Little Brown Jug.' Listen, this is 'Chattanooga Choo Choo.'" And because he never could whistle to save his life, he began making weird trumpet-sounding noises.

"You kidding me? That's 'A String of Pearls.' Maybe 'Tuxedo Junction.'"

"You're just naming songs."

"You're just making noises."

When they transitioned into a weird mash-up of "In the Mood" and Louis Armstrong's "What a Wonderful World," Gracie waved her hands and yelled, "What is happening right now?"

"We're working on the memoir," Noah said as if it were the most obvious thing in the world.

"This is not working on the memoir. *This*"—she waved her finger back and forth between them—"is putting me at a high risk for a stroke."

Noah lifted his hands in surrender. "You're right. Time to focus. No more Glenn Miller showdowns. How about we both just take a breath for a minute? You drink some tea. I take a shower. We start fresh in a half hour."

Not a bad idea. She reached for her teacup. "Fine. Reconvene in a half hour. Maybe then you can tell me what Chattanooga is all about."

"I thought Glenn Miller was off-limits. Oh wait. Do you mean *charcuterie*?" He stepped to the desk and tapped on the paper full of his scribbles.

"That says *charcuterie*?"

"Probably spelled it wrong, but yeah, see?" He ran his finger along the next bit of chicken scratch that may as well have been written in Greek. "It ties into this metaphor I thought up about baseball. But I was trying to get it written down so fast that now I can't tell what I wrote. Shoot, now I can't even remember how it all tied together."

"Get out." Before she dumped the cup of tea on his head. Which, after hearing about Rachel's beer experience, honestly didn't sound like a bad way to handle things.

"All right. Be back in thirty. Unless . . ." He paused in the doorway, his voice full of nonchalant innocence. "You want me to switch that shower into a bubble bath for two?"

Gracie threw a pen at him. He smirked and disappeared from the doorway, making ridiculous trumpet sounds to the tune of Bobby Darin's "Splish Splash" all the way down the stairs.

If Gracie smiled, it was only because he was stupid. And annoying. And a tiny bit appealing in his flannel button-down shirt that smelled like autumn leaves and outdoor work and all sorts of good memories, including cool fall days that ended in a bubble bath for two.

She shook off the thought. Better to focus on the stupid and annoying aspects so she could remain the ice queen—even if it did feel like that ice queen was slowly melting beneath bubbles the more time she spent with the man.

She glanced at the time. All right. Thirty minutes and they'd get down to business. This day wouldn't be another total waste.

She reached for the tea Noah had brought her. By now it'd cooled off enough that she could gulp it all down in one long swallow. So that's what she did.

Whew. She blew out a breath. The tea was stronger than she expected. Not bad. Just . . . *whew.*

She hiccuped and looked at the clock. Twenty-six minutes to go. And he better not be a second late getting back.

After a few more minutes, she hiccuped again. And again. She clapped a hand over her mouth. What was wrong with her? She never got the hiccups. *Never.*

Only time she ever had them was back in high school, which happened to coincide with the only time she ever gave in to peer pressure. Between her dad finding out she'd been involved in underage drinking and blowing the worst gasket she'd ever seen, followed up with three miserable days of nonstop hiccups, Gracie had sworn off alcohol ever since.

Hiccup. Gracie looked at her empty teacup. Noah wouldn't have . . .

Gracie sniffed it. *Hiccup-hiccup.* Would he?

She slammed down the cup. "Noah, what exactly is your definition of herbal?" she shouted.

37

Grace: Noah is poisoning me. I need you to come over here and kill him.

Matt: Can it wait until after supper?

Grace: Sorry. Meant to send that message to your mom.

Matt: So I'm off the hook for murder?

Grace: Unless I can't get ahold of her.

Matt: Have you considered calling the boys at the firehouse?

Grace: You're the worst.

Matt: Love you too.

Matt grinned as he slid his phone into his back pocket, reached for the drink carrier with one hand, the food with the other, then elbowed his truck door shut.

Things were clearly going well with Gracie and Noah's little memoir project. Now to get things moving along with his own personal little Matt-and-Rachel-should-be-more-than-friends project.

Ever since his breakfast with Noah and Abe yesterday morning, confessing his feelings to Rachel was all he could think about. *Tell her you love her, ask her to marry you, then promise to do whatever it takes to keep her safe and cherished for the rest of her life.*

Obviously he wasn't going to ask Rachel to marry him. Not yet. That'd be crazy.

Unless she was as head over heels in love with him as he was with her. Then maybe asking her to marry him by the end of the week would be the soundest decision he ever made.

The scent of juicy hamburgers and salted fries made his stomach growl as he juggled the drinks and sack to open the front door to his house.

"Hope you're hungry," Matt said, nudging the door shut with his foot.

He hadn't checked with Rachel before swinging through the diner on his way home from visiting Buck, but he didn't figure she'd be sad to see a sack full of greasy sustenance. Who would? Plus greasy sustenance felt like a great segue into discussing their relationship.

Sure, Rach, I'll take your extra pickle. Will you take my entire heart?

Okay, maybe not the best segue.

"Grabbed us a few burgers," he called out on the way to the kitchen. "Hope you wanted a lemonade. Wasn't sure if you'd want that or iced tea or—" He halted at the site of Rachel stepping out of the guest bedroom with her overnight bag slung over her shoulder. "Hey, what's going on? I just brought home dinner. You're not leaving, are you?"

Rachel's gaze bounced off the drinks and food. "Sorry. Should've texted you. I'm not all that hungry. I ended up eating a big lunch with Aimee today."

Aimee? "Oh. Okay. Sure you don't want some fries at least?"

Her stomach growled, obviously on board with the idea of fries. But Rachel shook her head. "No, that's okay. I just came back to grab my things. She dropped me off at my house earlier, so I could get my car and run a few errands."

Aimee?

"Yeah, Aimee."

He must've spoken that last bit out loud. "So you're just going back to your house now?" *For good?*

Rachel adjusted the strap of her bag along her shoulder, eyeing the bag of fries like a long-lost lover. "I'm sure you're ready to have your space back. Besides, my neck's way better. After this morning's chiropractor appointment, I can change clothes like there's no tomorrow. I mean, this is my third pair of pants today just because I can."

"And nobody's prouder of you than I am, but hey—" He tossed the sack of food on the counter and chased after her when it became apparent the fries weren't enough of a temptation to keep her at his house long enough for him to figure out how to tell her he loved her way more than a friend. "What about Ace?"

She paused at the front door. "What *about* Ace?"

"What if he shows up at your house?"

She wrinkled her nose and reached for the handle. "He's not going to show up at my house. Trust me."

"But what if he does?" He covered her hand to keep her from twisting the door handle.

"Then I'll call the police."

"After he hurts you?"

"He's not going to hurt me. Think about it, if he wanted to hurt me, he would've followed me home by now and slit my throat, then dumped my body where nobody could find it until it had decomposed so far beyond recognition that only my dental records would be able to identify me."

"Was that supposed to reassure me or . . .?"

"Bottom line, I can't stay here. Not if we're going to keep being friends." She shook off his hand and tugged open the door.

Matt followed her onto the front porch. "Well, of course, we're going to keep being friends. Why would we ever stop being friends?"

"If we turn out like you and Aimee, maybe." She hitched her bag higher onto her shoulder with a wince, then rubbed her neck as she proceeded down the sidewalk to her car parked in front of the neighbor's house.

Matt caught up to her side so that he could snag her bag from her shoulder and place it over his. "What, like broken up?"

"No, boring as all get out, and *then* broken up," she said, continuing to march to her car. "Oh my goodness, Matt. She droned on and on about your relationship, and I swear watching a two-hour documentary about how crabgrass grows in cement cracks would've been more interesting than what she described. Please tell me your relationship wasn't that awful."

She popped her trunk, then turned for her bag.

He twisted his shoulder back so she couldn't reach the strap. "Our relationship wasn't awful. Just . . . okay, yeah. Boring."

"Which is exactly why I have to get out of here. Before this gets any worse." She stepped closer to grab her bag.

He angled away to keep it out of reach. The closer she stepped, the more he turned. "What are you talking about?"

"Do I have to spell it out?"

"Apparently you do. And the sooner the better. I'm starting to get dizzy." Not only because they were literally spinning in circles next to her trunk. The girl was talking in circles. "What's the big deal about staying long enough to eat a hamburger and fries with me? I know you're hungry."

"The big deal is I've fallen in love with you."

Matt stopped turning. Her bag slipped from his shoulder and thumped to the pavement. "Are you serious?" *Please be serious.*

She nodded, not only looking serious, but tormented. The man walking his dog across the street probably thought she was admitting to some sort of heinous crime.

"Is falling in love with me not a good thing?" Matt asked, needing some clarification about the tormented look. "Because I happen to think falling in love with you has been one of the greatest experiences of my life."

"Falling in love with—" She sucked in a breath, and if possible, her face grew even more anguished. "Matt, no. This is terrible. Don't you get it? You're my best friend. My favorite friend."

"You're mine too."

"I hated not having you in my life for five years."

"Same here."

"I never want to go through that again."

"Me neither."

"So don't you see?"

See what? He was waiting for her to get to the terrible part. So far it sounded great. Like they were both ready to move on to the kissing part. "What am I supposed to see?"

"Why we can't ever be more than just friends. We'll turn into crabgrass!"

And with those words, she jumped into the car and sped away, the open trunk door flopping up and down until it slammed shut just as her car disappeared around the corner.

Matt met the gaze of the man walking his dog across the street. The man offered a little shrug. Matt returned it right back. Then he picked up Rachel's bag from the pavement and tried to recall the last time he'd ever felt this happy—Rachel had fallen in love with him!—and confused.

Crabgrass?

38

"Oh, would you calm down? It was one drop of peppermint oil. More like a half, really." Noah never imagined borrowing some of Mona's essential oils would cause such a big deal. The way Gracie ranted—when she wasn't hiccuping—you'd think the Poison Control Center needed to get involved. "It was supposed to help your muscles relax, not make you blow a brain aneurysm."

"What made you think serving me the equivalent of peppermint schnapps would help me relax?"

"What makes you think a drop of peppermint oil is the equivalent to peppermint schnapps?"

"Three days I'll be stuck in the belly of this whale," she moaned. "Three days!"

"Am I to assume the whale in this metaphor is the hiccups?"

Gracie lifted her head from her desk. "You're to assume I'm going to file a police report and you'll be spending the rest of your sorry life locked up in Sing Sing."

"For what? Serving you tea?"

"Spiking my drink!" Gracie dropped her head back to her arms and hiccuped. "Oh, I think the room might be spinning."

"One drop of essential oil, babe."

"Which is what? A fifth of a handle in drinker talk?"

"You're impossible." Noah rubbed his forehead. Maybe it wasn't too late to take up drinking himself.

Gracie angled her head on her arms to look at him. "You're the one making it impossible to get any work done on your memoir."

"Hey, I tried answering your silly questions, didn't I?"

Gracie held up the paper full of his scribblings. "Charcuterie metaphors? Is that what you call trying?"

She crumpled the paper and threw it at the trash can. "Come on, Noah. You haven't provided me with a single answer about your life since the day you stepped foot back in this house. Come to think of it, you never coughed up a lot of answers before you walked out of my life five years ago either."

"I walked out of your life? I'm sorry, *I* walked out of *your* life?"

"Good to know your hearing is still intact. Yes. You. Noah. Walked out of my life. And honestly, I haven't the foggiest idea what made you decide to walk back into it. I was doing just fine without you."

"Really? Sitting around here, stinking up the place in your dirty bathrobe while you wrote about time-traveling horses. That was you living your best life, was it?"

"Well, it certainly wasn't my worst life. Pretty sure that happened when my husband decided he'd rather spend another offseason working on his curveball instead of his marriage."

"Marriage? Please. That's the last thing we would've been working on. All you cared about was making babies."

"Well, that's part of marriage, isn't it?"

"It wasn't just a part of our marriage, it was your entire obsession. An obsession I watched slowly cripple you month after month, year after year. I needed a break. You needed a break. I wasn't trying to walk out of your life. I was just trying to not feel like a failure the entire offseason when I watched you cry yourself to sleep every night because your husband couldn't give you what you wanted."

Gracie tugged a tissue out from inside her sleeve. "Let's not do this again. Clearly nothing has changed. I'm still hurt and you're still delusional. Let's just figure out a way to get through this memoir."

Gracie's cell phone buzzed on the edge of her desk. She grabbed it, probably as grateful as he was for the distraction. Anytime they'd attempted this conversation before, it quickly nose-dived into a painful explosion of emotions and hurt feelings.

On a positive note, her hiccups were gone.

Gracie frowned when she looked at her screen. "The hospital left me a voicemail. I didn't even hear it ring." She swiped the screen and pressed the phone to her ear. She listened, then turned to Noah with wide eyes.

"Your dad?"

"No." Gracie spread her fingers across her chest, her breaths growing quick. "It's Matt. He's in the emergency room. They can't get ahold of Mona. I don't know where she'd be. She always has her phone on her."

"What's wrong with him? What happened?"

"I don't know. Some sort of accident. I hear lots of beeping in the background. That can't be good. Beeping?"

"I'm sure beeping is fine. It probably means his heart is still beating."

She covered her mouth and sobbed.

Noah rushed forward, crouched in front of her. "And of course his heart is still beating. He's got a strong heart. The beeping probably had nothing to do with his heart. It was probably a call light. Somebody probably just needed the bathroom." He had no idea what he was saying. "Why don't we drive over and see what's going on?" That sounded like a good thing to say—until Gracie started to rise, then sank back into her seat with a whimper.

"Shoot." She massaged her right hip. "I've been sitting too long. And I'm not even dressed to leave the house. It'll take me forever to get ready. Just go. I'll try calling the ER to get more information, but I want you to call me as soon as you get there, okay?"

"Everything's going to be fine." He tucked a strand of hair behind her ear, then kissed her forehead as he got to his feet.

Gracie held his gaze and whispered, "Thank you." Then, "As soon as you get there. I mean it. As soon as you get there. Noah—" Gracie latched onto his wrist before he could move away. "We can't lose him."

He leaned down, holding her face with both hands. "Babe, we're not going to. I promise." Then before he could stop himself, he dropped a quick kiss to her lips.

And yeah, she was probably just worried about Matt, but as he drove to the hospital, Noah couldn't help thinking that for a brief moment it'd sure felt like Gracie had kissed him back.

39

A penlight flashed in Matt's eyes. "Pupils look fine," an ER resident in blue scrubs said. "Can you follow my finger?"

Matt kept his head still and moved his eyes side to side as directed.

"Perfect." The resident shoved the penlight into her scrub pocket. "Headache?"

"Oh yeah."

"Not surprised. CT scan of your head looked okay, but I'd say you've definitely got a concussion." The resident undid the Velcro holding the rigid collar wrapped around his neck. "Any tenderness or pain?" She pressed with her fingers.

"Not in my neck."

"How about when you move your head side to side, or up and down?"

Matt did as she asked. "Feels okay."

"We didn't see any injury to your spine on the CT scan, so I think we're safe to remove this." She tossed the neck collar to the side. "Let me look again at those X-rays of your shoulder one more time. Might be wearing a sling for a while. All in all, though, I'd say you're pretty lucky. One of the EMTs showed me a picture of your truck." She let out a low whistle. "Can't believe the other driver just took off. Kind of shocked he was even able to."

Matt grunted. *Gotta love a hit and run.* "I won't have to stay, will I?"

"I'm okay with sending you home as long as you've got someone who can keep an eye on you and bring you straight back to the ER if you start having any worsening symptoms, which a nurse will go over with you here in a bit."

Matt gave a thumbs-up. Hopefully someone had gotten ahold of his mom or Aunt Gracie by now. If he was going to be miserable with a pounding headache, he'd much rather be miserable with a pounding headache somewhere far away from the sounds of other patients moaning and puking all night.

About thirty minutes later a nurse had his left arm and shoulder secured in a sling. "Sure you don't want some Tylenol? You look miserable."

"I'm afraid anything I try to swallow will only come right back up."

"I can give you something for nausea if that's what you're worried about."

He shrugged. The movement shot a bullet of pain through his shoulder. "You know what? Yeah. Give me whatever you got. Tylenol. Whisky. A belt to bite on. I'll take it."

The nurse chuckled. "Okay, cowboy, I'll see what I can come up with."

She returned with medicine that settled his stomach and eased the ache in his head enough that he was ready to ditch this place. "Were you able to get ahold of my mom?"

He'd lost his phone in the accident and the only two numbers he knew by memory were his mom's and Aunt Gracie's, which honestly should've won him a lot more points than just knowing the year and who the president was. If recalling someone's actual phone number these days wasn't proof he was good to go home, he didn't know what was.

"We've left messages with your mom and aunt. Is there anybody else we can try?"

Before Matt could answer, the curtain was shoved back and a wild-eyed Rachel raced to his stretcher. "Matt. Oh my goodness, what happened? Are you okay? Wombat texted me on my way out of work. Said you were in an accident. Was it bad? It looks bad. You're in a sling. Is that blood on your pillowcase? Why is there blood on your pillowcase? Did you hurt your head? Is that a staple? *Did they have to staple your head back together?"*

As happy as Matt was to see Rachel, she certainly wasn't doing much to improve his headache. "It's just a staple, Rach. I'm okay. They're actually about to send me home."

"Home? They can't send you home. What makes them think they can send you home? You have a staple in your head."

"It was just a superficial laceration," the nurse piped in. "The CT scan of his brain was fine."

"Sure. Fine *now*. But what about later? What if you have one of those secret head bleeds where everything looks fine, and then next thing you know you're dead and wearing a toe tag?"

The ER nurse took the green plastic barf bag that Matt never used and handed it to Rachel. "I think you need this more than he does." Then to Matt, she said, "Please tell me she's not your ride."

"Darn tootin' I'm not his ride," Rachel said, waving the plastic bag around. "No way I'm taking him home in this condition."

Darn tootin' she *was*. Matt reached for Rachel's hand. Squeezed. "Calm down. It's just a little concussion. Now grab me my shoes so we can get out of here."

"Little concussion. I don't think so. Only place I'm taking you is to the intensive care unit."

The nurse handed Matt his shoes. "Don't forget to make a follow-up appointment in a week or two with the ortho doctor so he can make sure the shoulder's healing okay."

"Ha! As if he's even going to be alive in a week or two."

"Any questions about the discharge instructions?" the nurse asked, ignoring Rachel.

"Oh-ho-ho," Rachel chortled like a deranged Santa Claus. "You better believe I've got questions. Starting with who is your supervisor?"

"No questions," Matt said, getting up from the stretcher.

"You sure there's nobody else you want me to call?" the nurse asked, sending a wary look at Rachel. "Like maybe security," she murmured.

"Thanks," Matt told the nurse as he sank back on the edge of the stretcher so he could put on his shoes. And maybe fight off a tiny wave of dizziness. "I'm good."

"Good?" Rachel said as soon as the nurse disappeared past the curtain. "You are not good. You're the exact opposite of good. You're clammy, you're pale, you're shoeless, you're circling the drain, you're—"

"*Rachel.*"

He didn't mean to snap at her, but good night, the girl was losing it. And he was about to lose his cookies if he didn't get some fresh air. "My head hurts, my body aches, and I'd really like to pee in something other than a jug." He pointed to the plastic urinal hanging off the side rail. "So stop acting like a girlfriend who's crazy in love with me and just be a friend who's here to help me put on my shoes so I can leave."

Outside the curtained room, voices carried, monitors beeped, IV pumps squawked, stretchers rolled past. Finally she took a deep breath, dropped her gaze, and nodded. "You're right. Sorry. I don't know why I'm acting like this. We're . . . we're just friends. And you're okay. Everything's okay."

Now that she'd gotten the hysterics out of her system, she actually made quick work of helping him into his shoes. A few minutes later, with her arm wrapped around his waist, she led him out the exit, across the ER parking lot, and all the way to the passenger's side of her car.

"Sorry I freaked out back there," she said, holding the door for him as he maneuvered into the seat, careful not to jostle his shoulder. "I mean, I know how I said I'd fallen in love with you, but I do believe we're better off as just friends, so I hope I didn't give you the wrong impression when I acted a little psychotic. I was only acting psychotic because we're friends. Not because I love you. I mean, I do love you. As a friend. The same way I love everybody. We're supposed to love our neighbors as ourselves, right? Do you think I should go back and apologize to that nurse and tell her I love her?"

Matt leaned back against the headrest and closed his eyes, wishing his world wasn't spinning like a slow-moving merry-go-round, making Rachel's ramblings that much harder to follow. "I think you should help buckle me into this seat and leave that poor nurse alone."

He heard her sigh. "I don't know what to do with you, Matt."

Did she mean tonight? Or life in general?

Because he was fairly certain "just friends" never helped each other out as much as he and Rachel had this past week. Or act the way she had inside the emergency room a few minutes ago. Or look at each other the way she was looking at him right now after she leaned over him to snap his seat belt in place.

He'd cracked an eye open and was peeking back at her. "I know exactly what I'd like to do with you," he said.

Her eyes widened and she leaned back a fraction. Whoops. Had that come out weird and creepy? It was supposed to come out smooth and sexy. And considering he couldn't pull that off on a good day, let alone after getting his head slammed around in a car accident, he should probably stick to just breathing and not dying for tonight.

She still hadn't moved.

Great, he'd freaked her out so much she was paralyzed. Matt started to open his mouth to apologize and blame his concussion when her weight settled on his lap and her lips were touching his lips.

Why were her lips touching his lips? Were they kissing?

Oh wow. They were kissing.

And now her lips were gone. Where'd her lips go? Why weren't they kissing?

It took his brain way too long to catch up. By the time he said, "Hey, wait a second," Rachel had already scrambled out of the car and was talking to Noah.

What was Noah doing here? Why weren't he and Rachel still kissing?

"Oh, thank goodness," Noah said, leaning into the car to unbuckle him—which for the record was definitely not as fun as getting buckled in by Rachel. "You scared your aunt and me half to death. So glad you're okay. C'mon, buddy." He helped Matt to his feet.

Why was Noah helping him to his feet? Why weren't he and Rachel still kissing?

"Let's get you home."

Before Matt knew it, Noah had loaded him into his Jeep, and he and Rachel were headed off in separate directions once again.

40

"She had her hands where?" Noah had already told her once, but Gracie wanted to hear it again as she checked the oven to see how the brownies were coming along.

"Everywhere. She was all over him."

"Oh my goodness." Gracie closed the oven door with a giggle. She was so relieved that Matt was okay—well, other than a concussion and shoulder injury—that she felt downright giddy. Which must be why she was giggling and gossiping with Noah like a schoolgirl.

It certainly had nothing to do with their little kiss earlier. Not even a kiss. A peck. Minor lip contact, really. And who gets giddy over minor lip contact from her ex-husband? Nobody. Definitely not Gracie.

Nope, she was just happy that Matt was okay. They still hadn't been able to reach Mona, but Gracie didn't care. She felt better having Matt under her own roof where she could keep an eye on him anyway—and maybe find out what exactly was going on between him and Rachel. "You sure they weren't just hugging?"

"I'm telling you," Noah said, grabbing a coffee mug from one of the hooks hanging on the wall next to the baker's rack. "When I got there, Matt had Rachel on his lap like she was his favorite teddy bear and he was never letting her go."

"Well, see? That just sounds more like a hug. They've always been good buddies."

"Mmm, I'm pretty sure there was a little lip action too. A car's headlights got in my way, so I couldn't tell for sure. But I do know this—buddies don't look at each other the way they were looking at each other. Trust me." Noah dipped his chin and hit Gracie with a tender, un-buddy-like gaze, before filling his mug with the coffee she'd brewed after he left when she needed something to do other than go crazy while she waited for an update. When that hadn't been enough, she'd started baking brownies.

"Wow," she murmured. "He was looking at her like that?"

"Like what?" Noah set the pot back on the burner.

"Uh, nothing." She shook her head. *Stop.* One little tap of the lips that lasted hardly a millisecond, and now she was imagining smoldering looks from her ex-husband.

Husband!

No wait, she had it right the first time. Ex-husband.

"I've always thought those two would be perfect for each other," Gracie said, needing to get her thoughts back on Matt and Rachel and far away from herself and Noah. "I was shocked when he asked Aimee to go to prom with him."

"He didn't ask her."

"Of course he did. I took pictures of them before the dance."

"But he thought he was going with Rachel."

"Why would he think he was going with Rachel if he was going with Aimee?"

"Because Rachel set him up with Aimee. He thought she was setting him up with herself, but no, turned out to be Aimee. The whole thing was a disaster. He was crushed."

"How do you know all this? He never said anything about Rachel or being crushed. I mean, good grief, he dated Aimee for what? Five years? He couldn't have been that crushed."

"He told me about it the other day. Said he never loved Aimee. He's always loved Rachel."

"So then why isn't he doing anything about it? Rachel's wonderful."

"He is doing something about it. Or at least he's trying to.

Sometimes these things take time. Especially when there's a strong-willed woman involved." He hit her with another one of his smoldering, un-buddy-like gazes.

She really needed to figure out how to make him stop doing that. The smolder. The lip contact. All of it.

Maybe if she treated him more like a buddy, she'd douse these unwanted sparks.

Maybe the buddy system would also help them navigate the rough terrain they still had to cover in his memoir too. Instead of arguing, they could just be two platonic friends on a sole mission to finish the memoir.

Well, maybe their sole mission tonight could be to finish making brownies and work up a plan to help Matt and Rachel move beyond the platonic to something special.

But after that, first thing tomorrow—the memoir and only the memoir.

41

Matt didn't know how long he had slept. An hour? Two? Twelve?

If he didn't have to use the bathroom, he would have gladly gone on sleeping another hour, two, or twelve. Sleep had never felt so good. Not nearly as good as kissing Rachel had felt, but . . . yeah, pretty close. Which was more of a reflection on how badly he needed the sleep.

He blamed the headache for his sluggish response in the car. When she leaned across him to fasten his seat belt, all he'd wanted to do was drag her onto his lap and kiss her senseless. His brain didn't know what to do when she plopped onto his lap and started kissing *him* senseless. By the time he realized what was happening, she was leaping off him like he was on fire—well, he sort of had been—and looking for any excuse to wipe her hands clean of him.

Why did it always look so easy for men like Noah? A few days after coming home and he was already hanging out with Aunt Gracie just like old times.

Matt shuffled to the toilet and relieved all the fluids the hospital had pumped into him during his short stay. Thoughts of Rachel were going to be much harder to get out of his system. What was it about her? No matter how hard he tried, he just couldn't shake her.

Granted, he hadn't really tried all that hard. But still. Even now, he could still taste a hint of her cinnamon gum on his lips. Feel her soft hair beneath his fingertips. Hear her trademark snort-laugh.

Wait.

He finished washing his hands and paused. He *did* hear her laugh. Her voice. Here. Now. Downstairs.

Matt crept to the top of the staircase. The lights from below weren't all that bright, but it pierced through his skull just the same. He squinted his eyes and inhaled a few deep breaths while the voices continued floating up from the kitchen.

"Isn't it great," Gracie said. "My dad's favorite dialysis nurse is the same girl Matt's taking a shining to. I think that's just great."

A shining to? Really, Aunt Gracie?

"I love Buck. Everyone does. He's one of our favorite patients. But anyway," Rachel's voice continued carrying up the stairs. "I didn't mean to interrupt. Matt left his discharge instructions in my car, so I just wanted to drop them off."

"You're not interrupting anything," Gracie said. "Stay. Drink coffee. Eat a brownie. They're a little overdone because Noah didn't trust me when I said it was time to take them out of the oven, but they're edible. Mostly."

"I did the toothpick thing and they weren't done yet."

Matt continued hobbling down the stairs as quick as he could, which was not all that quick. He clung to the banister to steady his balance. He needed to catch her before she left. Try to redeem himself somehow. Hopefully work out the potential for another chance at that whole kissing scenario—preferably when his head wasn't spinning or his stomach threatening to revolt.

"Hey, is it okay that he's sleeping?" Noah asked when they stopped arguing about toothpicks and brownies. "I remember an episode of *Wings* once where they couldn't let the one gal sleep all night because she'd had a concussion or something."

"Well, if you saw it on *Wings*," Gracie said, "then by all means rush on upstairs and wake him up. Did *Northern Exposure* happen to have any episodes about pelvic injuries? Is that why you thought you knew how to take care of me?"

Rachel giggled. "I think it's okay to let him sleep."

"Don't dis my shows," Noah said.

"I'm not dissing your shows," Gracie responded. "I'm dissing your medical knowledge. It's a wonder I survived more than forty-eight hours under your care."

Matt finally made it to the bottom of the staircase and rounded into the kitchen.

Rachel's eyes widened. "Hey. You're awake." She sprang out of her seat. "I just came by to drop off your discharge papers. I forgot about them when we were . . . um . . . talking."

Matt pretended not to see the way Noah's eyebrows wagged up and down at Gracie while Rachel motioned to her vacant chair. "Take my seat. I was just getting ready to leave."

"No, you weren't," Gracie said. "You were going to stay for coffee, remember? Hey Noah, grab the pan of brownies. And probably some steak knives."

"They are not that burnt."

Gracie smiled at Noah, and Matt did a double take. Gracie's smile actually seemed genuine. Like she was teasing Noah and enjoying it.

Nah. Probably just his head injury playing tricks on him.

Matt slid into Noah's empty seat, glad to be off his feet. Bed was already sounding good again.

"So any idea who hit you?" Gracie asked.

Matt adjusted the sling on his left arm, then dropped his forehead into his hand. "Police are looking into it."

"Person probably panicked," Noah said. "Maybe didn't have insurance or something. Fool could have been drunk. Who knows?"

"Either way, they really need to do something about that curve. It's such a bad spot for accidents." Gracie nibbled on a brownie. "Where were you coming back from?"

"Ace's bar."

"Who's Ace?" Gracie asked the same moment Rachel sputtered on her coffee and Noah said, "Rachel's Ace?" Which made Rachel sputter harder while Gracie asked, "Who's Rachel's Ace?"

"You went and saw Ace?" Rachel wheezed out in between more coughs and sputters.

Gracie handed her a napkin. "Wait, Ace? As in beer-on-the-head Ace?"

"What did you say to him?" Noah said.

"Did you pour beer on his head?" Gracie said.

"Did he pour beer on your head?" Noah said.

"Are you insane?" Rachel wheezed out.

Matt was about to be, if they kept firing off questions without ever giving him a chance to answer. He scooted his chair back. "I told him if he ever thought about hurting you again, just be sure to direct it at me because I'd much rather suffer than ever see you get hurt again. Or something like that. I don't remember. I've been in an accident since then, and to be honest, everything's a little bit fuzzy now. Except for you kissing me in your car. I remember that."

Rachel's cheeks flushed. Gracie clapped her hands together. And Noah said, "I knew I saw something."

Then Gracie and Noah both rose at the same time. "Hey, Grace, didn't you say earlier we needed to—"

"—do that thing," Gracie finished. "Yep. That's what I said. We should definitely go—"

"—do that thing. Yep. That's what I thought you said." Noah nodded. "Probably should do it in the other room."

"Right now."

"I should probably go too," Rachel said.

"No," Noah and Gracie both said at the same time. "You should do this thing," Gracie said as she stumbled toward the back kitchen door.

"In this room." Noah slipped an arm around her waist before she tripped over her own feet and fractured something else.

"Right now," they both added before slamming the back kitchen door shut behind them.

"Subtle, aren't they?" Rachel smiled.

Matt tried to return it, but even just moving facial muscles hurt his head at the moment. "Rachel, I—"

"Don't say anything." She held up a hand. "I can tell you're miserable, and right now I don't feel like I can yell at you the way I want to yell at you for seeing Ace until your head feels better."

"I don't feel like I can kiss you the way I want to kiss you until my head feels better."

Her cheeks flushed even darker. He smiled, not caring how much it hurt his head. "Wow, Rach. I don't think I've ever seen you so blushy before. At least not back when we were just friends. Maybe now that we're—"

"Nope. We're not having that conversation right now. Not when your brain is making up words like blushy. Right now we're just friends." She started for the front door.

"I love you."

"Stop it," she said, spinning around. "We'll figure this out later."

"Hey, pretty sure a medical professional said I might have one of those secret head bleeds where I'll be wearing a toe tag by midnight. If that's the case I want you to know for sure and for certain that I love you."

"Great. Now I know. But not another word about it until you've gotten some rest. I can't have the man I love puking all over my shoes."

The man I love. A slow sensation of warmth spread inside Matt's stomach, a welcome exchange for the nausea. He could almost believe his head even hurt a bit less. Almost. "You love me?"

"I didn't say that."

"You did say that."

"Okay, I might've said that. But it doesn't mean I mean what you automatically think I mean."

"What does that mean?"

"It means you need to go to bed and rest. We'll talk about this later."

"When?"

"When you're not about to drop dead."

"I'm not about to drop dead." But the whole puking-on-the-shoes scenario might have some validity. Matt gripped the doorknob, waiting for the ground to stop moving.

"Matt," Rachel whispered. Her hands gently pushed him away from the door. "Go to bed."

"I love you so much."

"Would you knock it off? We'll talk later." She squeezed through the door, then met his gaze with another rosy blush, and murmured, "Please don't die tonight," before clicking the door shut behind her.

Matt made it to the stairs, then sank onto the bottom step and cradled his head in his hands. He took it all back. He was about to drop dead.

Footsteps approached, followed by Noah's voice. "Well, don't you look pathetic."

"Just bury me right here on these stairs."

"And now you sound pathetic." Noah got under Matt's good arm and hefted him onto his feet. "Come on, partner. I'd say you've got too much left to live for to get buried on these stairs tonight."

"Isn't Rachel so pretty?"

"She's a doll," Noah grunted, dragging Matt up the remainder of the stairs to the spare bedroom. "You ever heard of picking up your feet?"

"My head hurts."

"What's that have to do with your feet?"

Matt dove for the bed. Either that, or Noah shoved him. Hard to say. Matt grabbed his head and groaned. "Rachel kissed me."

"I know. You told everyone about it ten minutes ago." Noah cracked his back side to side.

"I didn't kiss her back."

Noah turned in the doorway. "Why not?"

"My head hurt."

"Well, I wouldn't worry. Judging by the way she was looking at you tonight, I think you'll get another shot at it soon."

"I just never imagined it could hurt this bad."

"Concussions?"

"Love." Matt rolled onto his side, still clutching his head. "How did you do it? How did you survive after losing Aunt Gracie? I know you guys went through some stuff, but I just don't get it. How could you guys love each other and not stay together? I thought I understood when I was with Aimee. I thought I knew how it was supposed to be. But now . . . with Rachel."

Matt rolled flat on his back. "With Rachel, I feel like I can't breathe at the thought of her not being with me." He dropped his hand and met Noah's shadowed gaze in the doorway. "How have you been breathing all this time without Aunt Gracie?"

42

How have you been breathing all this time without Aunt Gracie?

Good question. Noah tossed a broken eggshell into the trash. He grabbed another shell, finding bits of yolk scattered across the counter next to giant clumps of chocolate batter. "What are you grinning about?" he said when he looked up and caught Gracie smiling as she returned to the kitchen from using the bathroom.

"Nothing. I guess making the brownies just reminded me of the time you thought you'd surprise me with one of those flaming lava cakes for Valentine's Day."

Now Noah was smiling. "Well, you can't say I didn't surprise you."

"Coming home to find a fire truck parked in front of the house certainly carries the element of surprise."

"The firefighters were so worried I'd end up in the doghouse for charring one of the kitchen walls, they offered us a ride in the fire truck back to the station so we could eat the chocolate cake someone had dropped off for them. Remember that?"

Gracie pressed her lips together, then twisted them to the side. "Actually, I was the one who begged for them to do that. I knew you'd worked so hard trying to make our last evening together special before you had to head off for spring training the next day."

"Really? And to think all these years I've been giving credit to the boys at the firehouse for saving our Valentine's Day that year."

"Well, they did put out a fire in our kitchen, so . . . Plus you have to admit, their cake at the firehouse was amazing. Pretty sure I tried making the same recipe for us the next year and it turned out an even bigger mess than the brownies did tonight."

Noah pointed to the brown globs all over the counter. "I wasn't going to say anything, but I'm kind of amazed you managed to get enough batter into the pan to make any brownies at all."

"I was stress baking."

"So you painted the entire kitchen with brownie batter, I get it." He winked and tossed a wet dishrag at her.

"Might want to keep this," she said, tossing it right back.

"So I can wipe up your mess?"

"So you can wipe off your face." Before he realized what she was doing, she swiped a glob of leftover batter across his forehead. Then staring at him, she licked off her finger with a mischievous smile.

Okay, was it him or was Gracie acting downright flirty tonight?

When they'd gone out the back door earlier to give Rachel and Matt some privacy, she'd practically glued herself to his torso with the excuse that it was freezing.

It hadn't been freezing.

And now as he ran his finger across his forehead, she put zero effort into stopping him from transferring that batter into a smear across her right cheek.

"I've always heard brownie batter is good for the pores," she said with a shrug. "Personally, I think your nose could use a little skin care." She scooped up some batter from the kitchen counter and ran a chocolate-covered finger down the entire bridge of his nose.

"Thank you for looking out for my nose. But if I were you, I'd be more concerned about the pores on your left cheek. They're looking a little neglected." This time he cut out the middleman. Instead of using his finger, he leaned down and angled his brownie-battered nose against her cheek.

And then stayed there. With his nose pressed to her cheek. Which happened to leave his lips achingly close to her lips. "Remember the

Valentine's Day I asked you to marry me?" he couldn't stop himself from murmuring.

Gracie held still. "That one sort of rings a bell. As I recall you were leaving for spring training the next day after that one too."

Noah held still. "And as I recall you got chocolate all over my nice new shirt."

With both of them holding still, how had their lips managed to draw even closer? "Well, maybe you shouldn't ask important questions after a lady starts eating her dessert."

Was Gracie the one who'd moved closer?

Or had he?

Either way, she sure wasn't moving away. And neither was he. Not when he could feel her breath on the corner of his mouth.

He'd just angled his head so he could feel her breath over his entire mouth when the front door banged open. "Is he here?" Mona's voice yelled.

Gracie jerked away from Noah so hard that he had to grab her elbows to keep her from falling. "Is who here?" Gracie asked, pushing against Noah, then spinning away from him as soon as she regained her balance.

It might take him a second longer to regain his.

Mona rushed into the kitchen. "*Matt.* Who else would I be talking about? I was just driving home when I got the message he'd been in an accident. Something about a concussion. Is he okay? The ER said he wasn't a patient anymore. I tried calling him, but—"

"He's okay," Noah and Gracie said at the same time.

"He's okay?"

"He's okay." Certainly more okay than Noah at the moment. He'd been *this* close to getting to kiss Gracie again. Which meant he was *this* close to tossing Mona out on her ear for ruining that moment.

Gracie pointed to the ceiling. "Matt's resting upstairs. He hurt his head and shoulder, but I promise, he's okay." Was she breathless? She sounded a little breathless.

Mona collapsed into a kitchen chair and blew out her own long breath. "He's okay. All right. Good. I can breathe again. Why do you have brown goo all over your faces?"

"I made brownies," Gracie said.

Apparently that was a good-enough explanation. Mona nodded and stood. Took a few more deep breaths. "Okay, well. I think I'll peek in on him, then head home. Is it all right that he stays here with you?"

"Of course," Gracie assured her. "Hey, where were you by the way? I was actually starting to get a little worried that we couldn't reach you."

Mona fumbled her purse, then tugged it over her shoulder. "Oh. Ah. Dinner thing. I had my phone on silence."

"Some sort of work dinner?"

"Yes. Kind of. Dinner with a client. Well, former client. Sort of. Anyway, I should get going. I have a lot of things I need to do tonight." She headed for the door.

"I thought you were going to check on Matt." Gracie looked at Mona like she might be the crazy one covered in brownie batter.

"Right." Mona glanced at the ceiling. "You know what, if he's resting, I should probably just let him . . . you know, rest. Thanks for looking out for him. Tell him to give me a call, soon as he's feeling up to it, okay?"

The moment Mona closed the front door, Noah turned to Gracie. "You know what that was about, right?"

"What?"

"Your sister was on a date."

Gracie shook her head as if she were about to deny it, then her eyes filled with wonder. "You really think so?"

"Bet you an entire bowl of brownie batter."

"Oh my goodness. You might actually be right. No wonder she's been acting so weird lately. Man, there must be something in the air. First Matt and Rachel. Then—uh . . ." Gracie cleared her throat and wiped the brownie batter off her cheek. "Mona," she finished saying after another throat clear.

Us. She'd been about to say *us.* He hadn't imagined that near kiss.

He grinned and started filling up the sink with soapy water. "Well, Rachel seems like a great girl. I hope things work out for her and Matt. As for Mona . . ."

"God help the poor man who wants to make a go of things with her," Gracie said, plopping the mixing bowl into the sink.

Noah pretended to snap her with a dish towel. "Listen to you."

Gracie's lips tipped up in a small smile as she yanked the dish towel out of his hands and motioned to the sink. "You wash, I'll dry. And for the record, I hope things work out between Matt and Rachel too. He deserves to be happy."

Noah plunged his hands into the soapy water. "You think marriage will make Matt happy?"

"Sure. If he's got the right girl."

"You think that's what our problem was? We chose the wrong person?" He scrubbed the chocolate off a spatula.

"Our situation was completely different."

"So you do think we were right for each other initially?"

"I didn't say that."

"So you think we were wrong for each other." He rinsed off the spatula and tossed it onto the drying rack, then started on some measuring spoons.

"I didn't say *that.* Stop putting words in my mouth. This isn't about us anyway. I was talking about Matt. All I'm saying is I know Rachel will make him happier than Aimee."

Noah rinsed off the measuring spoons, then started on the mixing bowl. "And all I'm saying is it's not up to Rachel to make him happy."

"I know that."

"Do you?"

She didn't answer. He didn't press. Something had shifted between them this evening. Something good. Something flirty. Something like how things used to be between them.

If only they didn't have to dredge up the bad times to remember the good for his memoir.

He finished with the bowl and a few other random dishes sitting out on the counter, then pulled the drain in the sink, letting the water gurgle down to nothing as Gracie finished drying everything off.

She folded the towel over the oven handle. "I'm going to check on Matt, then call it a night. Thanks, by the way. For picking him up from the ER."

"Of course. I've always loved that kid like he was my own, you know that."

She gripped the back of a chair, meeting his gaze with a soft "I do" before heading out of the kitchen. At the doorway, she turned. "Tomorrow we really need to dive into this memoir project. So be ready. We've got to get this done before we run out of time."

As if Noah needed the reminder. He felt the clock ticking on them more than Gracie knew.

43

The next afternoon, after filling two of the largest coffee mugs she could find, Gracie ordered Noah into his seat, ready to use duct tape if necessary. "I need you to focus. No more getting distracted."

"Who's getting distracted?"

"You. Every time we attempt to work on this memoir."

"I was in the middle of making breakfast when we attempted earlier."

"Which turned out to be a twelve-course meal, apparently."

"Hey, toast might be enough for you, but Matt and I needed real food. And real food takes time. Especially when you're making up for lost calories."

Noah wasn't kidding. Gracie wouldn't be surprised if Matt had eaten a pound of bacon and an entire carton of eggs this morning. He'd obviously gotten his appetite back after fourteen hours of sleep. She'd been on the verge of checking for a pulse when he finally popped out of bed, saying he felt like a new man.

Something told her his rapid recovery had a lot to do with whatever was developing between him and Rachel. Didn't hurt that he was still in his twenties either.

Oh, to be young again. Here she was still walking with a limp more than two weeks after her tumble. "Okay, fine," Gracie said, powering up her laptop. "The big breakfast I get. But what on earth have you been doing in the garage that's so important?"

"Checking out Buck's old Chevy. After I dropped Matt off at his house, I realized he was going to need another car until his truck gets fixed. I decided to see if the old girl had any life left in her, and you know what, she does."

"Ha! You think Dad's going to let Matt drive his '65 Corvette?"

"Uh, yeah, actually I do." Noah reached for his coffee. "Because Matt and I already talked to him about it, and he said yes."

"What? Betty?" No way. Gracie yanked her phone off the desk and punched Buck's contact button. "Are you dying?" she said as soon as he answered.

"Aren't we all?" he returned in a sleepy voice.

"I mean today. Right now. Why are you letting Matt drive Betty? Betty's your baby. Nobody drives Betty but you."

He hacked a few times into the phone. "Well, now that I know what it's like to be trapped inside four walls, gathering dust, I've realized somebody needs to break Betty free. And it's not going to be me. Who better than Matt?"

Guilt punched Gracie's gut. She hadn't visited her dad in far too long. "I'm coming to see you. This afternoon. I'm sorry it's been so long. I'll be over in about—"

"No, no, no, honey, I'm fine." He gave another few coughs. "Noah told me you two were working on a new project together. You work on that. Let Matt use the car. Really, I don't mind. I'm good. Don't worry about me. I'm too tired for visitors today anyway."

"You sure?"

"You'd just be watching me sleep. Plus I think Mona's already on her way over."

"I thought you were too tired for visitors."

"That's how I get through Mona's visits. I sleep."

"Dad."

"I'm kidding. You know I love her. And I love you too. Now get back to work. We'll talk more later. Say good night, Gracie."

"Good night, Gracie." Gracie set her phone back on her desk. So much for focusing on the memoir. All she could think about now was her dad. And Betty. Trapped inside four walls. Gathering dust.

She really did need to go see him. But he was right. She couldn't today. Not when she desperately needed to make progress on this memoir. She shot Noah a look. "Ready to focus?"

"I'm here. I'm ready. Let's focus."

"I mean it."

"Me too, babe."

Babe. It was starting to sound so natural, she almost didn't catch it anymore. Her inner ice queen was slipping. "You know, sometimes I wish I was working with that silly horse from my rom-com novel instead of you," she muttered.

"Ah, c'mon. I don't bite. Plus I'm way cuter."

Yeah, that was the problem. The more time she spent with him, the cuter he got. Even when his nose was covered in brownie batter.

She slammed her eyes shut. *Come on, ice queen, get back on your throne. Your ex-husband isn't cute.*

Besides, they'd just been goofing around. Reminiscing a little. That's all. He hadn't been about to kiss her.

Okay, maybe he had. But she wouldn't have liked it.

Okay, maybe she would have. But only because she was a big fan of brownie batter. Not Noah's lips.

A loud slurping sound caught her attention. She opened her eyes to find Noah watching her from over the rim of his mug as he drank. "Is this part of the focusing process? Because I'm going to need a refill if we focus much longer."

"We're done focusing." Gracie grabbed her pen and tugged her notebook in front of her. "I mean, we're *not* done focusing. We are focusing, just not on the things we shouldn't be focusing on."

"Pretty sure I lost focus halfway through whatever you just said."

"Focus!"

"Got it." He smiled at her, then took another sip.

Good grief, even her inner ice queen couldn't deny his smiles had gotten cuter. Gracie shook the thought away and stared down at her notebook. "So here's what I'm thinking for the outline. The first chapter will be short. Touch upon the big game since that's the only reason readers are going to buy this book. Sort of a teaser. Then we'll jump back to your childhood in chapter two and—"

"My childhood?" Noah jumped out of his chair.

Gracie bit back a sigh. She really should've used duct tape. Less than a minute and he was trying to escape again. "Yes, Noah. Your childhood. Where else would we start a memoir about your life?"

"Not there. Nobody cares about my childhood. I don't even care about my childhood. Let's just focus on the one game."

Gracie yanked a pencil out of the blue plastic cup covered in stickers that she used as a pen holder, a gift from Matt when he'd been around four, and banged the pencil against the edge of her desk like a heavy metal drummer. "You want the entire book to be about that one game?"

"Isn't that the point of a memoir? To focus on one thing? I didn't think this was going to be my entire autobiography. Besides, you said yourself that one game is the only reason readers are going to buy this book."

"Buy it, sure. But like it? They're going to want more."

"Start in college then. When I quit and joined the minors. I've got some great stories from those days. Or we could go back to high school and talk about how we met."

"We're not talking about how we met. Our marriage isn't part of this story."

"Our marriage is a huge part of this story."

"But it's none of the readers' business."

"And my childhood is?"

"Absolutely. People will want to know what sort of childhood you had."

Come to think of it, Gracie wanted to know what sort of childhood Noah had. He'd glossed over it when they started dating. Gracie had always been the one to prattle on and on about growing up without a mom and having a bossy older sister who tried staking a claim on the role of mom despite not having a single maternal instinct.

But what about Noah? Sure, Gracie knew he had three brothers, all older. They weren't close, she knew that. When she and Noah married, Mikey came to the wedding. Benny sent a card. To this day, she'd never met Pete.

"What are your brothers doing these days?"

Noah set his mug down, then shoved his hands in his pockets and leaned against the wall, looking out the window above her desk. "Why? Is this for chapter three?"

Gracie tossed her pencil onto her notebook. "This is for me. Do you still keep in touch with them?"

He lifted a shoulder. Sunlight highlighted the crow's feet around the edges of his eyes. "Talk to Benny every now and again. He's usually pretty good about calling when he's strapped for some cash." Noah's mouth tipped up in a humorless smile. "Last I heard, Mikey was doing all right. Works for a logging company out in Oregon. Not sure where Pete's at these days. I'm assuming he's still alive." He quirked a brow as if he were joking, but Gracie had a feeling he wasn't.

"What about your dad? Did he—"

"He's gone."

"I know, but did he ever—"

"I don't want him to be part of the story." His tone left no room for argument. Noah squinted out the window, the lines fanning from the corners of his eyes etching deeper. With a quick sniff, he ducked his head and shoved off the wall. "I'm going to grab another cup of coffee. You want one?"

"You haven't even finished your first cup."

"I need some fresh air."

"Noah—"

"I'll be back in a bit."

"*Noah*—"

He spun at the door. "I'm not putting my family in the book."

"That wasn't what I was going to say." Gracie rose to her feet, a slight twinge in her hip, but nothing like before. A twinge she could live with. "I was going to tell you to wait for me."

Her dad and Betty weren't the only ones gathering dust inside of four walls. Other than sitting out on the porch a couple of times, Gracie hadn't left the house since coming home from the hospital. "I'm sure I could do with a little fresh air too."

"Should you be walking around out there? The ground isn't even. What if you tripped and fell? You barely just got back on your feet."

"I'm not an eighty-year-old woman. Besides," she used the desk to guide her away from the chair. "If I fall, my orthopedic surgeon is going to kill you, not me."

"Me? This was your idea."

"Not the way I'll tell it. Now stop arguing and grab my sweater. I don't want to catch my death."

"You sure you're not an eighty-year-old woman, using expressions like *catch my death*?"

Gracie couldn't hold back a little laugh as Noah slipped her long sweater around her shoulders. She had missed this. Missed him. If only their marriage was like a '65 Chevy that just needed a little dust-off and bit of fine-tuning.

But too much time had passed for them. Too many wounds. Their marriage was full of broken parts that couldn't be fixed or replaced. It had already died in the walls of their past.

Noah linked her arm through his and said, "I've got some things I need to tell you. Things I should've told you a long time ago."

Why did Gracie have the feeling Noah was about to take a sledge-hammer to one of those walls?

44

Ten minutes into their walk, Noah was still struggling to find the right words. Same problem he always had when they were younger and she brought up his family. But something told him Gracie wasn't concerned about the right words. She simply wanted to hear his story. So after a deep breath, Noah started using the words he had, whether they were the right ones or not. "First thing I should probably tell you is I had another brother. Owen. He was younger than me. Died when he was eight." Noah let the words hang in the late afternoon air, swirling and dipping, before a crisp breeze carried them away.

"Second thing I should probably tell you is my mom had an affair." A flock of geese flew overhead. Gracie's grip on his arm tightened, her gaze focused on the ground, thankfully not him. Some information just came out better without having to look someone in the eye.

"My dad had no idea it was going on. Of course, when you're working sixty hours a week, how would you? Looking back, I wonder if my dad knew he even had five sons for a while. Poor Owen probably slipped out without him even realizing at first."

He sighed, watching the geese until they disappeared from sight. "Part of me gets it. Why my dad wasn't around much. Owen was born with some complicated health issues. So dad was working like crazy to cover the medical expenses. Equipment. Therapy. Even with insurance, I'm sure everything cost a ton. But when I say he was never around, I'm telling you he was never around. And since my mom's entire world revolved around caring for Owen, it didn't feel like she was around all that much either."

Gracie squeezed closer to his side. He half hoped she'd speak up and say he didn't need to keep going. But, of course, this would be the one time in her life she kept quiet and let him do all the talking.

"Things only got worse after Owen died. I can't say his death came as a shock. We all knew it was coming for years. Even so, I can't say any of us were ready for it. I mean, how can you ever be ready to lose someone you love? Doesn't matter what your brain knows. Your heart's just never ready. So we all took it hard. Dad completely disappeared for a while, and Mom couldn't get out of bed. Eventually she did, but it was just to crawl in someone else's bed. I guess having an affair felt better than missing Owen and trying to raise four rowdy boys on her own."

"Noah, I am so sorry."

He shrugged. "I don't want you feeling sorry. I just want you to see why this isn't my favorite topic. Definitely not something I want written down in a book for all the world to see."

Bad enough telling Gracie in the privacy of the backwoods that ran the line of their property. But now that he'd started, may as well get it all out there.

"She died from a ruptured brain aneurysm. She was with the other guy when it happened." Noah steadied Gracie as they passed some shallow roots from a tree. "By the time they got her to the hospital, there wasn't anything they could do."

"Is that how your dad found out about the affair?"

Noah nodded. "None of us boys knew the details, of course. Just that she'd collapsed. I knew my dad was acting weird, but . . ." Noah shrugged. "We'd lost Owen the year before. Now Mom had just died. We were all acting weird. Yeah, there were whispers at the time, but I was twelve. I had no idea what the whispers were about. Not until those whispers trickled from the adults down to the kids and became taunts at school."

"I can only imagine what that must've been like for you and your brothers."

"None of us handled it well, I'll say that. I guess instead of losing himself in his job Dad decided to start losing himself in the bottle. And my brothers . . . well, you name it. Drinking. Skipping school. Starting fights. Even set a few fires. All three of them landed in juvie before their seventeenth birthday."

"But not you?"

"See what a prize you landed yourself? The only Parker boy to stay out of juvie. No wonder you fell so hard for me."

She gave him a nudge. "What kept you walking the straight and narrow?"

"I don't know about straight and narrow, but there was one thing I had that my brothers didn't have. And that was baseball."

Gracie pretended to groan as she gave his arm another squeeze. "I should've known everything always comes back to baseball with you."

"And charcuterie. Don't forget that."

"I only wish I could forget that," she responded, offering a sweet smile. "So how did you get into baseball?"

"Found out I had a strong arm when I threw rocks to break out the windows at the old boiler factory in our town."

"You little scallywag."

"Told you I wouldn't say straight and narrow."

"How'd you go from rocks to baseballs?"

He reached for her hand still looped through his elbow. "Remember me mentioning Grandma Rosie?"

"The one who was obsessed with Glenn Miller?"

Seemed like Gracie's limp had grown heavier, so he stopped walking and turned to face her. "She wasn't technically my grandma. She was our neighbor. But she loved on me better than any grandma could. And in addition to Glenn Miller, she was obsessed with baseball. I think she saw the potential in me and knew I was going to slip through the cracks if someone didn't help me along, so she connected me with one of her nephews. He played in the minors for a while, eventually helped out coaching one of the college teams in his area. He took me under his wing. Told me it wasn't enough to have a strong arm and throw hard. You had to throw smart. Because all that separates you from getting a strikeout and getting your bell rung is a matter of inches. You can't afford to miss by an inch, he said."

A leaf had fallen and gotten caught in Gracie's hair. Noah brushed it away, then let his fingers linger on the bottom strands of her hair. "I knew what he was really saying. One inch off—whether that be a suspension, a demeanor, or taking things too far with a cute girl on a date—could end my career before it began. He's the reason I wound up here in high school. He knew I had to get away from my dad and his drinking, my brothers and their reputations. Shoot, I just needed to get away from that town. So he offered me the chance for a fresh start. And you know what, I thank God every day that I took it."

Gracie's hazel eyes, sparkling greener in the sunlight and full of more kindness than he'd seen directed his way in a long time, held his gaze. "Why didn't you tell me any of this years ago? You said you were an Army brat."

"I had half of it right at least."

She continued searching his eyes, obviously waiting for a real answer.

Noah let go of her hair. "I don't know, Gracie. I guess I felt like you were so far out of my league. Here you were this beautiful senior in high school with a great Dad. I mean sure, your sister was a little scary, but . . ." He reached for that strand of hair again, needing to touch her and stay connected to her and not lose her as he tried explaining something he wasn't sure he could even explain to himself.

He rubbed her hair between his fingers. "Truth is I felt like I'd hit the jackpot with you. From day one, I knew you were it for me. But I was scared to death thinking I may never be it for you. So when we started dating . . . I don't know. I guess I didn't want to blow it by dragging all these skeletons out of my closet. Then later on . . ." He shrugged. "All my family drama just never seemed that important."

"But they were your family." She shifted her weight and winced.

"Here." Noah spotted a fallen tree large enough for Gracie to sit on without having to bend much. He led her to it and brushed away the dried bark and leaves.

Once she was settled, she said, "I'm just looking back, trying to figure out how you avoided talking about them all those years we were together. Didn't you ever miss them after you moved here?"

Noah settled next to Gracie on the trunk. Inhaled a deep breath. Sighed. Then reached for her hand and cradled it between his on top of his lap, needing that connection again. Especially since he still didn't know how to explain it. Did he miss his family after he moved here?

"There was a game back when I was thirteen. Not just any game. The Little League championship. It wasn't my turn to pitch, but right before the game, our starting pitcher came down with a stomach bug. At first we thought it was nerves, but by the eighth or ninth puke, we realized he wasn't going to be spending any time on the mound. Another one of our pitchers had broken his arm two days prior, and our other pitcher just wasn't very good. So I knew it was going to be up to me to get us through that game."

Noah could still feel the sweat glazing his skin from the humidity and nerves hovering over the diamond. "I'm not lying when I tell you I felt as much pressure that night as any game I played in the majors. Maybe even more. The bleachers were packed. Felt like the whole town was watching. And yet in all those packed stands, I knew there wasn't a single person out there rooting for me. Not my brothers. Not my dad. Not even Rosie, since she was pretty much housebound by that point. I knew I was on my own."

"Did you blow it?"

He narrowed his eyes at Gracie. "Now as a writer, you of all people should know I can't just jump straight to the end. Where's the suspense in that?"

"I hate suspense. Did you blow it?"

"First few innings weren't pretty." Gracie huffed but tightened her grip as he continued on with his story. "I gave up a lot of runs. Thankfully our offense kept us in the game, but every inning was a battle. I kept getting down in the count. Batters kept hitting foul ball after foul ball, staying alive long enough to eventually earn a walk or a hit. Bases kept getting loaded, and I'd see no way I could possibly get out of the inning without giving up a dozen runs."

"Just tell me if you blew it."

He cracked a smile at her. "But then somehow, some way, I always got us out of it."

Her hand relaxed inside his as she let out a small, "Thank goodness."

"Inning after inning, I did that. All the way into extra innings. My arm was completely shot, but after eleven innings we won by a single run. I felt on top of the world."

"As you should have."

Without thinking, Noah dipped his head and kissed the skin on the inside of Gracie's wrist. "Thank you for that."

She didn't tug her hand free, so the kiss must've been okay. "I'm sorry someone wasn't there for you that night," she said in a soft voice, letting him return their clasped hands back to his lap.

"Someone was there." He felt her gaze on his profile as he continued staring at their hands joined together. "Soon as the game ended, I couldn't help myself. I looked at the stands. And that's when I saw him. My dad. It was the only game he came to all season. He was too drunk to come to any of the others. And you know what? I realized I couldn't care less if he was there or not. Because I couldn't care less about him. If I could show up on the mound and fight my way through inning after inning, why couldn't he figure out how to fight for his family?"

Noah dropped Gracie's hand and reached for his shoulder, massaging an ache there that refused to leave. "You want to know why I didn't talk about my family after I moved here? Because no, to answer your question, I didn't miss them. By the time I met you, I didn't feel like I had a family left to miss."

45

Grace: Are we sure my heroine shouldn't end up with the farmer?

Rachel: Him again? I thought you were supposed to be working on Noah's memoir.

Grace: I AM supposed to be working on Noah's memoir.

Rachel: Then why are we still talking about the farmer?

Grace: Because my heroine's heart is in serious trouble and I should be working on helping her, not Noah's memoir!

Rachel: Just for the record, I'm pretty sure I saw this "farmer" in person the other week and he didn't look fat or portly. He looked old. Shouldn't we be calling him the elderly farmer?

Grace: 51 is not elderly!

Rachel: So we are talking about Luke. I knew it!

Grace: We're talking about my heroine!

Rachel: Fine. But I thought we already agreed your heroine needs to end up with the real hero at the end.

Grace: What if the real hero broke her heart in the past? What if he wasn't there when she needed him? What if she didn't like the bitter, angry person she was turning into, so she pushed him away because she didn't know how else to get rid of her pain? What if the farmer is the only safe bet she has for never getting her heart shattered again?

Rachel: What if she's never stopped loving the real hero? What if he's worth risking her heart for again? What if the farmer deserves someone who will love him as much as the heroine loves her real hero?

Grace: What if the heroine's just not brave enough?

Rachel: Then I guess I only have one thing left to say. I completely understand.

46

Hey Rachel

Matt deleted his text.

Rachel, hey

Deleted it again.

Hey

Hi

Ho

"I thought you were getting the bananas." Mona dropped two boxes of cereal and a loaf of bread into his shopping cart.

"Huh? Oh. Bananas. Yeah. I was just about to grab them." Matt clicked his phone off and slid it into his back jeans pocket. "What?" he said when his mom continued to stare at him.

"Nothing. Just wondering if you're feeling okay. You haven't moved from this spot since we stepped inside the grocery store. Head feeling okay? You're not dizzy or anything?"

"I'm fine. Just . . . thinking about bananas." He started pushing the shopping cart toward the produce section.

Mona grabbed the cart and stopped him. "You still remember what they look like, right?" She lowered her voice. "Honey, do you know who I am?"

"You're the loudmouthed Realtor who sold me my house."

"Just checking." She punched his shoulder, then immediately

started petting the flannel material of his shirt. "That's not your bad shoulder, is it?"

"Well, it certainly is now." Matt rotated it with a dramatic groan.

"Oh, stop being a baby." She winked and pointed to a stand full of apples. "Grab some of those on your way to the bananas. I told Gracie I'd bake her a pie. Noah made one the other week and I guess it turned out terrible. I'm going to run over and grab a gallon of milk. Meet you at the checkout aisle in a few minutes."

"Got it." Matt made his way to the apples, picked out some shiny ones since he wasn't sure what sort of apples worked best in a pie. Then made his way to the bananas. He was just reaching for a bunch that was green when he heard her voice.

"Green bananas. You must really be on the mend then."

Matt's gaze whipped up. Rachel stood on the other side of the banana stand with all the organic produce. They hadn't spoken for days. Not since his accident. He cleared his throat, but for some reason he still couldn't seem to make it past the *hey, hi, ho.*

Mostly because he didn't want to press her. These past couple days he'd wanted to give her space. And yeah, take a little time to recover from that whole minor concussion thing. But mostly give her space. Make sure she was on board with taking her "I've fallen in love with you" to the next level. Maybe even the *next* next level.

He actually didn't know how many levels there were, at least in Rachel's mind. But he knew in his mind he was ready for the "I'll love you forever, through sickness and health, for richer or poorer" level. Which could freak a girl out if she was still on the "I guess we can start calling each other boyfriend and girlfriend and say we're in an exclusive relationship, but let's not rush things too fast and just sort of see how things go so that we hopefully don't turn into crabgrass" level.

Hence, the space the past few days and his current restraint not to climb over the banana stand this very second and say *Will you marry me?*

She frowned at him. Why was she frowning at him? He hadn't said that last thought out loud, had he?

She pointed an organic banana at his left shoulder. "Where's your sling?"

Phew. She was just frowning about his sling. Except why was she frowning about his sling? What sling? It took him a second to transition from marriage to orthopedic equipment. "Oh. My sling. Right. Yeah. I didn't like it. I took it off."

She aimed the banana at him like a gun. "You can't just take off your sling."

"It wasn't doing anything."

"But you were supposed to wear it until you saw the ortho doctor. When's your follow-up appointment?"

"Never made one."

"What?" She threw her banana into her basket, then reached for another one. "What do you mean you never made an appointment? You were in a car accident."

He really hoped she was planning to make banana bread, because the way she kept slamming those bananas into her basket wasn't going to leave them in great shape for anything else.

"So? Doesn't mean I need to start wearing slings and scheduling follow-up appointments."

"It does if that's what the doctor said you needed to do. What's wrong with you?"

"Nothing. Which is why I'm not wearing a sling or scheduling any follow-up appointments."

"Excuse me," a short, older woman said, reaching in to grab some bananas. "Do you mind grabbing those five for me from the top row? Yep, the ones right there."

Matt reached for them and caught a whiff of the woman's floral perfume. His nose tingled with the beginnings of a sneeze.

"Oh, everything's fine, is it?" Rachel marched over next to him. "Then how come just reaching for a few bananas is making you cry?"

"Oh my. I didn't mean to cause you any pain," the older lady murmured.

"It's not you, ma'am," Rachel said, taking the bananas from Matt.

"It's just him being stubborn." She lowered her voice into what he could only assume was supposed to be an impression of him and not a very bad attempt at Clint Eastwood. "Look at me. I'm Mr. Tough Guy. I don't need to wear a sling."

Matt's eyes watered and his nose continued to burn. Why wouldn't this sneeze just come out already? "Hold on a second." He was talking to Rachel, but Banana Lady must've thought he was talking to her. She scooted closer with her cart and said, "Yes?"

"I'm not the one who's stubborn."

"Okay," Banana Lady said.

"Are you saying I'm stubborn?" said Rachel.

"I'm not saying anything," Banana Lady said, looking back and forth between them. "I just want my bananas."

"Why is it so hard for you to admit you love me?" Matt sneezed. *Finally!*

"Bless you," Banana Lady said.

"I *have* admitted I love you. Twice!"

"Yeah," Matt said wiping his nose with the tissue Banana Lady dug out of her purse for him. "Then run off immediately afterward, not wanting to talk about it. Twice!"

"Well, I'm sorry, but the first time I was a little freaked out and needed some time to process. And the second time, well . . . I guess I was still a little freaked out and needed time to process. But you'd just been in an accident and could barely stand on your own two feet. It wasn't exactly the time for a heart-to-heart conversation, you know?"

"Well, I'm standing on my own two feet right now, aren't I?"

"Without your sling, though," Banana Lady said as if she even knew anything about his sling.

"Did you need anything else, ma'am?" Matt grabbed the bananas from Rachel's hands and plopped them into Banana Lady's cart. He'd really like to finish this conversation without a sneeze-inducing audience.

"I could use a few sweet potatoes."

"Wonderful. They're over there. Now what part is freaking you out?" Matt said to Rachel once Banana Lady had vacated the banana stand.

"Honestly?" Rachel reached for an orange and tossed it into her basket. "The same thing that's been freaking me out for years. Ever since high school to be exact." She added a lemon.

"Since high school? Wait, you're not saying you've loved me since high school, are you?" That *had* to be what she was saying.

"Why do you think I was so excited about setting you up with Aimee?"

Okay, he had no idea what she was saying. "Rachel, would you stop throwing fruit in your basket and just talk to me? Do you love me? Do you not love me? Do you want to be more than friends?"

"Of course, I want to be more than friends, but . . ." She looked at the grapefruit in her hand, then at Matt. "What if we don't make it?"

"Why wouldn't we make it?"

"Because nobody makes it. Look at my sister. Your mom. Half of anyone who gets married if certain statistics are to be believed."

"First off, don't ever base our relationship off anything to do with your sister or my mom."

"Fine. But what about Gracie and Noah? I used to think they had the type of marriage a person could only dream of. They were always so crazy about each other. Always cracking jokes, teasing and flirting, even when they argued. In some ways, they kind of reminded me of us. You know, if we ever decided to take things to the next level. So when things started falling apart for them our senior year, I don't know. It kind of freaked me out. What if we risked our entire friendship only to turn out like them—loving each other, but for whatever reason, unhappy and apart? I'd rather see you happy with a girl like Aimee and know that we could still be friends at least."

"But I wasn't happy with a girl like Aimee."

"You should have been. In theory at least. She's kind and sweet and gorgeous."

"Well, I don't want kind and sweet and gorgeous in theory. I want you in heart, body, and soul."

"Matt—*shhh*." Her cheeks blushed a shade darker than the ripened peach she was currently squeezing into a pulp. They were seriously going to have a lot of ruined produce to pay for by the time they left the store. "You can't say stuff like that. Not *here*. Not in a *grocery store*."

"Why not?"

"Because . . . well, it makes me want to leap into your arms and kiss you. But people are looking at us, and I can't leap into your arms and kiss you when people are looking at us."

Matt glanced around. Sure enough, customers were shooting them the side-eye as they filled up their carts. Banana Lady was staring at them straight on from next to the sweet potatoes.

Matt settled his focus back on Rachel. "Did you forget that most of this town has already seen me without any pants on? You think they'll care if they see me kiss the woman I'm madly in love with? Anybody here care?"

"Nah, I say lay one on her," a guy gathering radishes and carrots yelled from across the produce section. Several murmurs of agreement followed. Even Banana Lady was offering a nod of encouragement.

"See? They're all for it. They know we're in love. I mean, we *are* in love, right? We're both on the same page here? We're both ready to take things to the next level? Even if we're scared, even if it's risky, even if people are watching? You know I'll be patient as long as you need me to be, but please *please* tell me we can at least move to the level where I can start introducing you as my girlfriend."

"No."

"No?"

"No." Rachel dropped her juicy peach into her overflowing basket of fruit, then dropped the entire basket into his cart. "I don't want to be your girlfriend."

Matt heard several gasps. One might have come from his own lips. "You don't?"

"No." She clutched the fabric of his shirt and tugged him closer. "You're not the portly farmer, Matt."

"I don't know what that means."

"It means you're my real hero." She was definitely getting sticky peach juice all over his shirt, but when she smiled he didn't care. And when she said, "I want to jump straight to the level where you introduce me as your fiancée," someone could've dumped an entire container of peach juice over his head and he wouldn't have cared. Or even noticed.

Because he was only thinking about one thing. And this time he was ready for it.

He didn't wait for her to start kissing him. He swooped in and claimed her lips, lifting her off her feet and making sure she knew just how much he meant that body, heart, and soul comment.

By the time he set her down, they were both out of breath and every grocery shopper in the store was clapping and whistling. Even his mom was smiling from next to the deli counter as she shook her head and rolled her eyes, muttering something like, "I should've known."

"You know what I think," Rachel whispered, burying her face against his neck. "We should get to the level where you introduce me as your wife as soon as possible."

"You know what I think," Matt whispered back, planting a kiss on the top of her head. "I should've worn the sling. Making out with you really did a number to my shoulder."

She playfully punched him in the stomach. "You just make sure it's in good working order by the honeymoon, okay?"

Honeymoon.

Matt pulled her back into his arms. Oh yeah. They were definitely getting married as soon as possible.

47

Grace: How's the recording coming along?

Noah: What recording?

Grace: What do you mean what recording?

Noah: What do you mean what do I mean what recording?

Grace: You're supposed to be recording stuff for the memoir!

Noah: Why do I have to record stuff when I can just walk over and talk to you about stuff?

Grace: You ever heard of multitasking? I need you to be recording more stories while I write, so I can listen to those recordings later and we can get this done as quickly as possible!

Noah: I thought you only had to turn in the first 3 chapters.

Grace: Now. But eventually I'm going to need to turn in ALL the chapters. And to do that I'm going to need more stuff!

Noah: So why don't I come over right now and just tell you more stuff?

Grace: Because I won't be here! Oh my goodness, why are you being so difficult?

Noah: Where are you going?

Grace: The animal shelter. I volunteer once a month and forgot until two minutes ago that this is my day to help out for a few hours.

Noah: I'll come with you.

Grace: No! You need to be recording stuff for the memoir!

Noah: Why can't I help you out at the shelter while we talk about more stuff for the memoir? Goodness, Gracie. Haven't you ever heard of multitasking?

48

Three hours later Noah wouldn't blame Gracie for being a little annoyed with him. He'd walked a dozen dogs, fed twice as many cats, cleaned more crates than he could count, and in all that time said zero stuff about anything to do with his memoir.

Which is why he'd swung through her favorite sandwich shop in Alda on the way home and was slowing to pull into one of the town's little neighborhood parks right now. A little park that just happened to be his favorite park in Alda.

"What are you doing?" Gracie asked, her voice full of suspicion as she secured the bags of chips and sandwiches on her lap when he made the turn.

"Weather's nice. Figured we could talk and eat our food while we work on the memoir here for a bit."

Some of the happy endorphins from cuddling and cooing over kittens all morning must've still been circulating in her bloodstream. She didn't argue. But she did keep shooting him a curious glance from the side of her eye as he followed the curve of the narrow one-way road that wrapped around the park. Other than a couple moms chatting on one of the park benches while their preschool-aged kids played nearby on a swing set, the park sat empty.

"Man, I'm starving," Noah said as he parked his Jeep next to the tennis court. "What?" he added when he looked over to find Gracie staring at him straight on now with one of her eyebrows slanted.

"What are we doing here?" The suspicion in her voice had been replaced with an amused sort of annoyance.

"I already told you. Multitasking. We can work on the memoir while we eat. If you want, I can even record everything we say." He set his phone on the console, then grabbed his sandwich off her lap.

"Right. But what are we doing *here*?" She rapped a knuckle on the window.

Noah shrugged with mock innocence. "Something wrong with here? Can't think of any reason you'd get all weird about a park. I mean it's just a park. Nothing special about it except—oh, wait. You're not thinking about what I think you're thinking about, are you? Oh, I see. You *are* thinking about that."

Now Noah offered her a look of mock sympathy as he swiped his barbecue chips off her lap and pulled apart the top. "That's probably all you can think about, isn't it?"

Her lips pressed to the side, the way they always did when she was trying to hide a smile. "Uh-huh, and just what am I thinking about?"

"Obviously the most exciting thing that's ever happened in this park, probably even the entire town. Our first kiss, of course. Right there on the tennis court. And hey, now that I think about it—" He started unwrapping the brown paper from his turkey sub. "Weren't we eating sub sandwiches on that date too?"

She wasn't even trying to hide her smile now. "You've got it so wrong."

"Which part? The sandwiches or the tennis court?"

"The whole first kiss part," she said, unwrapping her own sandwich.

He paused on his way to take a bite. "What are you talking about?"

"Don't you remember our first date at the movies?"

"I remember a movie. I don't remember any kiss."

"You kissed my cheek before you dropped me off at home."

"A cheek kiss?" Noah bit into his sub, speaking around his mouthful. "Babe, no man alive is going to count that as a first kiss."

"Well, I'm counting it as *my* first kiss. I loved that kiss."

"Just goes to show what an amazing kisser I am." He winked,

started to take another bite, then lowered his sandwich. "Hold up a second. Out there on the tennis court—the night of our first *real* kiss—you told me your first kiss was at a summer camp to a boy named Dustin. Just how many first kisses are you going to count?"

Gracie lifted the long bun away from her BLT the way she always did to make sure there weren't any secret pickles hidden inside. "There was a summer camp. There was a Dustin. I sort of made up the whole bit about us kissing."

Apparently reassured that her sandwich was pickle free, she bit off a huge chunk and tried to chew without smiling. Her lips didn't even stay pressed to the side for two seconds before she was giggling. "What?"

Noah handed her a napkin before she shot BLT all over his Jeep. "Do you have any idea how jealous I was that this Dustin kid got to kiss you first?"

"Dustin wasn't even a kid," she said, her face turning red from trying to chew and swallow and not laugh. "He was one of the camp counselor's dogs. It was the first name I thought of."

"Are you kidding me?" Noah wadded up his napkin and bopped it off her forehead. But he couldn't stop grinning. And she couldn't stop giggling.

"I don't even know why I said it. I think I was just nervous."

"So you lied about making out with a camp counselor's dog?" She laughed harder just like he'd hoped. Man, he'd missed that sound. "Why were you so nervous anyway? I was the only one who should've been nervous."

"*You?* Please. You were the cute, mysterious new guy—all the girls were talking about you. You had no reason to be nervous. But me— well, I was just . . . Gracie."

"Sure. Just Gracie. Just-the-most-beautiful-girl-I'd-ever-met Gracie. You're crazy, you know that? I can't believe you made up a kiss and never told me."

"Says the man who never told me he had a brother who died."

Noah dipped his head to the side. "You might have me there."

He poured a few chips from the bag straight into his mouth. After a few minutes of them both eating in silence, he said, "Hey, so tell me this then. If I was your first kiss, does that mean I'm the only—" He shook his head. "Never mind."

He actually didn't want to know the answer to that question. He uncapped his bottled water and took a long drink. If he thought he'd been jealous of Dustin, no telling how jealous he'd get thinking about some man Gracie might've kissed after their divorce.

Best not to even think about it. Ever.

Neither of them said anything while they finished eating their sandwiches and chips. It wasn't until they'd shoved all the wrappers into a sack and wiped off their fingers with some wet wipes Gracie found in her purse, then started back for the house that Gracie's soft voice reached across the console.

"Yes, Noah. To answer your question, it's only ever been you."

49

Gracie drummed her pencil against the edge of her desk. She'd made a mistake. Two mistakes. Well, more like a thousand mistakes if she wanted to get technical, but right now all she cared about were the two biggies she'd made in the past forty-eight hours. Especially mistake number two. The first mistake she could've dealt with, but mistake number two . . .

Oh boy. That mistake was a problem. A big problem. Because now it made the first mistake . . . well, a really bad mistake.

Her phone rang and Gracie answered before the second ring. "I've made a mistake."

"No, you didn't. I loooove it," her agent belted out in a singsong voice.

"I shouldn't have sent it."

"Yes, you should have. I loooove it."

"Will you stop saying that? We can't use those chapters. Any of them. Don't show them to anybody. Especially the editors."

"I already did. And guess what?"

"Don't say it."

"They loooove it."

She said it. Gracie tossed the pencil on her desk and clutched her forehead. "This is terrible."

Her agent laughed. "Sure. Awful. Worst thing ever. You might still have a writing career in a publishing world that's changing every minute. Prepare the funeral march. Dress in mourning. Do whatever you want. But me? I'm celebrating. Gracie, this is great stuff. I know it's a memoir, but I'm telling you, it has the same feel as your earlier writing. The emotion. The humor. The zing. People are going to gobble this up faster than chips and salsa on half-price margarita night."

"I promised Noah I wouldn't write about his childhood."

"Well, un-promise him. I don't give a fig about sports and even I teared up over the Little League game. What is it about baseball and dads? And don't even get me started on the parts about you two. The cheek kiss at the movies. Your little sandwich date on the tennis courts. So funny. So sweet. *So perfect.* I love how you're writing the memoir in both of your own voices. This is exactly what your publisher was looking for. Relatable down-to-earth heroes. And we haven't even gotten to the big game yet. Keep sending in more chapters once you've got them."

"Believe me, I'm working as fast as I can."

"I can tell. You're on a roll. Keep rolling, baby. No writer's block this time. Didn't I tell you this project would be good for you?"

She did. And it was. Gracie couldn't remember the last time words had flowed so easily onto the page. Not that she could take all the credit. All she was doing was writing down Noah's story the way he was telling it—and perhaps weaving in a few stories of her own based on the way she remembered it. When she could.

Until now she never realized how much of Noah's story she hadn't known.

When he showed up at her high school, they were a couple of teenagers with an undeniable spark of chemistry between them. Too busy flirting and making up kisses, Gracie hadn't spent much time poking into his childhood. Whenever she did ask questions, he'd find a way to answer without really giving an answer. But before Gracie knew it, she was so head over heels he could've robbed a bank in his past and she wouldn't have cared.

All she'd cared about was their future, which they rushed into with the speed of a hundred-mile-per-hour fastball.

"Look, I'm not saying this hasn't been good for me." Gracie could admit there was something surprisingly therapeutic about working on this memoir with Noah. They'd shared more laughs the past two days than they had the entire last two years of their marriage.

But why shouldn't they laugh? They were rehashing the good days. Early love. First kisses. New beginnings. Seasons brimming with hope.

Gracie knew all too well what awaited them in further chapters. Disappointment. Uncertainty. Separation. Loneliness. Seasons of heartache after heartache after heartache.

Which is exactly why the whole thing had been a mistake.

"I can't do this, Simone. I'm sorry. I never should've sent you those chapters. I never should've agreed to write this story."

"But the story is beautiful, Gracie. I don't understand."

Neither did Gracie. Not after she'd worked so hard to build a wall around her heart. Not after she'd promised herself that she'd never go back to being the woman she'd been five years ago. The woman who couldn't stop hoping, obsessing, pining, *begging* God to make her a mom only to get crushed month after month, year after year, when God wouldn't answer her prayer.

The day Noah suggested it was time to move on was the day Gracie decided that was the only answer she was going to get.

So she'd moved on. Without Noah. Without God. Without the hope that was slowly killing her.

"Gracie? You still there? What's the problem with finishing this story?"

"The problem is . . ." Gracie shook her head. How had this happened? "I think I'm still in love with my husband."

"Ex-husband."

"That's what I said."

"No, it's not." Simone's voice softened into a gentle tone Gracie had never heard from her agent before. "You know the difference between a romance and a love story, right? A love story doesn't guarantee a happily-ever-after ending. Well, right now, Gracie, you're writing the greatest love story you've ever told, and no, a happy ending isn't guaranteed. But don't you at least want to see how it plays out, even if there's only the slightest hope for one?"

Gracie shook her head and sighed. "Fine, Simone. I'll finish the memoir."

But nobody, not even Simone, could convince her to start hoping for a happily-ever-after. Some things weren't worth the risk. Not this late in the game.

And one of those things was her heart.

50

Scotty: Are you awake? Probably not. I just remembered it's 3 AM your time. Okay, never mind. Go back to sleep.

Scotty: Actually, no. Wake up! I have to talk to you!

Scotty: You're not going to wake up, are you?

Scotty: That's okay. I'll just send you a million texts that you can read in the morning.

Scotty: Your memoir! Gracie's agent sent me some of the chapters. (Probably because I wouldn't stop texting her until she sent me some of the chapters.) And Noah . . .

Scotty: I'm blubbering! I'm literally blubbering in bed! I never blubber in bed! Or anywhere! I'm not a blubberer! But that Little League game! Your dad! I feel like I need to call my dad!

Scotty: Okay, I just called him and he yelled at me for calling him in the middle of the night blubbering about baseball. So I'll go back to blubbering to you. That game! So good! I'm going to keep reading . . .

Scotty: Uh-oh. Here come the blubbers again! Just read where you wanted to quit baseball and get a job doing HVAC cuz you two were barely making ends meet and you never thought you'd make it out of the minors, but Gracie told you to stick it out one more month and on day 29 you finally got the call to go up to the majors! (Remind me to send Gracie some flowers. I owe her one.)

Scotty: Bummer. I just finished the part about when Gracie flew out to surprise you at one of your away games (and make a baby—I can read between the lines) but you'd just gotten sent down to Triple A again and ended up never seeing each other because you were both stuck in different cities all weekend. I remember that weekend. You were very crabby that weekend. Pretty sure that was the weekend you got ejected from a game.

Scotty: Yep. Reading it now. (How did I not remember that you got ejected on Cowboy Monkey Rodeo Night?)

Scotty: Awww, now I'm reading about how Gracie was ready to quit writing cuz she thought she'd never get published, but you told her to stick it out one more story and that's the story that turned into her first publishing deal. (Remind me to send her some congratulatory flowers.)

Scotty: Are you awake yet? I ran out of chapters.

Scotty: Noah . . . I need more chapters.

Scotty: Tell Gracie if she wants any of my flowers then she better wake up and write me some more chapters!

51

Noah needed Gracie to stop writing so many chapters. At the pace she was going, she'd have the memoir finished in no time. He needed her to slow down. Especially since the only thing keeping him in her life right now was this project. An excuse that was growing flimsier by the day.

"Really," she'd told him at least three times yesterday. "We're way ahead of the deadline. You can go home, and we can just finish the rest of it over the phone or through recordings."

Go home to what? Didn't she know this was his home?

Well, not *here* at the cabin—cottage—whatever it was called.

Noah rubbed his fist over the condensation fogging up the tiny bathroom mirror after his shower. He didn't want to stay *here* alone any more than he wanted to fly back to Seattle alone. He was tired of living alone. What he wanted was to move back into the house and back into Gracie's life. For good.

Which is why he needed to up his game to more than just cute little sandwich lunches at the park. He tapped his razor against the edge of the bathroom sink, then ran the blades across his jaw. Time to take Gracie out on a real date.

Thirty minutes later Noah found her where he figured she'd be—sitting at her special writing desk in the spare bedroom upstairs, typing madly on her laptop. He gripped both sides of the doorframe, squeezing back all the pent-up energy buzzing up and down his body ever since his shower. "Mind if I ask you something?"

She gasped and whipped her gaze from her laptop screen. "Noah," she said on a shuddery breath. "I didn't hear you come in. But I know why you're here."

"You do?"

"And I'm sorry."

"You are?"

"I understand if you hate me."

Noah ran his finger over the spot where he'd nicked himself on the chin. He needed a new razor. "Mind filling me in?"

She pointed at her laptop. "I wrote about your childhood. All of it. Every last detail. Everything you said. Then I wrote a whole bunch of stuff about us and our relationship, and now it's all going in the memoir, and I can't take it back, and—"

"I know."

"—people are going to read it, and . . . Did you just say you know?"

He grinned, folding his arms and leaning against the doorframe. "It's my memoir, babe. Did you think they were leaving me in the dark? I already got an email from the editor and roughly two million texts from a blubbering Scotty. They all think it's great. And you know what? I do too."

"Really?"

"Really. Ever since I told you about Owen . . . I don't know. Guess it just made me realize that by ignoring all the bad parts in my past I'd swept out some good parts too. Like Owen's laugh. Man, that kid had the best laugh. I don't want to do that anymore. Ignore things. Not when it comes to my family. Definitely not when it comes to us. We had some bad times, sure. But we had plenty of good times, too, didn't we, Gracie?"

Her lips pressed together and rolled inward as she darted a gaze out the window then back to him. She gave a clipped nod. "You look nice," she said in an obvious attempt to change the subject. "Why do you look nice? Are you going somewhere?"

He shot a look down to his button-down shirt and dark jeans, then straightened from the doorframe and shoved his hands in his pockets, hoping his smile didn't look as insecure as it felt. "I am. And I'm taking you with me."

"Oh? And where exactly are you taking me?"

He shuffled from one foot to the other. Good grief. He hadn't felt this nervous since the first time he asked Gracie out on a date. Back then he hadn't thought he stood a chance since she was older, obviously more mature, and so, so beautiful. But for some reason she'd said yes. He took her to dinner and a movie, and to this day he had no recollection what movie they saw since he spent the whole two hours stealing glances, wondering if he'd get to kiss her.

"Noah?"

Right. He cleared his throat. "Dinner."

Gracie glanced at her phone on the desk. "A little early for dinner, isn't it?"

"Won't be by the time we drive down to St. Louis. Thought we'd go somewhere on The Hill. Whichever restaurant you want."

He held his breath. Driving down to St. Louis to eat at one of the Italian restaurants on The Hill was what they'd always done whenever they had something big to celebrate. An engagement. A major league contract. A book deal. A new start in their marriage?

"The Hill. Oh. That is a bit of a drive."

About an hour and fifteen minutes depending on traffic. "We'll get to fill our bellies with pasta," Noah pointed out quickly before holding his breath again.

"I suppose any distance is worth driving for that." Gracie looked down at her cardigan and sweatpants. "Give me a few minutes to change?"

Noah slowly exhaled, making sure to keep his hands tucked in his pockets and not pumping the air in victory. "Take all the time you need. But as far as I'm concerned, you already look great. Beautiful.

You could go as you are. Although it is The Hill, so you probably want to put on something special. And although I know you have a very special relationship with your bathrobe, I wouldn't suggest wearing—"

"The longer you stand there cracking jokes, the longer it'll be until we fill our bellies with pasta."

"Good point." His elbow racked against the doorframe as he spun to leave. "My arm's fine. Don't worry," he said over his shoulder.

"I was more concerned about the doorframe," she called after him.

"Thirty minutes. I'm starting the clock now," he said halfway down the stairs.

"You can't rush a lady."

"I can if we have reservations," he hollered from the bottom of the stairs.

"I thought you said I got to pick the restaurant," she hollered back.

He turned at the front door. "I made Scotty get us reservations everywhere just in case."

"This is getting serious."

"You have no idea," he muttered as he closed the door shut behind him.

52

A couple hours later, seated in a hardwood booth, listening to Dean Martin classics with a curvy glass pitcher of water slowly disappearing between them, Noah allowed his shoulders to finally relax. "Want another piece of bread?"

"I do. But I could barely squeeze into this dress as it was."

And don't think Noah didn't notice how fabulous she looked squeezed into that dress. He sliced off another piece of bread for himself as Gracie nestled back in her seat, her gaze sweeping across the room. "That old couple over there must recognize you," she said with a smirk. "They keep whispering and looking this way."

"Nope. That's all for you."

"Please."

"It's true. I met the husband in the bathroom. He couldn't stop yammering about how much his wife loved your last book and how she's read it so many times, the cover is falling off."

"Now I know you're lying. Nobody loved my last book. I didn't even love my last book." Gracie's eyes peeked in their direction. "She's waving at me."

"Told you so."

Gracie slowly lifted her hand and waved back.

Noah leaned across the table. "Put a nice lady out of her misery and just go over and say hi."

Gracie's eyes narrowed like she still thought this might be some sort of practical joke. But when the lady wouldn't stop waving, she slid from the booth.

Noah watched her introduce herself to the couple. The woman waved her hands in grand gestures that Noah interpreted to mean how grand her love was for that book.

When Gracie returned to the booth a few minutes later, her cheeks looked flushed with equal parts embarrassment and satisfaction. "She loved my last book. She named a chipmunk they like to feed in their backyard after the lead character."

Noah lifted his wine glass. "To your fans."

Gracie laughed and raised her glass. "To the one of them that's still left."

"Hey, you know I'm still a fan. Pretty sure the FedEx lady is too."

"The FedEx lady, I can believe. You? Not so much. Pretty sure my stories were never 'up your a' as Mayor Abe would say."

Noah nearly choked on his water. "I'm sorry, up my what?"

"Alley. A."

"I'd definitely advise sticking to the entire word if you're going to use that expression."

She laughed again. "I didn't think it sounded right when I said it."

"Let's just hope that's the last time you ever say it." Noah grinned and lowered his glass, praying what he said next flowed as easily as the banter and water. "Gracie, don't you think it's time we talk about that game?"

Judging by the way Gracie squirmed in her seat, she knew exactly which game. "You mean for the memoir?"

"I mean for us."

"I don't know. Feels like the wounds from our marriage are finally scabbing over. Do we really want to make those wounds start bleeding all over again?"

"Pretty sure those wounds are infected, and the only way for them to ever heal is to expose them so they can get treated properly. Which is why I think it's time for you to tell me your version of what happened."

Gracie leaned back as the server set her plate filled with shrimp over pasta on the table, then handed Noah his plate full of spaghetti. After the server left, Gracie met Noah's gaze. "All right. We can talk about the game, but only if we can agree on one thing."

"I'm listening."

"Whatever happens, whatever wounds we reopen, whatever purulent drainage splashes all over the table—"

"Maybe it's time to switch to a different analogy while we eat our meal."

"I want you to promise me one thing." Her hazel eyes lifted from the pasta and hit him with a serious gaze. "We're not leaving this restaurant until we order a slice of Death by Chocolate. I don't care how tight my dress is by the end of the night."

His shoulders relaxed as he reached for his fork. "Now that idea is definitely up my a."

53

Stuffed from supper, Gracie fiddled with her dessert fork, ready to finally dive into talking about the night of that game. "Did I ever tell you about the cat I had back when I was a kid?"

Noah squinted an eye in thought—or more likely confusion about what her version of the game had to do with a childhood cat. "Pepper?"

"That was the neighbor's dog who bit me. No, I'm talking about Morris. As a kitten he reminded me of that book about Morris the moose, so that's what I named him."

Gracie paused while the waitress delivered their chocolate dessert before continuing her story. "I picked Morris out of a litter from the neighbor's house. Same neighbor whose dog bit me. I think he felt bad, so he let me take a kitten for free. Although I'm not really sure how much of a deal that was, considering he was begging people to take one."

Gracie shrugged and dug her fork into the mound of chocolate. "Point is I loved Morris. I put cute little bows on him. Dragged him around town in my bicycle basket. Carried him with me everywhere I went. You get the idea."

"You loved that cat."

"I *loved* that cat."

"What happened to him?"

"MaryAnn Merkle happened to him." Gracie exchanged the fork in her hand for the mug of coffee, the memory of that woman as bitter as the brew. "In all the time I grew up, my dad never dated anybody. Mona didn't mind. She remembered my mom and never wanted anybody to replace that role. Plus, Mona had taken the responsibility of my surrogate mother and queen boss and I'm pretty sure she never wanted anybody replacing that role either."

"Why does that not surprise me?"

"But no matter what Mona said, I wanted a mom. I used to ask for one at Christmas every year, even long after I stopped believing in Santa Claus. And when MaryAnn Merkle moved to town and became my fifth-grade teacher, I thought it was finally going to happen. She was so pretty and nice. She wore these fashionable outfits, always smelled like fancy perfume, and she wasn't married. It seemed a no-brainer to me. I started doing bad on my schoolwork just so she and my dad would have reasons to talk to one another."

"Quite the little matchmaker."

"You could've called me Emma. You know, Jane Austen? Never mind. The point is even Mona couldn't find fault with the lovely Miss Merkle. I figured I'd have a mother in no time. Until the fateful night she stopped over to return my coat, which I, of course, had left behind in hopes of her stopping by to return it."

Noah stabbed a bite from the cake, then nudged the plate toward her, so she could take another bite when she was ready.

"At first everything went according to plan. She handed my dad the coat. He thanked her. They started talking. Joking. Laughing. He invited her in. Then that was the moment when everything went downhill. Fast."

"Let me guess. Miss Merkle was allergic to cats."

"Worse. Miss Merkle was terrified of cats."

He quirked a brow at her as he wiped his mouth off with a napkin.

"The way some people feel about snakes, that's the way she felt about cats. She screamed and ran right out the door."

"Because of a cat?"

"A cat wearing a cute red bow. I guess something happened in her childhood, I don't know, she tried explaining it to my dad, but whatever it was, she couldn't get past it and said she'd never feel comfortable stepping foot in the same house as a cat, which meant she'd never be comfortable entering into a relationship with a man with a cat."

Noah cracked a smile. "Poor Buck."

"Poor Buck? How about poor Gracie? I'm the one who ended up giving the cat away."

Noah swiped his finger across a thick layer of frosting. "Yeah, but I can only imagine the drama of dealing with you and your sister at those ages. How'd he talk you into giving up the cat?"

"Please. Have you met my dad? He'd never have the heart to tell a daughter of his to give away the love of her life. No, that was all Mona."

"I thought she didn't care about having another mom."

"Turns out she cared a great deal about having another mom. She wouldn't stop badgering me. *Wouldn't you rather have a mother instead of a cat? A cat's average life expectancy is only fifteen years. Miss Merkle is bound to live a lot longer than that.* To which I'd point out our first mother didn't make it very long. To which she'd point out how I played a factor in that, since her death did occur shortly after childbirth, and didn't I owe it to everybody to make a sacrifice after all they'd done for me."

"Your sister is something else."

"She's certainly good about getting her way. Eventually I gave in. I handed Morris over to a classmate who lived out on a farm. She said her parents wouldn't notice another barn cat. Can you believe that? A barn cat. My little Morris with bows became a barn cat. And for what? Nothing."

Gracie shoveled a bite of cake into her mouth, covering her mouth with her napkin as she spoke. "Miss Merkle never married dad. She started dating the town dentist."

"I caught something about a dentist."

"Sorry." She wiped her lips off and swallowed. "She married the dentist the following summer and moved to Chicago. And you want to know what happened to Morris?"

"I'm guessing something not good."

"Eaten by a pack of coyotes."

"For real?"

Gracie shrugged. "Eaten by something. My classmate said he disappeared. She had the decency to bring me back his bow, which was all mangled and dirty. If I'd taken a DNA sample, I'm sure I would have found it covered in coyote saliva. Either way, I couldn't give him a proper burial—not that anybody bothered showing up for his funeral."

"You had a funeral for your cat?"

"Tried to. I buried his bow and attempted a eulogy, but I couldn't really get much out past the tears. But I at least got out more than Mona. All she had to say when I came home for supper that evening was, 'Oh well. He was just a cat.' She never cried. Never cared. She didn't even seem that upset over losing Miss Merkle to the dentist, to be honest. When I complained to my dad, his only response was, 'Well, kiddo, sometimes you just got to learn not to hold onto things too tight.'"

Gracie shoved away the last bit of cake, her appetite gone. "You asked about my version of that game. Well, as pathetic as it sounds, that's pretty much it. After I got off the phone with you, I felt like once again, there I was, standing by myself over a pile of dirt mourning something that nobody else seemed to care about."

"I wanted a baby too, Gracie."

"Sure you did. The way Mona wanted another mom. The way Dad wanted another wife. It would be nice, but hey, if it doesn't work out, oh well. Don't hold on to that dream too tight, right?"

Noah leaned forward. "That's not how it was for me."

"Sure. I could tell how much you cared by the way you never missed a single game every time the pregnancy test was negative."

"I still had a job to do, whether you got pregnant or not. And that's what it was, Gracie. A job. It wasn't me blowing you off for another poker night with the boys. It was my career. Our livelihood. We both saw what it was like living paycheck to paycheck, and you better believe I wasn't ever letting us go back to that again."

"I know. And that's not . . . I don't want to argue about this. You asked for my version of that game, remember? Well, this is me trying to explain."

When Noah's fingers grazed her hand, she tugged her hands into her lap. She couldn't explain with him touching her. Hard enough to explain with him just looking at her.

"I grew up without a mom. The one thing I wanted more than anything was to get the chance to be a mom. I would have done anything. I would have gone through any amount of testing. I would have given myself any amount of shots. I would have filled out any amount of paperwork. I would've flown anywhere. I would have done anything to hold a child in my arms that I could call son or daughter—so long as I could do it with you. I was too scared to do it alone."

"You wouldn't have had to do it alone."

"I was already doing it alone!" Gracie shot a glance around the restaurant and lowered her voice. "Sorry. I thought I could do this, but I can't."

54

Gracie saw Noah's hand reach across the table for her. "Gracie, wait. Let me help you."

"I'm fine." She wasn't. Not by a long shot. But she had to get away from him. Regroup. Somehow scrape her puddled ice queen back into a block of ice. "Just pay and I'll wait for you outside," she muttered, not even sure if he heard her over the music and din of conversation.

Her vision blurred as she rushed outside, cold air smacking her bare arms. Shoot, she'd forgotten to grab her coat. She started to turn, then batted her hand. Forget it.

"Oh, sorry," she said, nearly colliding into a young couple on their way into the restaurant. "Sorry." Limping away, she passed several more people on the sidewalk. Noah had dropped her off, so she had no idea where he'd parked. Hopefully somewhere this direction.

She kept walking, her hip throbbing from where she'd banged it against the table in her rush to escape.

She spotted Noah's Jeep parked on the side of the road at the same moment she heard his voice. "Gracie, hold up."

The warmth of her coat settled over her shoulders just as she reached the passenger's side. Without turning to face him, Gracie hugged herself and spoke. "I didn't mean to call you before the game that day."

Wind whipped a slice of her hair against her cheek. She attempted to tuck it behind her ear, only for the wind to slap it right back in her face.

"I was going to wait until the next time I saw you in person. Or at least wait until after you'd pitched. I told myself not to call. Then I told myself just to wish you good luck. I didn't mean to tell you—" Her words clogged in her throat, but the memories refused to be tamed any more than her hair in the wind.

She'd kept the pregnancy test results a secret for weeks. After so many negative readings, she hadn't wanted to jinx the first positive. So she'd kept quiet. Waited for her first appointment, planning to surprise Noah with the ultrasound photos afterward. Their dream had finally come true. A baby. They could finally turn that spare bedroom into a nursery.

For the first time in a long time, she had more than hope. She had an answer to prayer.

But that absent heartbeat had changed everything.

"I knew it was a mistake as soon as I hung up the phone. I thought about what a jerk move that was, giving you news like that right before your game. But I think part of me was hoping you wouldn't pitch. Part of me was hoping you'd come home. I didn't want to be by myself, but I didn't know where to go. I didn't know what to do. Somehow I found myself driving to St. Louis."

"You came to my game? You were there that night?"

Gracie nodded. "Everyone assumed I was there because of that boy. It was the only thing anybody talked about. How often you'd visited him at the hospital during his treatments. How close you two had gotten. How you had promised him to 'win big' that night. And sure enough, I watched you pitch inning after inning, true to your word. You were his hero. Everybody's hero. But all I could think about the entire drive home was that I needed you to be mine.

"Later that night was the first time I started thinking you were right. It was time to move on. Let go of this whole motherhood dream. Let go of our marriage. By that point it felt like you already had."

"Gracie." Noah turned her around, forcing her to meet his gaze. "I never wanted to let go of anything. Definitely not you. I just didn't know how to make things better."

"I know, I know. And you know what—it's fine. Really. It took me a while, but I'm finally starting to see how our divorce worked out for the best. It was the only thing that allowed me to move on. The only thing that eventually allowed us to be friends again."

"We are not friends."

"We've practically been living under the same roof for almost a month without killing each other. How many divorced couples can say that?"

"We are not friends."

"Now we're working on this memoir project together. Sharing a nice dinner out. We're not letting things get complicated between us."

This time he didn't say anything. Just slid his hand around the back of her neck and tugged her mouth against his. He wasn't holding her tight. She could have moved away.

But Gracie didn't want to move away. She wanted to move the complete opposite of away. She molded against him and slid her hands to his back, wanting to get closer.

He tasted like chocolate frosting and coffee and everything familiar. Everything she recognized. Everything she missed.

He deepened the kiss. They must have been spinning because he nudged her backwards, pressing her against his Jeep and trapping her there. Not that Gracie minded. She had no desire to escape. If she was going to fall off the wagon with kissing her ex-husband, she was going to enjoy every blessed moment of it.

And apparently so was Noah. He didn't seem to mind the fact they were kissing on a busy public street any more than she did at the moment.

"We are not friends," he whispered next to her ear, dropping a trail of kisses down her jawline and back to her lips for another long taste before murmuring against them. "And that's why things will always be complicated between us. We were lovers, Gracie." Another kiss. "Husband and wife." More kisses. "We shared a bed. A life. And I thought we shared the same dream for a family, whatever that ended up looking like. Whether that meant a dozen kids or just you and me, at the end of the day that was all I ever wanted."

Before she got lost in his lips again, she palmed his chest and pushed him a fraction back. "Then why didn't you fight for it?" He froze long enough for her to shove him further away. "You talked about your dad not fighting for his family, why didn't you fight for yours? Why didn't you fight as hard for us as you did for any of your baseball games?"

"I didn't know how to. That doesn't mean I didn't want to. C'mon, Grace. Give me another chance to figure it out. Give us another chance to figure it out."

But what if they still didn't figure it out? What if their marriage still fell apart?

She pushed Noah further way. No. She couldn't go through that again.

She needed space. She couldn't think with his body pressed flush against hers. Definitely couldn't think when he kissed her. She needed him to go away.

When her phone started ringing in her coat pocket, she couldn't get to it fast enough. She didn't care if it was a call about extending her car warranty, she was answering and staying on the line the entire drive home.

Mona's name flashed on the screen.

"Hello?" Gracie said, relieved Noah had stepped back, giving her a little breathing room.

But it sounded like her sister was the one who needed help in the breathing department. "Mona, what's wrong?" All Gracie could hear was her hyperventilating into the phone. "Is it Dad?"

Please don't be Dad.

Gracie reached for Noah, already needing him back in her space again. His hand settled on her lower back. Solid. Steady.

"Mona, say something!"

Strangled words finally broke through all the panting. "Matt and Rachel are getting married. *In a week!*"

55

Noah couldn't tell if he'd made any progress with Gracie or not. While it certainly felt like progress when their lips were all over each other in St. Louis five nights ago, Gracie had been so wrapped up in helping Mona plan for Matt's wedding ever since that she'd barely had time to speak to Noah, let alone engage in further heart-to-heart discussions about their marriage.

Personally, Noah would've settled for a short lip-on-lip session if she didn't have time for a heart-to-heart, but it seemed Gracie was too busy even for that.

At least that's what Noah kept telling himself. Loudly. Especially when his other inner voice tried suggesting that Gracie was just avoiding him, plain and simple.

Not even using the memoir as an excuse to spend time together had worked. When he brought it up this afternoon, she texted him a list of questions and told him to make a recording of all his answers.

Yeah, well, he'd done plenty of that already this week. He had a much better idea for how he'd like to spend his afternoon, and it had nothing to do with listening to the sound of his own voice.

Noah rapped his knuckles on the open door to Buck's hospital room. "Hey, old man. You still alive or should I come back later?"

A low rumbled voice answered. "Noah? Good grief, boy. About time you came for a visit. I was starting to get a complex."

Noah rounded the curtain and stood at the foot of Buck's bed. He made a show of scrutinizing him over from head to toe and back up again. "Shoot. The way everybody was talking, I expected to find a corpse in the bed. You don't look half bad."

Buck swung a thumb to the window that offered a view of a parking garage. "Must be all the natural lighting."

"Or the gourmet food."

"The rubbery meatloaf alone has given me a new will to live."

Noah tapped Buck's leg with a rolled newspaper and sat down on the edge of the bed. "How are you? Really?"

Buck adjusted the nasal cannula against his nose. "I've seen better days. But I've got a feeling you have too."

Noah scrubbed a hand down his face, his scratchy face already due for another shave. "Five strikeouts. Can you believe that? Another outing or two on the mound and I could've set an all-time team record."

"I wasn't talking about baseball."

Yeah, Noah didn't figure he was. He tapped Buck's leg again, then hopped from the bed. "So do I need a voucher or something to get you out? I've been here five minutes and I'm already depressed. How do we leave?"

"It's not so bad." Buck cocked his head to the curtain. "Shorty—he's at dialysis and boy is he going to be sorry when he finds out he missed you—he and I can spend a day chewing the fat pretty well. But I wouldn't turn down the opportunity for a change of scenery. Is it nice outside? Last couple of times Matt visited, it rained."

"You sure do have a crummy view, don't you? Yeah, it's gorgeous outside. Let me scrounge up a wheelchair. It'll give us a little practice for when we break you out of here for Matt's wedding."

Buck laughed and started coughing. "Have to give the boy props," he said when he recovered enough to talk again. "After dragging his feet all these years, he's sure not wasting any time getting that girl down the aisle now."

"No, he's certainly not." Noah couldn't help the punch of envy thinking about how stupidly happy he and Rachel both were about this upcoming wedding—even if it was *completely* insane.

Fifteen minutes later, Noah had Buck situated in a wheelchair. He pushed him outdoors to a path that meandered to a small garden. The flowers had all withered and a cracked fountain in the center sat dry, but the view was still better than anything the inside of the hospital had to offer. Noah parked the wheelchair and sat down on a cement bench next to Buck.

"How often do you get a break from this place?"

Buck shrugged. "Used to get out every Sunday and join the girls for church and lunch. But it wears me out so much anymore. And I know it's hard on the girls, too. They don't complain, but I know it's a burden. Shoot, Matt's the only one strong enough to get me out of the wheelchair anymore. I've gotten so weak, it's stupid. When you reach the point you can't get on a toilet without your grandson's help, you start making excuses to hang back, you know?"

Noah nodded. "Getting old is no fun, but it's better than the alternative, right?"

Buck leaned forward, his nasal cannula hissing soft oxygen from the portable tank. "There reaches a point when the alternative doesn't sound too bad. I'm about to that point."

Noah hated to ask, but he had to know. "You're not hanging on just to see Gracie remarry someone like Luke, are you?"

"I'm hanging on because it's the top of the ninth and this game isn't over yet." Buck winked, then tugged out a tissue from his pocket to cover his mouth during another coughing spell.

Soon as he recovered, he said, "Am I hoping I'll get to see Gracie happy again before I go? Sure. Nothing would make me happier."

"What do you think will make her happy?" Noah kept his gaze focused on the weathered angel in the center of the fountain, not sure he wanted Buck to see the hope in his eyes. The hope that Buck would answer something to the tune of Gracie ending up back with Noah.

Buck took his time answering. "Did she ever tell you about Morris?"

Noah gave a slow nod, trying to figure out how a dead cat was going to factor into the key to Gracie's happiness.

"Did she ever tell you I tried giving her another cat at least half a dozen times afterward?"

Noah held Buck's pale-blue gaze. "She failed to mention that part."

"Because she's too much like her dad. Stubborn. The girls didn't know it, but that Merkle lady never stood a chance. Their mother was the love of my life. I never learned how to let go of her. Took me a lot of years, though, to realize I could still hold on to her without holding on to my pain. Gracie's cut from the same cloth, I'm afraid."

"That's why she never got another cat?"

"That's why she's never moved on from you. I think, whether Gracie realizes it or not, she's never stopped clinging to you because deep down she knows you're one of the best things that's ever walked into her life. But she's never figured out how to let go of the heartache either."

"So what does that mean for me?"

Buck leaned forward in his wheelchair. "Don't you get it, Noah? You're Morris. But you want to know the difference between you and that cat?"

Noah could think of a few things.

"You're not dead, son. Figure out a way to make this marriage work. And soon. I'd like to see my little girl happy before the bottom of the ninth rolls around."

56

Mona: Please tell me we're not really going to let them go through with this wedding.

Grace: The wedding we worked our tails off to put together? That wedding?

Mona: I was only trying to be supportive. I didn't think they'd actually go through with it! How do we stop them?

Grace: Have you seen the way they look at each other? There is no stopping them.

Mona: What if this turns out to be a huge mistake?

Grace: Then that will be their mistake to own. In the meantime let's not make the mistake of not doing everything we can to support them.

Mona: I am being supportive!

Grace: You are being the very definition of supportive!

Mona: Thank you for supporting my supportiveness!

Grace: You're welcome! You know who else I bet would be a very supportive support system at the wedding tomorrow? The guy you're secretly dating.

Mona: Goodnight.

57

Even after sitting through the ceremony, Noah couldn't believe it.

Matt. Married. To Rachel. In a week.

Noah shook his head. Crazy. Nuts. Insane. And pretty much just how Noah and Gracie had been back at their age. They hadn't seen the merits of a long engagement either. But at least they'd made it a whole month before getting hitched.

One week!

A loud country song blasted across the five-thousand-square-foot barn serving as the reception hall. With fresh wood paneling and giant bay windows along the walls, white sheer fabric floating across the open ceiling beams, and three round rustic chandeliers hanging down from the ceiling, the place held a magical glow. Certainly didn't look like any barn Noah had ever stepped inside of before.

Apparently Mona had pulled every string she had to land the venue on such short notice. There'd been a brief—and chilly—ceremony outside beneath a pavilion next to a pond, followed by a long—and probably even chillier—photo session for Matt and Rachel all over the venue's ten acres of property, ending now with a dance-the-night-away reception in the barn.

He caught Gracie watching him from the other side of their table. Or maybe she'd caught him. She glanced away, but he continued to stare. He'd barely seen her this week because of all the wedding crazi-ness. But he was sure looking at her now.

And he couldn't help thinking Matt had the right idea. Maybe it was time to get a little crazy and seize the day.

Noah rounded the table and reached out his hand. Wiggled his fingers. "C'mon, babe. It's Matt's wedding. We can't just sit here all night without busting out any moves. And by moves I of course mean orthopedic-surgeon-approved moves."

Gracie tightened her sparkly shawl around her bare shoulders as her lips twisted to the side in an attempt not to smile. "This isn't really my type of music."

"Don't worry. I made a request. Next song is going to be right up your alley. Notice, by the way, how I got the expression right."

This time her lips lifted in an undeniable smile. "Fine. But only because it's Matt and Rachel's wedding."

She grabbed onto his hand and let her shawl fall onto the seat when she stood.

Noah weaved his fingers between hers and let out a low whistle. Piece of fabric should be burned for what it had been hiding all eve-ning. Gracie's dress hugged every blessed curve, shimmering a pretty shade of blue that reminded him of the ocean.

"Ready?" He led her onto the dance floor just as brass instruments started up with a swinging tune that was definitely not country.

She met his eyes and laughed. "Chattanooga Choo Choo."

"Hey, you finally got it right," he said with a smile as he dropped a hand to the curve of her hip, dancing slow because of her recent injuries—and also because shimmery ocean dresses made a man want to move slow. And close.

He pulled her in a little tighter than a song like "Chattanooga Choo Choo" probably required. But Gracie didn't seem to mind as they slid right into their own tempo. Which was obviously a much different tempo than the one Matt and Rachel were keeping.

Matt grunted as he lifted Rachel. "Almost there."

"Almost where? What are you doing, other than making sounds

like you're lifting a Buick again?" Rachel said, her feet hovering off the floor.

"I'm Patrick Swayze in *Dirty Dancing*. I'm lifting you above my head. Oh, forget it," Matt said, plopping her back to the floor, then immediately dipping her backwards and nearly onto her head. "There. Much better."

"Maybe we should just stick to conga lines," Rachel wheezed, her face turning red from all the blood rushing toward her head.

"Good idea." Matt straightened her and they immediately transitioned into a wild-limbed two-person conga line.

"They're really terrible dancers, aren't they?" Gracie said with a laugh.

Noah grinned back. "I'm not even sure what I'm seeing right now." Other than two lovebirds having the time of their lives.

Had Noah ever seen Matt look so happy? Everyone tonight looked happy. Even Mona was laughing and clapping as she spun Buck around on the dance floor in his wheelchair.

Noah traced a slow trail with his fingertips from Gracie's hip up to the middle of her shoulder blades, wishing that when the song ended, there'd be another one. And then another one. And that he could just go on holding Gracie like this forever and everyone stayed happy.

He pressed his cheek against her hair. "Remember the first time we ever danced together?" he murmured next to her ear.

"You were even worse than Matt," she said with a chuckle.

"But you taught me the steps, and you have to admit, I was a fast learner." He leaned back to catch her eye.

"Pretty sure you taught me a few moves that summer too," she said with a saucy grin.

He stared at that grin, wanting to gobble it up as much as he had back when she was teaching him to dance. He dropped his forehead against hers. "Whatever happened to those two kids, Gracie?"

He felt her tense, then start to push back just as one of her ankles must've twisted in her high heels. "Ooh." She stumbled to the side.

Noah grabbed her waist. "You okay?"

"I'm fine." She clung to his upper arms, not meeting his gaze as she tested her weight on her foot. "Should've known better than to wear these shoes. Maybe I should find some ice."

"Let me—"

"No." She waved him off. "No, I'll get it. I'm fine. You just . . . stay here."

"Gracie—"

She limped off the dance floor, weaving in and out of tables. Wouldn't take more than a few quick strides to catch her. But he wasn't so sure whether he should catch her. One of these days she had to decide to stop running away from him on her own.

A pointy fingernail jabbed him in the back. Noah turned and found Mona's sharp gaze locked on him. "Well?" she said.

At some point "Chattanooga Choo Choo" had ended and a song he didn't recognize with a heavy bass beat had started up. All of Matt's friends rushed back onto the dance floor, brushing past them. "Well, what?"

Mona rolled her eyes and dragged him away from the commotion of dancers, then propped her hands on her waist. "Are you really that big of an idiot?"

"I think you of all people know the answer to that one."

She inched closer, her voice as hard as her gaze. "You're about out of time, bub. Are you going to make a move or not?"

"I've spent nearly a month with her. Not sure I have any moves left. And wait a second—what are you saying? You want me to go after her?"

"What I want is for my sister to be happy. Didn't she ever tell you about Morris?"

"It really does all come back to that cat, doesn't it?"

"I never should have made her get rid of him. I didn't realize at the time how much it would cost her because it didn't cost me any-thing. And I hate to say it, but I think I did the same thing with your marriage. I encouraged her to let go and move on without realizing how much that would cost her. To me you were just a stupid cat who wasn't worth the grief, but to her? Well, you're like Rachel is to Matt. You're the love of her life—even if you are an idiot."

"Wow, Mona. That was almost supportive."

"It's a new thing I'm trying," she said with a quirk of her brow. "Now go. Fight for my sister. I've seen you down in the count before. I don't know why you're acting like this is any different."

Because it *was* different. If Gracie didn't give him another chance, he wouldn't be losing a game. He'd be losing all hope.

58

Taking Mona's advice, Noah tracked down Gracie. She'd gone outside and was hiding in the shadows of a pergola attached to the back of the barn. "You're missing the Electric Slide."

She glanced over her shoulder, the lights from inside the barn spilling out enough to highlight her soft smile. "Never did care for that one."

Noah wrapped her shawl around her shoulders. "You know, the other night on The Hill, I listened to your version of that game, but I never did get a chance to tell you mine."

"I don't know that I want to have that conversation again."

Noah turned her around to face him. They *were* having that conversation again. No walking away this time. "Gracie, don't you understand that pitching through that game was the hardest night of my life? The hardest decision I've ever made? You called me, heartbroken. I was heartbroken too. Of course I wanted to be with you. But I didn't know how to help you. For so long I'd felt like I didn't know how to help you. So when an eight-year-old boy who was probably never going to make it to his ninth birthday had already asked me to do the one thing I knew how to do—show up on the mound and pitch—I couldn't say no. He reminded me so much of Owen. I had to show up for him. I couldn't not show up for him."

Gracie shook her head, refusing to meet his eyes.

"I did something great that night, Gracie. You know it. I know it. It's the whole reason we're writing this blasted memoir together. And I'm sorry I couldn't be there for you that day. I'm sorry you felt so alone. I am. I'm truly, truly sorry. But . . . when will you forgive me? When will you realize I'm here for you now? I'm right here, Gracie."

She still wouldn't meet his gaze as her shoulders sank with a defeated sigh. "I do forgive you," she whispered. "I forgive you, Noah. But now I need you to realize that sometimes you just have to let go."

"What if I can't let you go?"

"Then you better figure out a way how to. Because I can't be with you again. I can't go back to the person I was before."

"What person was that?"

Her hair was falling out of her pins. She wiped a strand from her eyes, her lips quivering as she took in a few breaths before continuing. "I'm almost forty-two, Noah. I know time's not on my side, but I also know the desire for a baby is still there. Waiting. And if we get back together, I know how I'll be. I can't . . . I just can't go through it again. Not when I've finally reached a certain level of peace about it all. I'm better off alone."

"We don't have to try for another baby, Gracie. Why can't we be happy, just you and me?"

"What if we're not happy, just you and me? It's too much of a risk."

"So what? We risk it anyway. Come on, Gracie. This isn't one of your romances where everything gets tied up in a neat bow by page three-twenty-two. This is life. This is love. The pages keep going. And sure, it's risky and messy, and yeah, we may not always be happy. There'll be heartache and disappointment and probably more tears. But that doesn't mean we should just end the story here. Give up. Not fight for another chapter."

She shook her head, more hair falling across her temple. "I need to get back to the reception."

"Don't leave me, Gracie."

She dipped her head and stepped past him, leaving him alone in the dark.

59

Mona's hand latched onto Gracie's wrist as soon as she stepped inside. "There you are. Good. Matt and Rachel were just getting ready to leave and wanted to say goodbye."

"Oh." She fought the temptation to turn back for Noah. "Did they, uh, figure out where they were staying tonight?" Shouldn't she turn back for Noah?

No.

Thankfully she couldn't have turned back even if she tried the way Mona was dragging her by the hand. "St. Louis, probably. I don't know. Didn't ask. Matt said he had it taken care of. Now hurry. My feet are killing me. The sooner they leave, the sooner I can go home and take a hot bath. I'm too exhausted for any more of this nonsense."

"You're such a sentimental fool."

Mona snorted. "Don't think I'm not two seconds away from bawling my eyes out right now. That's why I bought uncomfortable shoes. I knew it would keep me distracted from the fact my baby boy just went and got himself married. You should try it sometime."

Gracie didn't think there were shoes small enough to take her mind off everything tonight. They found Matt and Rachel surrounded by friends. When Matt spotted Gracie, he slipped away from the group.

"Thanks for everything, Aunt Gracie," Matt said, giving her a tight hug. "Everything."

She leaned back and palmed the sides of his face. "I'd do anything for you, you know that." And she would. He'd always been more like a son than a nephew.

"Anything?" He leaned down next to her ear and whispered, "Then give Noah another chance."

What a twerp. She never could stand the kid.

Others cut in to hug Matt and clap him on the back. Gracie backed away, bumping into Rachel. "Oh. Sorry, honey."

Rachel smiled and wrapped her in a hug. "I hope you know how grateful I am. I owe you so much."

Gracie's eyes stung. "For what? I haven't done anything."

"You've been cheering us on since the very beginning. You don't know how much it's meant to know we've always had someone in our corner. I mean, without you, who knows?" Rachel leaned back and gave her a wink. "I may have settled for a farmer."

Great. Now in addition to the stinging eyes, a boulder had lodged in her throat. Gracie grabbed Rachel's hands. "I'm sorry your sister couldn't make it."

"It's fine. Better that she didn't. I didn't want her getting anywhere close to Ace again anyway. Matt and I are going to go visit her as soon as we get the chance."

"Good." Gracie gave Rachel's hands a final squeeze. "Now get out of here. Go have some fun. You two deserve it."

Matt swooped in, wrapping his arms around Rachel. "Ready?"

"Oh yeah," she whispered.

Whoops and hollers escorted them outdoors and into Buck's Corvette. Not bad for a getaway car. But they could probably ride off together on a mule and be happy tonight. Gracie watched them leave, waving goodbye even after she knew they couldn't see her anymore.

You don't know how much it's meant to know we've always had someone in our corner.

She used her finger to swipe a tear before it spilled over. Is that what happened between her and Noah? They stopped being in each other's corner?

The rest of the guests made their way to their cars and headed out. Gracie remained outside, wrapped up in her shawl. Wrapped up in her thoughts.

When the sound of footsteps drew closer, she didn't have to look behind her to know it was Noah. She could feel his presence the moment goose pimples rose on her skin.

He stopped next to her with his hands in his pockets, the indoor lighting showing off half of his ridiculously handsome face.

"You can't just ignore what's happening between us, Gracie."

"I'm not ignoring anything." Okay, half of her was ignoring everything. The other half was trying to figure out what to do about everything.

"Do you still love me?" Noah asked, his voice deep and steady.

"That's not the issue. I've already explained it."

"Then you're going to have to explain it again." Noah stepped in front of her, dipping his head so she was forced to look him in the eyes. "Did you not see those two kids ride out of here just a little bit ago? That was us, Gracie. Twenty years ago, that was us, head over heels in love. And you can't tell me you wouldn't move heaven and earth to see those two kids from twenty years ago make it the same way you want to see Matt and Rachel make it today."

Give Noah a chance.

Why did it feel like everybody was ganging up on her tonight?

And why did it feel like maybe they were right? Maybe she should take the risk. Give Noah another chance.

Headlights angled up the drive to the barn and flooded over them. Gracie lifted her forearm to block her eyes. Noah turned and did the same.

Soon as the car rolled to a stop, a tall, shadowed figure stepped out. For one panicked second Gracie thought it was Luke. But then a voice she hadn't heard in five years said Noah's name.

Dusty? What was Noah's manager from Seattle doing here?

Apparently Noah wondered the same thing. His voice, deep and steady a few moments ago, now croaked out hesitant and hoarse. "What are you doing here, Dusty?"

"Seeing if you're ready to be a hero again." Dusty tossed something in the air, and when Noah caught it against his chest Gracie realized it was his baseball glove. "You're back on the roster, kid."

60

Simone: Noah's agent is blowing up my phone. What's going on? Did something happen to Noah? (Please tell me he didn't die.)

Grace: His manager showed up about 20 minutes ago and told him he was back on the roster for the World Series.

Simone: WHAT?! Oh wow! Okay. Some of these texts are making a lot more sense now. Scotty's right! This could bring a whole new level of closure to the memoir. (Definitely better than the current "and then he got old and was kicked off the team" ending we have now.)

Simone: Hey, just reading through more of Scotty's texts. (Sometimes I regret giving that man my number.) He says if Seattle wins the World Series then the manager will probably retire. And if he retires and if Noah pitches well then Noah could be a strong contender for getting hired on as their new manager. I know that's a lot of ifs, but . . . this could be a big win for both of you. Noah back to doing what he loves. You finally getting your ex-husband out of your hair. (And a great memoir for the rest of us!) Sounds like the perfect happily-ever-after to me!

Simone: Okay, I'm turning my phone off now. Scotty is driving me crazy.

61

"You're kidding me, right?" Noah paced back and forth on the empty dance floor where just a short while ago people had been bouncing and flailing their arms to that Otis Day and the Knights song "Shout."

Well, right now Dusty was making Noah want to shout. "A little over a month ago you told me I was too old and worn out to keep going. Now you're telling me I'm your last hope for winning the World Series?"

Dusty sighed and sank into a chair. Propping his elbow on the table, he lifted his ball cap enough to start massaging his forehead like he was the one too old and worn out to keep going. "Listen. I get that you're ticked."

"I'm not ticked." Maybe he had been a month ago, but not these past few weeks—as long as he didn't think about it. And he'd been doing a pretty stellar job of not thinking about it until Dusty showed up here with Rooster, Noah's former teammate and catcher, who had apparently scrounged up some of the wedding cake because he was diving into his second piece now.

Other than the three of them, the barn had cleared out.

"Look, guys, I'm sorry to tell you this, but you're wasting your time. I'm not—"

"You want me to beg?" Dusty interrupted. "Is that it? Fine. I'll beg."

"I don't want you to beg." *Not entirely. Maybe a little bit.* "I just want you to understand that—"

"Aw, c'mon, Noah. Stop playing so hard to get," Rooster mumbled around a mouthful of cake. "It's the World Series, for crying out loud."

Noah stopped pacing. "Exactly. The World Series. So why on earth are you guys coming to me?"

Dusty held up a hand. "Hear me out. We've had more extra-inning games this postseason than any other postseason in history. I've used and abused our bullpen to the point that their arms are darn near falling off. These guys aren't going to make it another seven games if that's what it comes to. We need a fresh arm to get us through a few innings at the very least. We don't need a perfect pitcher. We just need a little relief. Some experience. We need you."

Rooster grunted in agreement, digging into another bite. "Got that right."

"Dusty, I haven't been following the postseason at all. My arm might have gotten some rest, but my head—"

"Will be back in the game as soon as you step on the mound. You've been a pitcher longer than anybody I know. You don't forget that kind of experience."

Dusty tugged his ball cap back into place. "Look, I never should have dropped you out of the rotation. It was the wrong move. These young guys are struggling. They need a steady presence to keep them calm. You've always had a great way with keeping the nerves in the clubhouse down. It's the World Series, Noah. *The World Series.* Come back. Who knows? Pitch a few innings and you might even get that record. Maybe this will even open some doors for a management position. I don't think it's a secret that this is probably my last season."

Noah looked back and forth between Rooster and Dusty. Five strikeouts was going to take more than a few innings for him. It was going to take a miracle.

Is that what this was? His chance at another miracle?

He had to admit, even if they didn't win the World Series, it would be awful nice to end his career with a record under his belt instead of the absolute *nothing* he had from his baseball career as of right now.

Noah rubbed his thumb over his fingertips. He couldn't deny the itch to rub them over the seams of a baseball again. To stand on the mound one more time.

But those days were gone. Baseball was his past. Gracie was his future.

Hopefully. He still hadn't convinced her.

What if he never convinced her?

Then what would he do with the rest of his life? What if baseball was the only future he had left? What if he could spend the next several years managing a team in the majors?

But Gracie . . .

"I'm sorry. Thing is—"

"Come on, man," Rooster said, licking frosting off his thumb. "You know this may be the only shot at a World Series some of us players ever see. Plus, think what a great story it'll be." Rooster waved across the air like it held an invisible headline. "Old fogy pitcher comes back and saves the day." He smacked Noah on the arm with a grin as he walked past to toss his plate in a trash can.

"He's going to be there, you know." Dusty stood and adjusted his cap. "The boy. The one from your perfect game. He's been in remission for over five years. They're saying it's a miracle he survived. When he wrote a letter to the team, our PR person got ahold of it and made some calls. He and his dad have seats to all the games. I know it'd mean the world to them to see you on the mound again. It'd mean the world to all of us."

Man, Dusty wasn't pulling any punches, was he?

"Can I think about it?"

"Think fast. First game is in St. Louis tomorrow."

"I don't even have everything I need. I'd need to go back to Seattle first." Was he actually considering this?

Rooster tapped his fist against Noah's shoulder. "We already got your glove and your uniform. What else do you need? Lucky socks?"

Noah patted his chest. No, but there was definitely something else he never pitched without. And he could kick himself for not following his gut instinct to bring it along with him. Especially since the whole reason he came back was to win another chance with Gracie. "I'm going to have to fly back to Seattle." He was really considering this, wasn't he?

Which meant he needed to find Gracie. Now. Give her a chance to talk him out of it. Convince him to stay. Tell him the one reason he should throw the biggest career opportunity of his life away.

One word. That's all he needed from her. One word and he'd stay.

"Let me make some calls and get the flights arranged, so you're back in time for tomorrow's game." Dusty walked away with his phone already out.

"Make it two tickets," Rooster called after him. "That way I can make sure this guy doesn't get any cold feet. Not that you will," he said, slinging his arm around Noah's shoulders and guiding him toward the exit. "You've always managed to do the right thing when it counts. Besides, what do you have keeping you here?"

When Noah stepped outside the barn, he found Gracie waiting for him with her arms clutched around her middle. Before he could say anything, she lifted her chin and said, "You need to do it. You need to go. It's the only way for us to finish this memoir with the right ending—which is you back on the mound with your ball and your glove. We both know baseball is where you've always belonged."

What did he have keeping him here?

Sounded like the answer was the same one he'd been hearing the past five years.

Nothing.

62

Luke: Hey Gracie, I just heard about Noah getting added back to the roster for the World Series. That's wonderful news. I don't have his number, so will you tell him good luck from me? Take care.

Wombat: Hi Miss Gracie. It's Wombat. Tell Noah the boys at the firehouse are all cheering him on! (Even the Cardinal fans, but they said not to let that get around.)

Abe: GRACIE! OH MY GOODNESS! LIZZY AND I ARE GOING CRAZY!

Simone: I don't know how you're still making progress on the memoir when there's SO. MUCH. EXCITEMENT!!! I swear I can't go anywhere right now without hearing Noah's name! But anyway, just wanted to let you know your editors couldn't be more pleased with everything you've sent them. (They also hinted that if you need someone to go with you to any of Noah's games for research on the memoir's ending, they'd be happy to assist.)

Scotty: Grace! Did you get the flowers I sent you?

Unknown Number: Hey kiddo. Mert Adley here. Bowling league wants to know when Noah's pitching. Also Bobby the Barber says to let Noah know all his haircuts will be half-price if he helps Seattle beat St. Louis.

63

Gracie dropped an armload of clothes into her suitcase. She had to get out of here. Find a place where nobody'd ever heard of Noah, baseball, and text messages.

Nine days.

Nine days since she'd told Noah to leave.

Nine days since she'd told herself it was for the best.

Nine days of trying to forget that man, only to have every single one of her thoughts consumed by that man.

The fact she'd been working around the clock to finish that man's memoir probably didn't help. But how else was she supposed to move on? She *had* to finish the memoir.

Thankfully all of the chapters were written now except for the ending. For the first time in her writing career she was way ahead of her deadline. She could take a long break. Escape. Write the final chapter after all the World Series hubbub died down in a few weeks. Maybe by then she'd know whether to include if Noah gets offered the manager job in Seattle or not.

If he did get the offer, he'd accept it of course. All Noah had ever cared about was baseball. From the first moment she met him, baseball, baseball, baseball.

At least up until her silly little horse accident last month. After that he kind of acted like all he cared about was her, her, her.

But *before* that it was always baseball, baseball, baseball.

And what did he ultimately choose nine days ago? That's right. Baseball.

Okay, sure. She may have given him a little push in making that decision, same way she pushed him to stick it out years ago when he was ready to walk away from baseball completely. But she didn't want to think about that. She didn't want to think about anything right now except packing plenty of clean underwear, underwear, underwear.

She grabbed a handful from the dresser and added them to the growing pile of clothes in her suitcase.

When a FaceTime call chimed, she paused long enough to answer and prop her phone on the dresser before adding a fistful of socks that hopefully matched onto the clothes heap.

Mona's face appeared on the screen. "I couldn't understand anything you said in your voicemail earlier. What's going on?"

Mona cradled a steaming mug in her hands. Probably tea. Gracie could practically smell the herbal scent of it through the screen. It reminded her of the day Noah had fixed her his special mint brew. A sound between a laugh and a sob, closer to a sob, burst out of her chest. "Peppermint schnapps," Gracie wailed as she dissolved into a blubbering mess.

Mona plunked her tea down and leaned closer to the screen. "Have you been drinking? Why does it look like your bedroom's been ransacked?"

"I thought Noah tried spiking my tea with peppermint schnapps."

Mona frowned. "When? How? He's been with his team all week in the World Series."

"I don't want to talk about the World Series." Gracie picked up a sock with a hole in the heel and tossed it onto the pile of clothes that needed to be thrown away. "All I've been hearing about is the World Series. I'm sick to death of the World Series. How many stinking games is the World Series going to last?"

"Seven. Last one's tonight. Noah's pitching."

"I said I don't want to talk about—Wait, what? Noah's pitching?

What do you mean he's pitching? Like as in he's the starting pitcher? For game seven? Tonight? Why? He hasn't pitched all week."

"I thought you didn't want to talk about it."

"I don't! Those were all rhetorical questions." Gracie dug out several T-shirts from the middle dresser drawer, gave them a quick glance, then dumped them into the donate pile on her bed.

Mona shook her head. "Okay, seriously. What are you doing, other than destroying your room?"

"Packing."

"Why?"

"Because."

"Great answer."

A generic painting of a seashore and lighthouse hung on the wall behind Mona's head. Must be in a hotel. Probably another speaking engagement. Gracie had been lost in such a memoir fog these past nine days, she had no idea what was going on in anybody else's life. "Where are you, by the way?"

"Out of town."

"Great answer."

"Speaking of great answers, I'd really love to know the answer as to why you blew a whole bunch of dough on a plane ticket to nowhere last week."

Gracie's head snapped up from her dresser. How could Mona know that? How could anyone know that? Not even the FedEx lady could've known that.

"Seven hundred dollars? Just to tell Noah goodbye?" Mona smirked. "Sounds like a pretty romantic thing to do for someone you don't want to talk about."

"I wasn't . . . No. That's not . . . No." Gracie continued shaking her head as she sank onto the edge of her bed. She didn't have to explain herself. She was a grown woman. If she wanted to go to the airport and blow a stupid amount of money on a ticket just to see her ex-husband before he boarded his flight, then decide at the last minute she *didn't* want to see him and she had no earthly idea what had possessed her to think she *did* want to see him, then leave without ever seeing him, she could. That's what grown women did.

"Why won't you just admit that you still love Noah? Why won't you give him another chance?"

Gracie jumped from the bed. "Why are you doing this? You never liked Noah. Now you're suddenly the president of his fan club? For crying out loud, you're the one who introduced me to Luke and told me I should move on with Luke."

"I know. But . . ." Mona sighed. "Did it ever occur to you maybe I'm wrong sometimes?"

"It's sure occurring to me right now." Gracie stomped to the closet and grabbed an armload of clothes, hangers and all, and hurled them at her suitcase.

"When I told you to move on it was because I thought you were miserable. Then Noah came back, and you were different. Both of you were different. And it took me a while to realize that you weren't actually different. You were the same. Except maybe a little different. Or maybe I'm just the one who's different."

"Have *you* gotten into the peppermint schnapps?"

"Just hear me out."

"Then try to make sense fast. I'm hitting the road in five minutes." And she was going to need every one of those five minutes to figure out how to get her suitcase closed.

"Wouldn't you want Morris back if you could have him?"

Gracie tried bouncing her knees on her suitcase to close it. "Talking . . . about a dead cat . . . from my childhood . . ." Oh forget it. The suitcase wasn't closing. ". . . is not what I had in mind when I told you to make sense."

"What I'm saying is I'd forgotten what it was like when you and Noah were together. How much fun you had even when you drove each other crazy. It used to drive me crazy. But I don't know, seeing how happy Matt is with Rachel . . . Seeing how you two looked dancing together at their wedding . . . It just made me think there's still reason to hope."

"For what?"

"A happily-ever-after. And not just for you. For everyone. Even me."

Gracie shoved half of the clothes out of her suitcase so she could start tugging the zipper closed. "Well, don't waste your hopes on me, Sis. Hate to break it to you, but Morris is dead. And so is my marriage."

Gracie ended the call, lugged her suitcase to her car, and drove to the hospital. After a quick visit with Dad, she was driving to Tennessee, finding herself a quiet little place to stay, and hunkering down until all the World Series hoopla was over.

But twenty-five minutes later, as soon as she stepped into Buck's room, she knew she wasn't going anywhere.

64

Sports talk radio:

David: Have you ever seen a crazier World Series than what we've witnessed this past week?

Brad: Never in my life.

David: What do you make of Dusty's surprise move to not only bring Parker back on the roster for this final series, but place him as the starting pitcher in the eleventh hour?

Brad: You know, the way I see it, it's the type of move that can only go two ways. Either Dusty walks away with a World Series ring and looks like the most brilliant manager to ever wear a baseball uniform. Or he walks away looking like the world's biggest village idiot. Basically it all boils down to how Parker performs tonight.

David: And how do you think he's going to perform?

Brad: Well, that's the million-dollar question, isn't it? He hasn't pitched in over a month. Last six games Dusty has kept him locked up in the bullpen. And you have to remember, Parker was getting his butt handed to him on a platter by the end of the regular season. So why start him tonight in St. Louis? I don't know. On the one hand, he's had a month off. His arm ought to be rested. On the other hand, he's been gone for a month! Nobody even knows where he's been. What's he been doing? Is he even ready to pitch?

I guess we'll see. All I can say is hold on tight. This wild ride isn't over. Not by a long shot.

David: You've got that right. Stay tuned, listeners. When we come back, we want to hear from you. What are your thoughts on tonight's game? Does Grandpa Parker have what it takes to pull off a World Series win and be a hero one last time?

65

Noah's ears still rang from the rock music that had blared earlier in the clubhouse. Hey, whatever pumped up his teammates. He propped his foot on the bench next to his locker and tied his cleats, glad for the silence. The solitude.

The nice thing about being the starting pitcher for game seven of the World Series is when you tell everyone to leave you alone and not talk to you, especially reporters, they listen. Well, everyone but your catcher.

"How you feeling?" Rooster straddled the bench next to his foot.

Noah shrugged. "Good. I think."

"Head's in the game?"

Noah shrugged again. Not really. But hopefully Dusty was right. Hopefully once he stepped on the mound, it would be. Past nine days he felt like he'd been walking around in a fog.

Rooster smacked Noah in the leg with his glove. "You've had a lot going on lately. Wouldn't blame you if you needed a little time to adjust. Just remember you don't have any time to adjust. This is it."

Noah dropped his foot and grabbed his glove. "The only thing I'm worried about adjusting is my slider against Marshall. That guy's been on fire."

"I say we bean him first thing. Right on the butt."

Noah smiled. "You want to start a brawl the very first inning and get both of us kicked out?"

"Might be worth it just to know he won't be able to sit on anything but an icepack the next few days."

Noah smacked his glove on Rooster's shoulder. "Let's save it for the fifth inning. I'll be ready to be pulled out of the game by then—if I even make it that far."

"You will. I can always tell by the look in your eye whether you're in the zone or not. You're in the zone. I see it."

He hadn't even thrown a single warm-up pitch, but okay. He was in the zone. He nodded at Rooster. "Let's do this." After a few steps, Noah patted his chest and stopped. "Shoot. I'm missing something. Go on without me."

"What is it? I can wait."

"Nah, I'll find it. Go on. I'll catch up with you in a minute."

Rooster tapped his shoulder with his glove. "Win big."

"Win big." The click-clack of Rooster's cleats disappeared toward the dugout as Noah turned back for his locker.

Call him superstitious but he never pitched without wearing his wedding ring on a chain beneath his jersey. That was the whole reason he'd had to fly back to Seattle last week. He'd worn it throughout all his time in the minor league, whenever he pitched in the majors, including the night of his perfect game, and every game that followed even after they'd divorced. He wasn't going without it tonight. He never should have gone without it at all.

He dug into his bag, his fingers grazing his phone as he unzipped the side pouch where he kept the ring and the chain. He paused, tempted to call Gracie. It was the same temptation he'd been battling every hour every day since he stood in the airport about to board his flight to Seattle. If Rooster hadn't grabbed him and shoved him past the boarding gate all the way to his seat, Noah might never have found the strength to walk away from the crazy hope that she'd come running toward him any second like they were filming the final scene of some cheesy romance movie.

"Noah, you coming?" Rooster's voice echoed off the walls of the clubhouse.

Noah shook off the memory and pulled out the chain with his wedding ring. "Be right there," he called, sliding the chain over his neck, then patting the ring beneath his jersey.

Okay. He had what he needed. Time to play ball.

He stood there another full minute.

"Noah!" Rooster shouted.

"One second," Noah shouted back. He crouched down and dug out his phone. Started to pull up Gracie's contact, then dropped the phone back in his bag. What was he doing? He had a game to pitch. He should be focusing on that, not—

His phone started ringing and Gracie's name flashed on the screen. "Hello?"

"You answered."

Noah's knees buckled with so much relief at the sound of her voice, he slid down his locker all the way to the floor. "You called."

"I didn't think you would answer."

Noah held up his index finger when Rooster stomped back toward him with a *what the heck's going on* expression.

"Bro," Rooster said in a no-nonsense voice with his hands propped on his waist. "You are the starting pitcher. You cannot be sitting on the floor right now."

"Everything okay, Gracie?"

She was so quiet on the other end that for a moment he thought they'd lost their connection. Then she whispered, "Dad's not doing well." He heard her sniff. "He took a turn for the worse. I don't think he's got much time left." A shuddery breath. "Sorry. I shouldn't have called. I don't know why I called. You need to pitch. Sorry. I shouldn't have—I'm okay. Don't worry about us. Just . . ." Her voice grew stronger. "Focus on the game. Everybody's already so proud of you, Noah. You were right all along. Baseball is who you are. You're right where you need to be. I know you'll do great. The memoir's going to be great. Whatever happens, I just want you to know I . . ."

"You what, Gracie?"

"I wish you the best." She ended the call.

And before Noah knew what was happening, Rooster was lifting him off the floor and hustling him from the silence of the clubhouse—and the memory of Gracie's voice on a similar phone call five years ago—to the sound of forty thousand fans who were all waiting to see if Noah was ready to be a hero or not.

66

The sound of oxygen hissed in the tiny room.

"So basically we have two options here." The doctor, a young man with curly hair and tired eyes, pulled a chair up next to her dad's bed and propped his arms on his thighs, leaning forward to include both Gracie and her dad in the discussion.

"We put you on a ventilator and throw everything at you, including the kitchen sink, for the sole purpose of buying you whatever time we can, regardless of quality. Or . . ." He shifted in his seat, clasping his hands together. "We do not pursue any further aggressive forms of treatment, including dialysis, and instead focus on keeping you comfortable, knowing full well this will greatly reduce the quantity of time you have left."

"I'll take it."

"Dad," Gracie said, stepping closer to his bed and grabbing his hand. "Let's think about this."

"I don't need to think." He tugged the oxygen mask from his face and worked to catch his breath. "I've thought long enough. I'm done."

"Okay, shh, okay." Gracie slid the mask back over his nose and mouth. "I understand. You're exhausted. I just thought—" Her voice hitched. She thought what? Her dad would live forever? They'd known this day was coming. "I just didn't think it would be now. Tonight."

Why did it have to be now? Tonight? When she felt completely alone.

Why did it always feel like she was completely alone?

"I need to call my sister. Call my nephew. We need to get everyone here. I'm not sure how quickly they can get here. I'll tell them to hurry. My phone," Gracie said, spinning in a circle. Where had she put her phone?

"It's okay." The doctor held up his hands. "Nothing needs to happen right this second. We've still got a little time."

Gracie glanced at her dad, the way his shoulders lifted and dropped, using every last bit of reserve to move air in and out. Whatever time they had, it sure wasn't much.

"Here's what I think." The doctor pressed his stethoscope to her dad's lungs, listened to a few breaths on each side, then draped it back around his neck and focused all his attention on Buck. "I think we give you a little morphine to take the edge off. Keep you comfortable. Should help with your breathing." He looked to Gracie. "In the meantime, you make whatever calls you need to make."

Gracie nodded. "Morphine. Breathing. Calls. Got it." Why was she acting like she had no idea what to do? She knew how this needed to play out. Get the family here. Let her dad go out with peace. With comfort. With—

"Can I watch the ball game?" her dad's voice croaked out.

Anything but that.

The doctor laughed. "Of course. Man after my own heart."

Before Gracie could stop him, the doctor grabbed the call light and switched on the TV mounted to the wall, finding the game in two clicks. "Oh good. Haven't thrown out the first pitch yet. Mind if I watch for a minute?"

"Pull up a chair," her dad, treacherous man that he was, told the doctor. And the doctor, treacherous man that he was, did as her dad suggested.

Unbelievable. "I'm going to go make those calls. You know, the calls to let everyone know you're *dying*."

Neither man acknowledged her. Just as well. She didn't need either of them witnessing her reaction the moment her eyes landed on Noah.

A tsunami couldn't have bowled her over as much as the wave of emotions crashing into her at the mere sight of him. She couldn't look away. The camera lingered on a close-up of his face, capturing every bit of warrior in his eyes. The determination. The focus.

The man she'd talked to a short while ago on the phone had sounded like a normal guy. This man standing on the pitcher's mound didn't look like that guy. No, this Noah was ready for battle. This Noah wasn't taking any prisoners. This Noah was a hero.

And yet, she could still see it. This guy was also just plain old Noah Parker, Gracie's fella. The guy she should've clung to with all her might and never pushed away.

"Oh, Noah," she whispered.

"Ma'am?" the doctor said.

"Huh?" Gracie swiped the moisture that had gathered on her cheeks. Both the doctor and her dad were staring at her.

"Something wrong?" the doctor asked, then immediately winced. "Right. Stupid question." He stood and patted her awkwardly on the shoulder. "Your dad's in good hands. I promise. We're going to do everything we can to—"

"She's married to the pitcher," her dad interrupted. "That's why she's crying." He gave a weak laugh that led into several coughs.

"You're married to Noah Parker?" The doctor's eyes lit up like a kid at Christmas. "No way! That is so cool. Wait—what are you doing here? Why aren't you at the—oh, right. Of course." Two red splotches flooded his cheeks. He cleared his throat and patted her shoulder again. "How about I find a nurse to bring in that morphine?"

"Thank you," she mumbled as the doctor rushed past the curtain and she moved over to help her dad readjust his oxygen mask.

His coughing spell subsided just as a commercial break started. "You need anything before I step out?" Gracie asked.

"New body?"

"I was thinking more along the line of some ice chips."

He held her gaze. Patted the space next to him. "Stay. Watch the game with me."

"I can't."

"You'd deny a dying man his last wish?"

A commercial for chicken wings filled the screen. Why couldn't his last wish be a bucket of those? "I need to call Mona. Tell her what's going on."

"Call her from right here."

Before she could come up with a good excuse, the announcers were back on the screen, surrounded by a flood of noise. "What a night for a ball game," one of the announcers said as the camera swooped over the stadium with an aerial view. "Game Seven. Seattle and St. Louis. Listen to those fans."

Gracie's legs shook. "I'll be back in a minute."

Racing from the room, she darted down the closest stairwell, out of the hospital, and didn't stop rushing until she'd crossed the entire parking lot and a black metal fence blocked her from going any further.

Too much. She clung to the rails and gasped for air. This whole thing was too much. Dad. The game. The hospital. *Noah.*

She dug her phone from her purse and tried calling Mona. When the call went to voicemail, Gracie hung up and tried again. Then again.

"Where are you?" Gracie yelled after the fourth attempt went to Mona's voicemail again. She sent three back-to-back text messages to CALL ME! then reached for the fence rails. Tried slowing her breathing. Tried pushing down the panic.

"God, I can't do this," she whimpered. "I need someone." Where was her sister? Where was anybody? "I can't keep doing this. Not by myself."

I never said you had to.

"What?" Gracie twisted. Who'd said that?

She peered across the dark parking lot, not seeing anyone beneath the pale splotches of security lighting. A motorcycle backfired and rumbled down the street a block over. Otherwise, silence. Until her phone pinged with a message.

Mona: What's wrong?

Finally! Gracie texted back. Call me!

Gracie stood still and waited for her sister to call. Another text pinged through.

Mona: Can't. What's wrong?

"What's wrong is I need my sister to call me," Gracie muttered, texting furiously. Dad's dying! CALL ME!

Nothing came through for several seconds. Not even the little bubble dots to show her sister was responding. Finally, after a good three minutes, Mona called. "Is Dad okay?"

"When does the word *dying* ever mean that someone is okay? It means they're *dying*! And where are you? I can barely hear you."

"Sorry. I'm trying to find a quiet spot. How bad is he?"

"What part of the word *dying* don't you understand?" Gracie forced herself to take a breath. "Sorry. I'm sort of freaking out right now. He doesn't want anything more to be done. He just wants to be made comfortable." Gracie snorted a half-laugh, half-sob. "And watch the stupid ball game, of course."

"Gracie . . ."

"Seriously. Where are you? It is so loud."

"Gracie . . ."

"Why do you keep saying my name like that? Like you've got something to hide? If I didn't know any better I'd think you were at the—" Gracie's breath whooshed out of her. "No. You are not there."

"I didn't want to upset you."

"You. Are. Not. There."

"Noah was able to get us tickets. He figured you wouldn't want one. I'm here with Matt and Rachel and um . . . well, Gus. We've sort of been seeing each other."

"Gus? You're dating a boy from the firehouse?"

"He's not a boy, he's a man, thank you. And hey, that's not the point."

That *wasn't* the point. "I can't believe you guys are all at the game."

"We never said anything since we know how much you hate base-ball. Plus we had no idea Noah would be pitching tonight. Can you believe Noah is pitching? Did you know? Gracie, say something."

"What am I supposed to say? What am I supposed to say to Dad? Sorry, Dad. Nobody can make it. They're all at a baseball game. Go ahead and die. Better luck next time."

"No, you'll tell him we'll get there as soon as we can. You'll tell him we love him. Then you'll tell him if he's ready to go . . ." Her voice broke. "It's okay to go."

"How can you say that?"

"Honey, he's been dying for the past year. You don't think we've said our goodbyes to him by now? We're at peace. Don't worry about us. You just get back to his room and find yours before it's too late."

"Mona?"

"Yeah?"

Gracie looked to the dark clouds in the sky, unable to stop herself from asking. "How's he doing?"

Her sister didn't have to ask who she meant. "So far? Amazing."

Tears leaked down Gracie's face. "I'm glad. I really want him to finish well."

"I think that's all any of us can ever hope for."

67

Raindrops freckled the skin of Noah's arms as the stadium rumbled with the chant of forty thousand fans. *Win Big! Win Big! Win Big!*

The dirt on the pitching mound vibrated with energy. His fingers caressed the seams of the ball. *Win Big! Win Big! Win Big!*

Noah zeroed in sixty feet six inches from where he stood. A flash of two fingers, down and in. Noah nodded. Rooster adjusted his stance behind home plate and held up his target. *Win Big! Win Big! Win Big!*

No runners on. Two strikes. Two outs. Noah stared at the catcher's mitt. The same target he'd been staring at for the past thirty years. Better to stare at that than the stands. The seats. The empty spot he used to hunger for his dad to fill. Then eventually Gracie.

Noah stepped back, lifted his arms above his head for his windup. His arm rotated, wrist flicked. *Thump!*

Noah didn't have to hear the umpire's call to know it was a strike.

He walked off the mound. Players ran past him on their way to the dugout. Raindrops fell faster. His first baseman shouted something, but Noah couldn't hear.

His ears hummed. Rock music, voices, hands clapping, feet stomping. He couldn't hear anything except for the defeated voice of one man, haunting him still, all these years later following that one Little League game.

Good game, Son.

Noah should have said something at the time. Should have responded. Should have looked his dad in the eye. Acknowledged him. Responded to his messages later. Answered one of his calls. Read one of his letters.

He shouldn't have stayed away until he received the call years later that his dad was running out of time.

Lightning flashed.

Because by the time Noah had shown up, he'd been too late.

Just like with Gracie.

68

Buck's eyes drooped, his breathing less labored. The morphine had helped. Had also made him groggy. Gracie reached for the remote and flipped the TV off.

"Don't you dare," her dad growled, eyes still closed. "I'm seeing how this plays out if it's the last thing I do."

"Why?" Gracie sighed, tempted to do a little growling of her own. "The game's been in a rain delay for over an hour. There's nothing to see."

She stood from her chair and paced to the window. Torrents of rain pummeled the parking lot below. A storm similar in velocity to the one raging in St. Louis had settled over the hospital. Where was her sister?

"Turn it back on."

"Why is it so important? It's just a *stupid* game. I don't get it. People are more important than games. People shouldn't be at games. They should be here. I just—I don't—why isn't anybody *here*?" Instead of *there*.

"Gracie . . ." His eyes were open, barely. They'd exchanged the oxygen mask for his regular nasal cannula, which was hissing. "It's not just a stupid game." His voice weakened with each word. "It's love."

"Love? Please." Gracie batted tears from her cheeks.

"People love the game . . . because they love people." He coughed, a small rumble in his chest. "Noah . . . what he did . . . it was about that boy. That was the only way . . . Noah knew how to love."

Gracie's eyes burned with more tears. "What about me? That night was the hardest thing I've ever had to go through. I needed Noah to love me."

"He did. He does. Don't you see he wants to be your hero too? Now—" Her dad jabbed a finger at the TV. Gracie huffed a big sigh, then punched it back on.

"If he wants to be my hero, he sure has a funny way of going about it."

"Men usually do." Her dad grabbed her hand, his grip weak. "But don't you think it's time to stop pushing him away?" His grip trembled and he worked to catch his next breath.

"Dad? Are you okay?"

"I will be. If I know you don't blow it in the final inning. I'm begging you, Gracie . . ." His next words came out no more than a whisper. "Go."

Dad couldn't be serious. She squeezed his hand. "I'm not leaving you alone. Especially not now."

"Sweetheart, I'm not alone. I've never been alone and neither have you. And right now it's not your hand that's going to get me to where I'm going anyway." Nodding his head to the door, he said, "But I know a man who might lose his way if you don't grab hold of *his* hand. Now go."

"Absolutely not." So what if her dad made a small point? So what if he made her think that voice she heard out in the parking lot had been real? So what if maybe all those times she'd felt alone had been more about her pushing everyone, including God, away rather than actually being abandoned? So what if a huge part of her right now at this very moment was aching to run as fast as she could back to Noah?

Now wasn't the time for epiphanies and grand gestures. Now was the time to be with her dad. "If I leave, who's going to stay with you?"

"Me." Shorty wheeled into the room. "I've put up with him for nearly eight weeks. What's a little while longer?"

"Same here." Wanda, the nurse they sometimes jokingly referred to as Nurse Ratched, stepped into the room. This time she wasn't wearing her white uniform. Just a pair of jeans and a sweater. "I'm off duty and I've got nowhere better to be," she said with a wink.

"See?" her dad said. "I'm surrounded. Give her the hat, Shorty."

"Dad, no. I mean it. *No.*" Shorty rolled over in his wheelchair and tugged her down close enough that he could plop a baseball cap onto her head. Noah must have left it behind after his last visit.

When her dad motioned her back over to him, he tapped the bill and whispered the words that did her in. "Win big. For me. For your marriage." Tears gathered at the corners of his eyes. "Win big for you. Keep holding onto hope, babe."

Babe. Her dad had never called her *babe* before. He sounded like Noah.

Why did he have to sound like Noah?

Made her consider leaving. Made her consider hoping. And the last thing she could afford right now was to hope. "Dad, you have to understand. Noah and me, we . . ."

"What?" her dad said, his voice sounding more tired by the second. "Love each other?"

"Belong together?" Wanda said.

"Are miserable every waking second you're not around one another?" Shorty piped in.

"Well . . ." She wagged her head in a sort of nod. *Yes, yes, and yes.* "Thing is, it's not as simple as that. I've been pushing him away for so long, what if it's too late now? I can't just run after him and tell him I'm sorry and I take it all back, can I?"

"Yes," all three of their voices responded.

"Really?"

"Yes," they said again, louder.

"Right now?"

"Yes," the trio shouted.

"But what about—"

"We're here," Mona's breathless voice interrupted from the doorway.

Gracie whipped her head around as Mona, Matt, and Rachel rushed into the room.

"We're here," Mona said again, tugging Gracie into a quick hug. "Would've been here sooner, but the storm slowed us down. Thankfully it's clearing up. If you leave now, you might be able to make it down to St. Louis before the game finishes. Go on. We've got this," Mona said, pushing Gracie toward the door.

"Are you sure?" Gracie looked back at Mona, then Matt, Rachel, Shorty, Wanda, and finally her dad. "Because I'm just not sure—"

"Go," the entire room chorused.

"We're here with Grandpa. Go be with Noah." Matt wrapped an arm around Rachel and pulled her close to his side. "Everybody needs at least one person in the stands rooting for them."

"Pretty sure I won't be able to make it past security to get into the stands," Gracie said with a watery laugh. But she'd do whatever it took to let Noah know she was back in his corner. "Oh, I can't believe I'm doing this." She rushed back to the bed and pressed a kiss to the top of her dad's head. "I love you so much."

He cradled one of her arms with his own. "I know you do. Now go love Noah."

After another kiss to his forehead, she backed away, ready to do just that.

69

Noah's cleated shoes scraped against the parking lot. Rain soaked into his jersey. Trailed down his arms. His steps stopped, uncertain. Was he too late? Again?

The glass doors to the hospital slid open and a woman wearing a ball cap ran out. Not just any ball cap. His ball cap.

Gracie.

She saw him the same second he saw her. "Noah," she said, her footsteps slamming to a stop. Her head shook back and forth as if she didn't trust what she was seeing. "You're here?" She took a tiny step forward.

"I'm here."

The moment the words left his mouth she started running. Or trying to. Her gait still carried a hitch from her injury. "You're here."

He didn't make it more than half a dozen steps before she was slamming against his chest and wrapping her arms around his neck. When he lifted her off the ground, it was his turn to say, "You're here."

"I'm here," she said with choppy breaths. "I'm sorry I pushed you away for so long."

"I'm sorry I stayed away for so long."

They clung to each other, not saying anything, just holding onto each other, as the rain slowed to a drizzle.

"Why'd you come back?" she finally asked.

"To see Buck." He pressed a kiss to her ear, not ready to let any space in between them just yet. "And be with you."

"But the game isn't over."

"It is for me." He finally leaned back far enough to meet her hazel eyes beneath the shadow of his old baseball hat. "Am I too late?"

She slid down from his grasp and reached for his hands. "You're just in time. Dad's still holding on."

"What about us?"

She looked at their clasped hands, then tipped her chin to meet his gaze. "I'd say we're still holding on too, wouldn't you?"

He would. He would definitely say that.

He turned his hat backwards, then did the same to hers. Buck could surely hang on long enough for Noah to kiss Gracie the way a husband really ought to kiss his wife. Which reminded him . . .

"Marry me again?" he murmured against her lips.

"Thought you'd never ask," she murmured back between more kisses. Then her lips froze and she pushed back. "I might still want to be a mom."

"Okay."

"That's it? Okay? You still want to marry me again?"

"I've always wanted a child, too, but Gracie . . ." He turned both of their hats forward to help block the dwindling sprinkle from running down their faces. "I can't promise it'll go any better this time than it did before. I can't promise we'll even be able to adopt. We may never have a child. If that's the case, all I can promise is to be okay with whatever happens, even if it's just you and me at the end of the day. Can you promise the same thing?"

She took a deep breath and blew it out. "I can't promise that I won't be disappointed if we never get the chance to be parents. But I can promise that no matter what happens, I'll do my best to let go of the disappointments and cling tight with everything I've got to the good in my life, which I know now is you. Our marriage. Matt. Mona. The boys at the firehouse," she said with a smile. "But most of all—"

"The FedEx lady, I know."

Her smile turned into a laugh. "I was going to say God, but yes, I suppose I better cling on to the FedEx lady too." She wiped a mixture of tears and raindrops from her cheeks. "And Dad. Speaking of which, we should get back inside."

When they reached Buck's hospital room, everyone did a double take. Everyone except Buck. His eyes remained closed, his breaths slow and shallow.

"What are you doing here?" Matt asked, looking back and forth between Noah and the TV on the wall. "Thought the game was still in a rain delay."

"Rain delay's over," Buck whispered.

He cracked his eyes open long enough to see Noah and Gracie clinging to each other, their hands clasped together, with no intentions of ever letting go.

Then he closed his eyes and sighed with a tiny, whispered "And not a moment too soon."

70

November 6 headlines:

WILD RIDE ENDS WITH SEATTLE VICTORY

PARKER DISAPPEARS DURING RAIN DELAY, MISSES CELEBRATION

WIN BIG OR GO HOME: PARKER GOES HOME, AGAIN

"No comment. You want the full scoop, you'll have to read about it in my memoir."— Noah Parker, Retired Pitcher from the Seattle Mariners

Epilogue

What's going on, Gracie? I thought we were done with the memoir.

The editor wants us to add on an epilogue. She needs it right away, so she said to just dictate one and she'll take care of typing it all up once she gets it. Now take a seat. I've already started recording. (Clears throat.) A little over three months have passed since Noah walked off the pitcher's mound under a downpour of rain—

And straight into a downpour of love. Hey, that's good. Maybe I should be the romance writer.

Are you done interrupting?

Just making sure you get the details of my memoir right, babe.

Oh, but this is *our* memoir now, babe.

Why do you think it's officially become my favorite story to tell? By the way, I love it when you call me babe.

I know you do. Now can we focus on finishing? These readers have lives, you know.

Couldn't be more focused if I tried. Oh shoot. I need to check on the special Valentine's Day dessert I'm making us. Go ahead and keep telling our story. And don't worry. The boys at the firehouse are already on standby.

That actually makes me more worried. Well, as you can see, dear reader, not a lot has changed between Noah and me. And yet, so much has changed.

The morning following that infamous rain-delayed World Series victory, Dad took his final breath on this earth. He was surrounded by his biggest fans and will forever remain one of my all-time favorite heroes.

I've heard bereavement experts say you should wait at least a year before making any big decisions after the death of a loved one. Well, don't tell the experts, but Noah and I remarried less than a month after Dad's death. In our defense it didn't feel like a big decision. It felt more like undoing the bad decision we made five years ago when we didn't know how to handle our grief at that time.

We're working on handling things better now. Which is to say we're working on handing things over to God better now. Both our griefs from the past and our hopes for the future.

What exactly are those hopes for the future? Good question.

We were able to hunker down and shut out the world for a little while after Dad's death, but it didn't take long for the world to start elbowing its way back in. And right now, the world wants Noah.

Before the parade confetti had even settled, the Mariners were offering Noah some sort of "special assistant to baseball operations" position, which they hinted would help pave the way to a future manager job. (Dusty decided to stay on and manage the Mariners one more year.) ESPN calls once a week, asking Noah to work as one of their MLB analysts. A few days ago Noah even got invited to be a future contestant on a dance competition reality show. (Matt and Rachel have both volunteered to go in his place, but I'm pretty sure not even reality TV is that desperate.)

So far Noah has turned everything down. But not because he's done with baseball. (Didn't I always say he'd never be done with baseball?)

Noah has it in his head he wants to build up the baseball program in our little Alda area. From T-ball to high school. A program that mentors and trains. He wants to upgrade all the little neighborhood parks with baseball fields and better playgrounds. He's even been talking about how to spruce up the hospital with a new recreational area named after Buck, so patients aren't stuck staring at the same gloomy walls every day.

When I asked him why this pressing desire to pour so much money and effort into a dot on the map the rest of the world couldn't care less about, he simply shrugged and said, "This is our home, Gracie. Whether we ever have kids or not, I still want to make it a great place where kids can grow up and couples can grow old together."

I'd say that's a dream worth sharing.

Okay. I'm back. Nothing's on fire yet. Did you start talking about the new story you're working on?

I'm still talking about you.

Readers have surely heard enough about me. Let's talk about something fun. Like the new romance you've been working on with your new special writing cat.

It's true. I have a cat now. Noah talked me into adopting him from the animal shelter a few weeks ago, and I couldn't love him more. Same way I couldn't love my new romance story more. My editors gave me a new deadline and thankfully the words are flowing this time. (Probably because there's no time-traveling horses this time.)

I came up with the title.

We don't have a title yet.

It's called *Rain Delayed Love*.

Probably won't be the title.

It's about a writer wooing back her super-sexy ex-husband.

Not at all what the story is about.

And they end up living happily ever after together.

That part is true.

What about our story? Don't you think it's time we wrapped up this memoir with our own happily-ever-after?

I don't know if we can. This is a memoir, not one of my romance stories. Pretty sure someone once told me that everything can't be tied up in a neat bow by page three-twenty-two.

Wise words indeed. But why don't you give it a shot anyway?

Okay then. (Clears throat.) This is life. This is love. The pages keep going.

So far so good.

There'll be heartache and disappointment and probably more tears. The end.

Well, they do say first drafts are always terrible. Want to try again?

Perhaps one more rewrite. All right. (Clears throat.) This is life. This is love. The pages keep going. No, we don't know what awaits us on those pages, but Noah and I do know this. Whatever happens in the chapters to come, we'll never stop clinging to God. We'll never stop clinging to each other. We'll never stop clinging to hope.

I'd say we found our perfect ending, babe. Now come on. Let's eat dessert and celebrate. We're finally done with this memoir.

But not with our story. And oh, dear reader, how we thank God for that.

A Note from the Author

Dear Reader,

Let's just address the elephant in the room. As a lifelong Chicago Cubs fan, how on earth could I possibly write a novel involving baseball that doesn't even include a whisper of the Cubs? To quote my husband, "Of all the teams, you sent the *Cardinals* to the World Series?!"

I know. I know. It pained me a little bit too, but sometimes you just have to do what's best for the story, and in this case, the Seattle and St. Louis locations worked best.

In my defense, I do include a whisper of the Cubs. Gracie's name was definitely inspired by my favorite Cubs player, Mark Grace. And the whole idea of a rain delay was heavily inspired by the greatest rain delay of all time—the seventeen-minute rain delay in game seven of the 2016 World Series between the Cubs and the Cleveland Indians.

I'll never forget sitting in my living room with my husband, my parents, and my in-laws as we chewed our nails down to nothing, watching that game. And I'll admit it: Before the rain delay, I was losing hope. I was already picturing the inevitable heartache that seemed to be a Cubs fan's lot in life and trying to steel myself for our biggest disappointment yet.

Then the rain delay hit.

I don't remember the exact words my dad said as we sat there, trying to regroup, in a very tense living room. But he gave a similar message to what it sounds like the Cubs players were hearing inside the clubhouse from one of their outfielders. Basically, *Stop acting defeated, guys! The game's not over! We've still got reason to hope!*

And in a nutshell, that's the message I hope you hear from this story. Whatever trials you go through, whatever disappointments you face, whatever delays you find yourself stuck in, I hope you'll take a moment to regroup, tighten your grip on God, and remember that this wonderful gift of life you've been given is not over yet. With Jesus, there's always reason to hope.

Acknowledgments

When it came to writing this story, a more accurate title would be *First Love, Seven Hundred Drafts*. And I'd be fumbling through draft number 701 right now if I didn't have the support of some truly wonderful people—starting with my truly wonderful team at Tyndale.

Kathy Olson and Elizabeth Jackson, thank you for working with me on another zany story and, once again, helping me find ways to dig deeper to make it better. (Which, yes, in this case included making sure my characters didn't run around in their undies all day.)

Libby Dykstra, one of my favorite days as an author is when I get to see your creativity and cleverness come to life on my book covers. Thanks for making that such a fun part of the writing process for me.

Andrea Garcia, thank you for your guidance and expertise in marketing my books, as well as your guidance and expertise in navigating Chicago last summer, two things that would normally make me a sweaty, anxious mess without such guidance.

Stephanie Broene, Wendie Connors, Andrea Martin, Jan Stob, Karen Watson, Stephanie Abrassart, and all those at Tyndale who have taken the time to cheer me on, pray for me, and offer encouragement (which sometimes comes in the form of sending treats to my dog), thank you! I'm so grateful for all of you.

Becky Yauger, Wendy Galinetti, and Jody Stinson, thank you for reading draft 547 and helping me keep this story headed in the right direction. Christina Myerly, I'm pretty sure you read a very unpolished draft 32, so thank you for encouraging me a few years ago to even keep going with this story in the first place. To the rest of my writing huddle group—Denise Colby, Lynn Watson, and Becky DePaulis—I'm always so blessed by our Zoom calls and emails. Thank you for navigating the writing world alongside me.

Rachelle Gardner, whenever I give my "how I got published" talk, one of my favorite parts is how you became my agent. Thank you for all you've done for me these past four years. Or has it been five now? However many it's been, I'm grateful.

Oh boy, now we're on to Dave, Maria, and Charlie. You poor people have suffered through listening to me talk about every single one of my seven hundred drafts and then some. But I know you wouldn't have it any other way. (Right? You wouldn't have it any other way? *Right?*) Either way, I love you three like crazy.

Speaking of crazy, a special thank you to Katie Geisler and Toni Yandell, who have listened to their fair share of crazy talk from me throughout all the various stages of my publishing journey. Your encouragement and listening ears mean the world to me.

To all the booksellers and librarians who place my books on your shelves—thank you, thank you, thank you. And to all the readers who have taken the time to read my books, leave reviews, and spread the word about them—thank you, thank you, thank you.

Last but not least, I am forever grateful to God for giving me another story to tell and allowing me the opportunity to share it.

Discussion Questions

1. At the opening of this story, we see that Gracie has a hard time accepting help. Is that something you can relate to? If so, why do you think that is?

2. If you got injured and had to completely rely on someone from this story to take care of you for a week, which character would you choose?

3. Part of Gracie's struggles as a writer stem from trying to write an upbeat, humorous story when she's emotionally stuck in a place of bitterness. How can we keep disappointments and setbacks from turning us bitter?

4. In addition to Noah, Gracie, Matt, and Rachel, this story has a lot of secondary characters. Did you have a favorite supporting character? Who was it and why?

5. Have you ever gone through an experience that has left you feeling like Gracie—that it's better to accept defeat and move on, than to keep hoping for something that may never happen? How do you determine when it's time to hold on versus when it's time to move on?

6. Morris the cat clearly made a big impact on Gracie as a child. Did you have any childhood pets that made a big impact on you?

7. In Noah's case, sports were a big part of his childhood. Were you athletic growing up? Did you play on any teams? If so, how did those experiences affect you?

8. Gracie mentions that she hates writing "love triangle" tropes in her romances. Are there any particular romance tropes you don't like reading? Any tropes you especially love?

9. What parallels do you see between Matt and Rachel's relationship and the relationship between Noah and Gracie?

10. Would you ever want a memoir written about you? Like Noah, are there parts of your life story you would prefer leaving out of a memoir?

About the Author

BECCA KINZER lives in Springfield, Illinois, where she works as a critical care nurse. When she's not taking care of sick patients or reminding her husband and two kids that frozen chicken nuggets is a gourmet meal, she enjoys making up lighthearted stories with serious laughs. She is a 2018 ACFW First Impressions Contest winner, a 2019 Genesis Contest winner, a 2021 Cascade Award winner, and an all-around champion coffee drinker. Visit Becca online at beccakinzer.com.

CONNECT WITH BECCA ONLINE AT

beccakinzer.com

OR FOLLOW HER ON

@beccaannkinzer

@BeccaKinzer

@Becca_Kinzer